I0628344

Christmas Love and Mercy

When Grace Comes Down

WELL OF LIFE
PUBLISHING

Christmas Love and Mercy

Christmas Hotel Series
Book Five

by

Saundra Staats McLemore

Christmas Love and Mercy

When Grace Comes Down

Christmas Hotel Series Book Five
by
Saundra Staats McLemore

Paperback ISBN: 978-1-7336122-2-7

Also available as an eBook
eBook ISBN: 978-1-7336122-1-0

First published by
Desert Breeze Publishing 2016
© Saundra Staats McLemore 2016

This new and revised edition 2019
Content Editor: Chris Wright
Cover Artist: Jenifer Ranieri

All scripture verses are taken from the KJV of the Holy Bible. An excerpt from the song *Somewhere Out There* (James Horner, Barry Mann and Cynthia Weil 1986) Mendelssohn's Wedding March
Amazing Grace (John Newton 1779)
How Great Thou Art (Carl Gustav Boberg 1885)
Lord, I Need Thee Every Hour (Annie S. Hawks and Robert Lowry 1872

Published by
Well of Life Publishing
Ohio
United States of America

http://www.saundrastaatsmclemore.com

Other Books by Saundra Staats McLemore

The Staats Family Chronicles Series

Abraham and Anna – Book One of Staats Family
Chronicles Series – Available now
Joy out of Ashes – Book Two of Staats Family
Chronicles Series – Available now

Christmas Hotel Series

Book One: Christmas Hotel
(New Edition) Available now
Book Two: Christmas for Lucy
(New Edition) Available now
Book Three: Christmas Redemption
(New Edition) Available now
Book Four: Christmas Pact (New Edition)
Paperback available now
eBook available October 11, 2019
Book Five: Christmas Love and Mercy
New Edition)
Paperback available now
EBook available November 01, 2019
Book Six: Christmas Hotel Reunion
(New Edition)
Available November 15, 2019

Dedication

Christmas Love and Mercy is dedicated to my Aunt Anna Dailey Parks and my friend Phyllis Mayne, both of whom are cancer survivors; and also dedicated in memory of my grandmother Maude Ellen Hendricks Dailey and my friend Joyce Fullum, who both succumbed in their early sixties to cancer. I pray 2020 is the year we find a cure.

Acknowledgements

I thank Franklin, Kentucky historian Denise Shoulders for info regarding businesses around the Franklin, Kentucky square in '87-'88. She graciously answered my questions, and much of the information I was able to use for the accuracy of pertinent information.

I would like to offer a special thank you to Sid and Jill Broderson for granting me permission to have my characters Christopher and Jerilyn Wright and their children, throughout the Christmas Hotel series, reside in their historical home at 210 South College Street in Franklin, Kentucky. This beautiful home is known in Franklin as the *Montague House* or the *Malone House*. The Italianate structure was built around 1860 by William Clement Montague.

Another special thank you to Barbara Beasley Smith for allowing me to have her father Dr. L. F. Beasley "visit" the story.

As always, I thank my husband Robert E. McLemore for his complete support, as I enjoy the passion I have for writing.

I would like to thank our Lord and Savior Jesus Christ for the inspiration He provides for every story I write.

"Let us therefore come boldly unto the throne of grace, that we may obtain mercy, and find grace to help in time of need."
Hebrews 4:16

Chapters

Prologue

Thursday
December 01, 1988

Chris tiptoed into the bedroom to check on her. She lay on her back, sleeping with a slight smile on her sweet face. She had kicked off the covers, so he straightened the quilt and tucked her in. His mother had made this quilt over a period of eight months. With a chuckle and the inevitable hug, Mom said, "It's my first quilt. I want you to have it. You're my youngest and my last, so you get my practice quilt."

Chris smiled, remembering the conversation. His mother had been his rock all through his growing up years. He loved his father, but there was something special about a mother's love. Her love was always unconditional. Not that he gave his parents cause for alarm, but he did engage in a few teenage pranks.

Although Chris and his nephew Brian were six years apart in age, and he being the older, they were the best of friends. On Halloween night, back in '71, when Chris was sixteen and Brian was ten, they toilet papered the trees of his biology teacher's home. Of course, as the older boy, he was the one to get in trouble.

"You did that why?" questioned his father in a stern voice. "Your teacher, Mr. McKinley paid me a visit. You were spotted by Lori Anna, who you know lives next door. Lori Anna thought it was funny, but her parents James and Carol Ann were not pleased. After all, Mr. McKinley is their neighbor. What do you have to say for yourself, Christopher Joseph Wright?"

Chris hung his head. He knew he was in deep trouble when either parent used his full name. "I'm sorry, Dad. I'll clean it up."

"You will do just that, *and* you will apologize to Mr. McKinley. I told him you'll also handle chores around his house after school three hours each day for a week. Therefore, there will be no work or pay at Christmas Hotel that week."

When he arrived to clean up the mess, of course Brian was a no-show to help him. Three-year-old Lori Anna stood behind a bush, watching him. Chris placed the ladder against the tree, climbed up, and began removing the paper. Thankfully, it didn't rain or snow or he'd have a serious mess. As he threw down the shreds of toilet paper, Lori Anna stepped away from the bush, picked up the shreds, and stuffed them in a large garbage bag Chris had left on the ground. He looked down and smiled at his little helper. She looked up at him and returned a smile, displaying her dimples. Her mom must have given her one of those home perms, because her normally straight black hair was in little ringlets all over her head. *What a little cutie.*

The phone rang, interrupting his reminiscing from the past and abruptly jolting him back to the present. He stepped out of the room, quietly closing the door. "Hello," he said into the receiver. "Yes, Mom, she's asleep. Yes, I'm okay. I'll probably take off a few days from Christmas Hotel. I think Mr. Hanover, Mr. Adams, Mr. Thompson, Mr. Clark, and of course you and Dad can make certain all shifts are covered. I just need to be here *and* at the hospital."

"I understand, son. Please let me help you more. You're wearing yourself out and spreading yourself too thin."

"I'm fine, Mom. I love you."

"I love you, too. Never forget that."

Chapter One

Lori Anna Stanley

*"I wait for the LORD, my soul doth wait,
and in his word do I hope."*
Psalm 130:5

One year earlier
Tuesday Morning
December 01, 1987

"Hey, Uncle Chris, did you just snap our picture?" Brian had been snuggling on a bench in Franklin's town square with his wife Christine.

Chris laughed, throwing back his head for a good guffaw. "I'm just photographing my annual Christmas pictures of the square. My, my, a picture of you snuggling with Christine will make a great picture for your little one someday. *And* quit calling me uncle! I'm only six years older than you."

"I know, but I just want to remind you now and then that you're getting old."

Chris grumbled. "It's more than now and then, so thanks a lot."

4

Christine smiled and rubbed her rotund belly. Her coat no longer completely closed; she appeared to be wearing a couple of bulky sweaters underneath.

Brian jumped up. "Give me the camera, Chris. Let me take *your* picture for a change."

"I don't think so, buddy boy. This is the latest Canon model. It's the RC-760 released this year. My parents gave it to me for my birthday in September. I know how camera-challenged you are. Why you couldn't even use my Polaroid from the sixties. You cut off everyone's heads."

"Ha, ha. I was a kid. By the way, why aren't you at your desk at Christmas Hotel? Since when does the senior manager have time off?"

"I do schedule a day off now and then. What about you? Shouldn't you be doing your detective stuff? Aren't you working on a big case?"

"It's all under control," Brian said with a smug grin and a wave of his hand before he returned to his seat, hugging his wife closer. He looked up at Chris with his cheesiest grin.

They all turned when they saw a camera flash nearby. A young woman snapped pictures about twenty feet away, and a well-trained Golden Retriever sat at her feet. When the girl walked a few paces, the dog obediently followed and then again sat at her feet. Despite the chill of the December morning, she wore no coat; just a bright green sweatshirt over black sweatpants tucked into her tall, furry boots. A multi-colored knit hat covered her head, but her straight black hair hung to her waistline. Every time she spun around for another picture, her long hair followed in a swinging motion around her lithe, petite figure.

Chris watched her, mesmerized. She gave extra special meaning to the phrase poetry in motion. She appeared to be around twenty, so he knew she was too young for him. It didn't seem right; a thirty-two-year-old man ogling such a young woman. However, he couldn't stop watching her and the dog. The dog anticipated her every move.

Brian jumped up and ran his hand in front of Chris's eyes. "Earth to Chris. Don't you know who she is?"

Finally, and reluctantly, Chris turned back to Brian. "I guess not. I thought I knew everyone in Franklin." He cocked his head. "Yet, there is a familiarity about her."

"You dunce," Brian said, landing a friendly smack to the side of Chris's head. "That's Lori Anna Stanley, James and Carol Ann's daughter. She's been away at the University of Louisville for the past two years, but she recently transferred to Western Kentucky University. I hear she's working part-time at the *Franklin Favorite*. Maybe that's why she's taking all the pictures. I think you've been cooped up at Christmas Hotel too much. You need to get out more often, so you can know what's happening."

Lori Anna. It's even worse than I thought. I'm gawking at a nineteen-year-old! He turned back to Brian, but he had rejoined Christine on the bench. Brian and Christine met three years ago, married a year later, and now had a baby on the way. Chris watched them laugh together, and Brian rubbed her very-pregnant belly. He turned back toward Lori Anna, but she and her dog had moved to the next block, snapping more pictures. *All my siblings are married with children, and were married by my age. What's wrong with me, Lord?*

Three hours later, Chris returned to the square, this time munching on his lunch sandwich and drinking a Coke. He had gone home to pick up his German Shepherd, Fritz. After seeing Lori Anna on the square with her dog, he realized his day off should involve Fritz. Finishing his sandwich, and tossing Fritz the last bite, he threw the wrappings in the trash receptacle. "Okay, boy, get ready to catch the Frisbee!"

Fritz pranced around in excitement, jumping and trying to steal the Frisbee from Chris's hands. Chris reared back and threw the Frisbee about twenty feet high, at a distance of about forty feet. Fritz ran and caught it with practiced ease. Chris and the three-year-old shepherd had been playing catch with a Frisbee or a ball from the time his dog was just two months old.

At the third throw, a golden retriever jumped, caught it, and the feminine laugh of a woman rang in his ears. Fritz tried to grab the Frisbee away from the dog, but the dog ran from him.

"Here, Bella. Bring it to me." Lori Anna laughed when she took it from Bella and threw it for Bella to catch it again. Fritz sat and cocked his head, and then he looked back at Chris, as if to say, "What gives, Master?"

Bella brought the Frisbee back to Lori Anna, and she in turn handed it to Chris. "Sorry, Chris. Bella wanted to play, too."

Chris checked out Lori Anna. She had put on a warm car coat and had on knit gloves, but no knit hat this time. She wore earmuffs instead. Her long straight hair remained loose and hung down her back. One side fell over her eye, and she quickly tucked it behind an ear, still smiling at Chris. She didn't wear the big-hair teased look most women of the eighties sported. Obviously, she didn't follow the crowd. He liked that about her, because he didn't either. He still wore his brown hair shorter than most men his age, and he bore no tattoos. She had the cutest dimples. She was so small, not over five feet tall. She could easily walk under the outstretched arm of his six feet two inch frame. Her voice was deeper than he expected from a nineteen-year old. Almost sensual.

He realized he was staring. He closed his eyes for

only a second to focus. "Uh ... not a problem, Lori Anna. I see Bella likes to play Frisbee, too. I think Fritz was just a bit confused, but he seems okay now.

"So, Lori Anna, you haven't been home for a while. Did you recognize me this morning when you were snapping pictures?"

"Yes, but I didn't want to intrude on your time with Brian and Christine. They seem like a happy couple. I've been gone for a couple of years, and I'm trying to get reacquainted with everyone."

"They *are* happy. As you could see, Christine is very pregnant with their first child."

"Do they know if they're having a boy or a girl?"

"No, they decided they wanted to be surprised."

During a lull in the conversation, they turned to watch the dogs playing, running, and jumping.

"Bella is two. How old is Fritz?"

"He just turned three. His lineage has been in our family since 1954, before I was born. First with Lydia Grace's first dog Bullet, and then his son Gabe. Fritz has cousins all over Simpson County."

Lori Anna smiled and motioned to a nearby bench. "Why don't we have a seat and watch our dogs play?"

"Okay." *Now what*, thought Chris, as he sat by her on the bench. *She's nineteen. I can't be attracted to her. However, she definitely is not a giggly teenager. She's very mature.*

"So, Brian said you transferred from the University

of Louisville to Western Kentucky University. Why the switch?"

She smiled again. "I forget how quickly news in a small town travels."

"I'm sorry. I didn't mean to pry." Chris knew his face reddened. It always did when he was nervous, to his mortification. Maybe he was being nosy.

"Oh, no, it's okay," she said as she touched his arm.

He felt the electricity shoot through him. He noticed a surprised expression cross her face.

Does she feel it, too? Okay, what am I doing? I'm sitting on a park bench in the square, and anyone in town who's nearby will see us. She's right, news does travel like wild fires in a small town.

"I was only teasing," she continued. She removed her hand from his arm. "Actually, I missed the small town atmosphere. Louisville was just too big for me, and I also wanted to be closer to my parents. Dad hasn't been well lately, and Mom's been worried about him. She did get him to quit the long-distance trucking. The short-distance runs permit him to be home nightly. In her words, 'That allows me to keep an eye on him.'"

She paused for a moment to watch the dogs. "With me attending classes in Bowling Green and working for the *Franklin Favorite* newspaper here in town, I can help out, too." Pausing again, she said, "By the way, I noticed you're into photography, too. I saw you with your camera this morning."

"Yeah, I've been taking pictures since I was a kid. It's been one of my dad's many hobbies, and through the years we've used photography as our special time together. I suppose I grew up with a camera in my hands. My dad's camera collection is huge. I think he has cameras back to circa 1920. However, I haven't been paid for photography, like you. It makes me the amateur and you the professional."

"Not a professional very long. The paper just hired me in September. I've only been into photography about ten years. I received my first camera at Christmas when I was nine."

The age difference hit him again. *Nineteen-year-old Lori Anna has been using a camera ten years, and me about twenty-eight years. Good grief, I need to get far away from her.*

He rose. "Well, Lori Anna, it's been a pleasure seeing you again. Please tell your parents I said Hi." Did he see disappointment flash across her face? "Oh! I should let you know Christmas Hotel now has a darkroom in the basement. I added it about ten years ago. If the paper is closed and you need pictures developed, please feel free to use it. Just tell the manager on duty where you'll be. We also have a full gym down there too, along with a men's and ladies' shower room. It's really for the guests, but the town's people are welcome. Both are available twenty-four/seven, three hundred sixty-five."

She rose with him. "Thank you, Chris. I'll probably take you up on both of the offers." She turned toward her dog. "Come, Bella," and Bella ran to her.

Chris walked to his 1986 black Ford F-150 pickup parked at the curb across from Christmas Hotel. Opening the passenger door, Fritz jumped in and sat on his side of the front seat. As Chris climbed in, he looked toward Lori Anna. She was heading in the direction of her parents' home. The lonely feeling gripped his heart.

Chapter Two

Beginnings

*"Wait on the Lord: be of good courage, and he shall
strengthen thine heart: wait, I say, on the LORD."*
Psalm 27:14

The next day
Wednesday morning
December 02, 1987
Chris awakened extra early, to work in Christmas
Hotel's darkroom before he was to report for front desk
duty at 5:00 a.m., relieving Mr. Thompson from his
midnight to five shift. Generally, his parents
Christopher and Jerilyn only worked at the front desk
of Christmas Hotel four or five shifts per week during
the afternoons. Mr. Hanover, Mr. Adams, and Mr.
Clark covered the other shifts.

With Fritz at his heels, Chris entered Christmas
Hotel, said hello to Mr. Thompson, and headed to the
basement. He wanted to develop yesterday's pictures
and then get a thirty minute run on the treadmill and a
shower before his shift.

Hanging his suit in the men's shower and dressing room, he entered the darkroom. Fritz lay down on his over-sized pillow in the corner to await his master.

After finishing the developing, and checking the quality of the pictures, he was pleased with the results. The black-and-white prints had been squeegeed off and now lay flat by the sink to dry. After closing the door to the darkroom, he patted Fritz's head, and walked toward the treadmill. Someone descending the steps caused him to pause and turn in the direction. *Probably an early morning guest.* He was surprised when Lori Anna smiled at him, holding a small suitcase in her hand.

"Good morning, Chris. I see you're an early morning riser, too." Fritz walked to her, tail wagging. "Good morning to you, too, Fritz." The German Shepherd sat in front of her while she scratched him behind the ears. He then rolled onto his back with all four of his legs flailing for the anticipated brisk belly rub.

"Lori Anna, I see you've stolen my dog's heart. He's not normally so quick to warm up to strangers."

Lori Anna stared Chris square in the eye. "But I'm no longer a stranger. I'm sure Fritz and I will be great friends. I thought I'd take you up on your offer to use the gym before work. If you don't mind, I'll use one of the treadmills for a quick run." She hung her coat on a wall hook and headed toward the treadmills.

"I don't mind at all. We have ten treadmills. Take your pick. I was just going to jump on one myself." He stepped onto the treadmill, programming it at warm-up speed, and placed a hand towel and a bottle of water in the proper slots.

Lori Anna hopped upon the one next to him, placing her towel and water bottle, too.

Chris nearly groaned aloud at her close proximity to him. Her long black hair was pulled into a ponytail, and she wore a blue and white body-hugging jogging suit, and blue and white jogging shoes. She was fresh-faced with no makeup, but none was needed. She flashed her dark brown eyes at him and smiled, displaying those amazing dimples.

They both sped up at the same time, running neck-and-neck for about twenty minutes, before beginning a five minute cool down. Simultaneously, they grabbed their towels, wiped their faces, and guzzled the water.

"I've got some pictures drying in the darkroom, but you're free to use it later if you like."

"Thanks, Chris, but by the time I get my shower and dress, the *Franklin Favorite* offices will be open. I'll develop the pictures I took yesterday in the darkroom at the paper. Then I've two classes this afternoon at WKU. Thanks for the offer, though."

"You're welcome."

They entered the separate shower and dressing rooms. Chris showered and changed, throwing his dirty clothes in a duffel bag. Entering the darkroom he checked the pictures, and decided to leave them until after his shift ended at 1 p.m.

He turned off the back light and closed the door. Lori Anna walked from her dressing room at the same time. Wearing a navy blue suit, white silk blouse, and navy heels, she stopped in front of him. She had washed and partially dried her long hair, which hung loose down her back. If she had applied makeup, it was very little, but she did have on pink lipstick. He sniffed a touch of heavenly cologne, but very subtle. His mother always said cologne should be a whisper and not a shout. Lori Anna's cologne was an intoxicating whisper. As usual, she looked stunning.

He realized he was staring, and she had a slightly amused smile on her face. *I think she can read my mind, and that's not good.*

She touched his arm, and the electricity shot through him again. The smile never left her face. "Thanks, Chris. I enjoyed our run together. We should do this more often." She bent down, petted Fritz, and he watched her until she disappeared up the steps.

Fritz whined, and Chris bent down and petted him. "Don't get attached, Fritz," but his own heart was racing as he said it.

Chapter Three

Mixed Feelings

*"And hope maketh not ashamed; because the
love of God is shed abroad in our hearts by the
Holy Ghost which is given unto us."*
Romans 5:5

Saturday
December 05, 1987
Lori Anna showed up at Christmas Hotel early
Thursday and Friday mornings: once for the treadmill,
and once for both the darkroom and treadmill. Chris
and Fritz were now used to her visits, so much that
when she didn't appear Saturday morning, they both
missed her.

During his treadmill run, Chris kept looking over
his shoulder at the basement steps. Fritz sat at the
bottom of the steps, until finally giving up and lying
down on his pillow. However, every time Fritz heard a
slight noise, he looked up, wagging his tail.

By 4:30, Chris realized she wasn't coming. He

showered, dressed, and rushed to the front desk by 5:00 to relieve Mr. Adams, who was on duty last night to give Mr. Thompson a night off.

It was the typical busy day in December. Happy families and couples, young and old, checked in for the week or a weekend. Although Christmas Hotel was nearly booked to capacity all year around, it was still at its busiest in December. Chris was thankful he had a wonderful crew of assistant managers, dining room staff, and room staff.

Normally he worked until one o'clock, but his parents no longer relieved him on Saturday. He needed to work until four o'clock when Mr. Hanover came on duty. Mr. Hanover arrived a little early, and he and Chris smoothly met the shift change.

"Come, Fritz," Chris called to where his dog slept in the back room.

Fritz followed Chris across the street inside the square, where Fritz quickly relieved himself. Chris held the doggy clean-up bag if needed. Out of the corner of his eye he saw Lori Anna walking toward them with Bella at her heels. He knew he probably looked ridiculous with the huge grin on his face, but he was happy to see her.

"Hi, Chris. Sorry I missed you this morning. I had planned to come, but my boss at the paper wanted me to take some pictures of the downtown squares of Bowling Green and Russellville. They featured

Franklin's Christmas decorations in their papers last week, so my boss wanted to reciprocate. My parents will be out of town tonight, and I'd like to invite you and Fritz over for dinner. I make a mean lasagna, if I do say so myself."

Chris guessed she must have noticed the surprise and hesitation on his face, because she quickly added, "As friends, you know, and a play date for Bella. Bella has no other doggy friends, so it would be doing her a favor. It will also be my way of thanking you for the use of Christmas Hotel's gym and darkroom."

"I'm ever so sorry, Lori Anna, but I promised my parents I'd have dinner with them this evening at Christmas Hotel. They spent part of the afternoon at my home cutting down the traditional Christmas tree for our family home, and I'm planning to help them decorate tonight. Brian and Christine will be at the hotel for dinner, too, along with my older sister Lily and her husband John. After dinner, we're all going back to my parents' house to decorate."

He watched her face drop with disappointment. He didn't think before he blurted, "Why don't you have dinner with all of us at Christmas Hotel. Then, if you like, you can help us decorate the house afterwards?"

Her face brightened. "I'd love that. I'll go home for a quick shower and change into something suitable for a Saturday night dinner at Christmas Hotel. Thanks, Chris, for the invitation."

She hurried away before he could say anything. *What have I gotten myself into, Lord?*

That evening, family and friends gathered in the Christmas Hotel lobby. Laughter and hugging commenced – as if the family hadn't seen each other for a while. Lily rubbed Christine's stomach. "Hello, baby, I'm your grandmother, and I can't wait to meet you."

Jerilyn was next to rub Christine's stomach. "Hello, baby, I'm your great-grandmother, and I can't wait to meet you, either."

The men just shook their heads, while the women talked the baby-talk to Christine's stomach. Jerilyn turned toward the men. "Okay, guys, Lily and I are just doing what you men want to do." She turned to her grandson, Brian. "I would be very surprised if you *didn't* talk to your baby every day. I know Christopher did when I was pregnant with our children."

Christine nodded. "Yes, he does. In fact, he also plays classical music several times a day for the baby. He always says, 'Maybe he or she will inherit the musical ability from Great-Grandpa Christopher, as did my mother and Aunt Lydia Grace.'"

A hush fell over the room when Lori Anna appeared. She walked straight to Chris, a wide smile on her face. "I hope I'm not late."

Chris had not had a chance to inform his family

that Lori Anna would be joining them. He saw the surprised expressions and then the smiles. *I know I'm going to have to explain. They're all going to jump to the wrong conclusion.*

"Hi, Lori Anna. You're not late. I suppose you know all my family, so I won't need to introduce you."

She shook hands or hugged, politely greeting all of them. While she did, Chris checked out her black knee-length dinner dress and black heels. Her heavy black wool coat was slung over one arm. She wore dangling ruby earrings, but no other jewelry, except a ruby jewel clip holding her beautiful upswept hair in place. She was breathtaking.

He glanced at Brian, and Brian gave him a, 'I know what you're thinking look' with one raised eyebrow, a slight nod of the head, and the discreet thumbs up. He knew his reaction to Lori Anna was going to be a problem. Later, he would be razzed by Brian. After slowly releasing his breath, a smug smile appeared on Brian's face.

The doors to the Christmas Hotel dining room opened promptly at six o'clock, and the guests filed through them, the women taking the offered arms of their men, which left Chris offering his arm for Lori Anna. The Wright family took their seats at their private dining table overlooking the beautifully landscaped courtyard. Although flowers were not in bloom this time of year, they could still look out at the boxwoods and the decorated evergreen tree in the middle. They had called ahead requesting seating for up to twelve, never knowing how many in the family might appear.

After the waiter took their orders, Jerilyn addressed Lori Anna. "It's lovely to see you again, Lori Anna. I had heard you left the University of Louisville when I spoke with your mom last week. She said you had transferred to WKU and working part-time as a photographer at the *Franklin Favorite*. I must say, Carol Ann is very happy to have you back home." She looked from Lori Anna to Chris and back to Lori Anna. "And I see you and Chris have become reacquainted."

Brian coughed and took a sip of his water, while Chris shot him the narrowed-eye look.

"Why, yes, indeed. I was shooting pictures earlier this week on the square with my dog Bella. The paper wanted me to get as many pictures as possible of all the businesses decorated for Christmas. As usual, the businesses didn't disappoint, nor the workers who decorate the square. Like my mom, I'm very happy to be home." She looked over at Chris.

Chris took up the conversation. "I was on the square that morning with Brian and Christine. I'm sure Lori Anna didn't realize she also snapped a picture of us." He watched her look down in her lap. "You *did* know. You said you were taking pictures of people on the square."

"Well, yes, I was, but I knew all my subjects, too." She laughed. "It's a small town, Chris. Everyone knows everyone, or at least a family member."

Brian jumped into the conversation. "I had to tell him who you were, when he was staring at you."

Chris did his best to send Brian his 'shut up' look with his eyes, but Brian rambled on, ignoring him. "Chris finally said you looked familiar. I put him out of his misery and told him who you were ... Lori Anna Stanley." Brian shot a look back to Chris with a quirky grin, wide eyes, and raised eyebrows.

The others around the table said nothing, but Chris noted the polite amused smiles, along with a few throat clearings.

Lori Anna also smiled and turned back to Jerilyn. "I returned later, and my dog Bella and Fritz met. Then Chris and I played Frisbee with them. Chris informed me Christmas Hotel now had a darkroom and gym in the basement, and he invited me to take advantage of both, which I have this week. Chris and I seem to arrive much earlier than the guests. My work and school schedule rarely permits me to jog outdoors, and I don't have a treadmill, so this is a wonderful treat for me."

She turned back to Chris flashing her bright white smile. "Thanks again for inviting me to the gym – and dinner tonight."

When she turned those beautiful dark brown eyes on him, he nearly melted, but quickly gathered himself, so hopefully, his family wouldn't see.

Too late. Brian saw, as usual, and continued with his annoying grin. Mom and Dad also exchanged knowing looks. Thankfully, dinner arrived, Christopher asked the blessing, and other topics of conversation were discussed.

Christopher held up one finger, swallowed, wiped his mouth, and addressed the group. "Lydia Grace called today. She and Jacob and Anthony are coming home on the Monday before Christmas."

Mom quickly blotted her mouth. "Oh, Christopher, I meant to tell you earlier. I talked to Carrie Emeline and Marcus. They promised to be here at least for a week around Christmas. They need to schedule their time off from the restaurant with Marcus's sister Sally. Ken and Loretta will drive down from Lexington on Christmas Eve, along with their brood. It's so nice they don't live too far away. Loretta is such a loving mother, homeschooling and organizing a great deal of family time with Ken and their girls." She realized her error. She jerked her head toward Lori Anna, her eyes pleading forgiveness. Chris knew his mom wished she could take it back.

"It's okay, Mrs. Wright. The few times I've met my biological mother here in Franklin, I'll admit it's been somewhat awkward, but I think it's awkward more for her than me."

The conversation hushed for a moment. Then Mom

continued by saying, "Lily and John, you'll be here for your father's Christmas Eve and Christmas morning service, won't you?"

"We wouldn't miss it, Mom. We always look forward to Dad's preaching. However, he doesn't preach as much in the chapel now as in the past." Lily looked at her father and smiled. "I wish you did, Dad."

"I know I don't, honey. I realize I'm not old at seventy-four, and the Lord still gives me plenty of sermons, but I like to give visiting preachers a chance. We seem to have more preachers stay at Christmas Hotel as the years go by. I rather think God is choosing the next preacher for the Christmas Hotel chapel. He chose Chris for the manager of the hotel, but so far I don't think Chris has the call to preach. Am I correct, son?"

"You're correct, Dad, but I promise you'll be the first to know if the calling comes."

After dinner, the families headed toward the Wright family home on South College Street. "Would you like to come and help decorate?" Chris asked Lori Anna. "Since your parents are out of town," he quickly added.

"I'd like that, Chris, but I need to sort my pictures I developed earlier, study for a final on Monday, and get to bed early for church in the morning."

He escorted her home, and at her door, Lori Anna rested her hand on his arm. "I'd still love to cook lasagna for you. How about you and Fritz come here at my place Sunday evening?"

"Well, Brian and Christine are coming over to my house Sunday evening. We're planning to have pizza and rent a movie for my Betamax." He saw the downcast look again. "How about you bring the lasagna around five o'clock, and you can bring Bella, too, to play in the backyard with Fritz. I'm sure Brian and Christine would love your homemade lasagna much more than the warmed up frozen pizza. I'll supply the Cokes."

"Perfect! I'll see all of you at five o'clock. Actually, I'll probably see you at church tomorrow morning, too."

"See you then." Chris turned and slowly walked back to his truck. *Did I just make a date, Lord?* He hurried on to his parents' home.

Chapter Four

An Evening to Remember

"But the path of the just is as the shining light, that
shineth more and more unto the perfect day."
Proverb 4:18

Sunday
December 06, 1987
Sunday morning, while Christopher and Jerilyn stood
out front of the First Methodist Church of Franklin,
visiting with friends, Lori Anna walked up and greeted
them. Chris parked his pickup and joined his family.

Jerilyn opened her arms and Lori Anna stepped in
for a hug. "It's really nice to have you back home in
Franklin and at church with us. How long will your
parents be out of town?"

"Oh, they should return sometime tomorrow
morning. At least that's what they said when they
phoned me last night. They're visiting Dad's brother in
Atlanta. Dad's health is better, but now Uncle Louis
hasn't been well."

"I'm pleased about your dad, but I'm sorry to hear
about his brother, honey. I hope your uncle is better

soon." Jerilyn looked toward Chris and turned back to Lori Anna. "With your parents out of town, please sit with Christopher, Chris, and me this morning. Unless, of course, you were planning on sitting with someone else."

Lori Anna glanced at Chris, and he smiled at her and nodded. Returning to Jerilyn, she said, "I'd love to join you and your family. Thank you for asking."

Brian and Christine arrived shortly after, and climbed the steps to the church with Christine leaning heavily on her husband, along with holding the railing.

At the top of the steps Pastor Chuck Mason and his lovely wife Linda greeted all of the parishioners, not only as they entered, but when they filed out after the service, shaking all their hands. Pastor Mason had taken over as senior pastor of the church following the leave of Pastor Palmer in 1975. Pastor Palmer and his wife were now missionaries in El Salvador.

Following the service, Lori Anna reminded Chris she was going home to cook the lasagna for all of them, bake the garlic bread, and prepare a salad. "What time do you want me there?"

"I think five o'clock. What about you two?"

Brian draped his arm around his wife. "Five o'clock works for me. What about you, honey?"

"That's good for me, too. I love homemade lasagna. Is there anything I can do to help?"

Lori Anna looked Christine over and shook her

head, "I think I'd rather serve you with your legs propped up on an ottoman." And they all laughed. "Someday, I'll let you reciprocate. Maybe a few months after *baby* is born."

Chris already had the address written down to his home on highway 31-W and handed it to Lori Anna. "Here you go. I think you'll easily find the house, but it does sit a ways back from the road. It's also closer to Bowling Green than Franklin. The address numbers are on the mailbox at the end of my driveway."

"I'll find it."

Lori Anna pulled her 1985 Chevy Caprice into the long gravel driveway and parked behind Chris's truck. She saw no other vehicle, so she must have arrived ahead of Brian and Christine. Fritz rounded the corner from the rear of the house, barking his greeting to the newcomers. Bella wagged her tail, pranced on the passenger seat, and barked, too. Lori Anna leaned in front of her and opened the passenger door so Bella could jump out and greet Fritz.

She stepped out of her car and opened the rear door. She had placed everything securely on the floor. She reached in just as Chris appeared. "What can I help you carry?"

She handed him the casserole dish wrapped in towels. "Careful, it's still hot. I'll get the bread and the salad."

They turned when Brian and Christine pulled into the driveway, parking beside Chris's pickup. Brian hurried around to the passenger side, opening the door for Christine. He used both his hands to pull her from the car, and she laughed. "I hope this baby arrives soon or Brian will need a crane to lift me out!"

As Lori Anna headed up the walkway, she noted the barn and the pasture behind the house. The white-frame house was small, but charming. *I suppose it might be considered a cabin, or a cottage.* She took in the light blue shutters at each window and the front door painted in a darker blue hue. A colorful Christmas wreath hung on the door. The neatly manicured flower beds held shrubs across the front of the house and down the side toward the backyard. In the front yard the American flag waved on the flag pole with two flood lights trained on the flag. A large circular flowerbed heavily mulched for the winter surrounded the flag pole.

Chris opened the front door for his guests to enter. A nicely arranged living room with a sofa and two end tables along one wall, two recliners with a table in-between facing the television, and a stone fireplace with a raised hearth along the outside wall met Lori Anna's gaze. A framed painting of Fritz hung over the fireplace and a beautiful painting of Christmas Hotel above the sofa. A double picture window provided a lovely view into the front yard.

She followed Chris into the kitchen and her mouth dropped open in amazement. "Wow! I think I've been transported back to the 1920s, or even earlier!"

Chris chuckled while setting the casserole dish on the large antique oak table. "You're not the first person to say that."

Brian chimed in from the living room, after lowering Christine into one of the recliners. "I've offered my help to bring him into the 1980s, but he always says he likes it this way. When was the last time you saw a wood-burning cast-iron cook stove?"

"I don't think … ever. Nor an ice box. Are they both still usable?"

Chris nodded, taking the salad and bread from Lori Anna, and setting them beside the lasagna. "Most definitely,"

Wood, brush, and twigs were neatly stacked beside the old wood cook stove, a pie safe along one wall and the ice box beside it. Opening one door of the ice box, Lori Anna saw milk, eggs, bacon, cheese, ham slices, and other items that would be stored in any refrigerator. Another door contained a block of ice and a bag of crushed ice.

She tilted her head, and her eyebrows drew together. "Where do you find the blocks of ice in this day and age?"

"There's an old general store over in Woodburn, a few miles from here. If they're out of block ice, I buy extra cubed or shaved ice, which I buy daily anyway for cold beverages. Evidently, there are a few others in the community who still use an ice box. However, I don't store much food because I eat most meals at Christmas Hotel, and one or two days a week with my parents at the family home."

Chris looked around the house as if seeing it through Lori Anna's eyes. "This place looks pretty much the way it did at the turn-of-the-century." He nodded his head, and swept his hands in opposite directions. "I want to keep it authentic. How about a nice roaring fire?"

Brian called out from the living room. "I'll tend to it. You help Lori Anna. I'm ready to chow down on the lasagna."

While Chris set the table, Lori Anna peeked in to watch the fire being built. This house captivated her. Brian opened the glass fire doors, looked up the chimney to make certain the flue was open, and then selected brush and twigs stacked near the hearth, making a neat pile in the fireplace.

Grabbing the match box on the hearth, Brian struck a match, and cupping the flame with his palm, he set the brush afire. Down on his hands and knees he leaned into the fireplace, gently blowing until the fire caught. He added more twigs until the fire was ready for a log. After adding the log, he closed the glass doors, stepped back, and nodded in appreciation of his handiwork. With a sigh of satisfaction, he turned around.

Lori Anna, along with Chris and Christine, had been watching him. Christine just shook her head and grinned. "That's my amazing hubby." Moments later, Chris finished setting the table, and the tinkling sound from icing the glasses for the Cokes.

"Time to eat," announced Chris.

Brian pulled his wife out of the recliner and helped her walk, as she waddled to the table. They all held hands while Chris asked the blessing.

Forty minutes later, Chris leaned back in his chair, patting his stomach. "Wow, that was excellent, Lori Anna."

"I second that," Brian and Christine agreed simultaneously.

Lori Anna jumped up and began clearing the table.

Chris grabbed her wrist. "Oh, no you don't. You cooked, so I'll clean."

"Well, I can help, can't I?"

"Let's just put them in the sink to soak in some hot soapy water. We can tend to the washing and drying after the movie."

Christine gave a little groan. "Well, I can't watch the movie until I go to the bathroom for the millionth time today."

"Let me help you up, my *little* wife who exaggerates a trifle."

"Don't get cute, hubby," Christine retorted but with a smile, and punched him on the arm. "It's entirely your fault, anyway."

He smiled wiggling his eyebrows. "Hmmm ...."After helping Christine down the hall to the bathroom, Brian rejoined Chris in the living room. Looking around, he asked, "Where's your girlfriend?"

"She's not my girlfriend. She's a girl and a friend."

"Yeah, right. I've seen you looking at her."

"She's outside checking on the dogs." He turned his back to ignore Brian's comment.

"When are you going to admit you like her?"

Moving into the kitchen, he began washing dishes trying to avoid Brian. Brian followed him and leaned against the sink. "She's too young for me, Brian. Let it go."

"Oh, hogwash. Age is a number. She likes you, I can tell."

"Maybe she's forgotten I'm thirty-two. If so, she'll eventually wake up and come to her senses. She'll look at me and say, 'Oh my, what an old man is Chris Wright!'"

"You're nuts." Brian walked back into the living room and checked out the Betamax. He teased Chris when Chris followed him. "When are you going to arrive in 1987 and buy a VHS recorder? How do you even find movies to rent for this antique?"

"Well, I think the picture quality is better on the

Beta. But yes, unfortunately, I will need to give it up one day. I'm having trouble finding some of the movies I'd like to see, and I really don't have time for movie theatres."

"Aw, you're just cheap."

"Thanks, Brian, but I *don't* resemble that insult."

The backdoor opened and closed. In walked Lori Anna, with Fritz and Bella on her heels. "They wanted to come in. Is it okay, as long as they behave?"

"Sure. Fritz usually winds up asleep in front of the fireplace. Bella will probably join him."

"So what's the movie for tonight, Uncle Chris?"

Chris tapped Brian lightly on the head with the movie tape. "Quit calling me uncle."

Brian feigned injury with his hands on his head and stepped backward, but laughed while doing it.

Brian grinned when Christine wobbled up to him. "Are you okay, honey?"

"I waddle like a duck, my ankles are swollen, and I live in the bathroom. Am I okay? Yes. Am I ready to have this baby? Yes, *again*."

Placing an arm around her, and hugging her to his side, Brian whispered, "Weebles wobble, but they don't fall down."

Christine glared at him. "That's not nice."

"Remember, I love you, dear."

She looked up at him. "I love you, too, Brian. Now please help me back into the recliner."

"Yes, dear." Brian lowered Christine into the chair, and asked Chris again, "What's the movie tonight ... Chris? Did you notice I didn't call you uncle?"

Chris turned around and smiled. "We're going to watch *Back to the Future.*"

Brian claimed the other recliner, leaving Chris with no choice but to join Lori Anna on the sofa. He caught Brian's self-satisfied look, and hoped Lori Anna didn't see it.

Thirty minutes into the movie, Christine announced she didn't feel well. Chris paused the tape.

Brian leaned toward his wife and touched her arm. "Should we head home, honey?"

"If Chris doesn't mind, I'll just lie down in his spare room. It's just some cramping that's been happening on and off all day. I'll be fine."

"Certainly, feel free to use the spare room. Can I bring you anything? I've got a heating pad."

Christine nodded. "Thanks, Chris. A heating pad sounds wonderful."

Chris retrieved the heating pad from his room, handed it to Brian, and Brian settled his wife into the spare room. When Chris returned to the living room, Lori Anna was not on the sofa and both dogs were asleep by the fireplace. He found her in the kitchen washing the last of the dishes.

She turned to him when she heard him enter. "I'm almost done." She threw the hand towel at him. "Here, make yourself useful and dry the dishes."

"It doesn't seem right for a guest to cook all the food and then wash the dishes."

"I'll tell you what. Next week *you* can cook for me on that old iron stove, and I'll let *you* wash the dishes, and I'll dry."

Brian returned before Chris could reply. *Planning dinner together next week sounded too much like a date.*

"How's Christine?" asked Chris.

"She appears to be comfortable, and she insists we finish watching the movie."

"She's just in the next room if she needs you, buddy."

"I know, but she should probably be at home in our bed. She just doesn't want to spoil our evening. God certainly blessed me with the kindest woman and the most unselfish. She's only twenty-one, but so mature for her age." He must have remembered Lori Anna and quickly amended his comment. "Uh ... present company with the same attributes, of course."

"Thanks, Brian. Compliment accepted. I agree that Christine is pretty exceptional. You two have a wonderful relationship."

Brian simply nodded in agreement.

They all settled back in their places, and Chris restarted the movie.

An hour and a half later, Brian growled. "Grrr, I

hate it when a movie ends in a cliffhanger."

"Well, it appears there's going to be a sequel," Chris said in response.

"I wonder how long we'll have to wait," added Lori Anna.

Chris picked up the remote and began the long rewind. A loud moan from the bedroom propelled Brian onto his feet and down the hall before Lori Anna and Chris could move.

Lori Anna's eyes reflected fear when she looked at Chris. "What should we do?"

"I'm calling my mother."

Thirty minutes later, Jerilyn rang the bell. The first thing his mother asked was, "Chris, how far apart are her pains?"

"I don't know for certain if she's in labor. She moaned, and Brian ran to the guest bedroom and hasn't returned."

Jerilyn hurried down the hall and politely knocked. "It's Grandma, Brian. May I come in?"

The bedroom door opened and closed.

"It'll be okay now Mom's here. She's helped birth many babies ... *if* Christine *is* in labor."

Lori Anna settled back on the sofa. "I've heard about your mom and delivering babies. In fact, my mom has told me the story of when I was born. Your mom was there, and assisted Dr. Beasley."

"Really. That's a story I didn't know about my

mom."

"You know your mom is an amazing woman and loved by a great many people in Franklin. She stood by both my adoptive mom Carol Ann, and my biological mom Loretta."

"I knew that Loretta, my brother Ken's wife, was your biological mom. So, why was Mom at your birth?"

"The story told is that when Loretta was in labor, at my mom and dad's home, she wanted Dr. Beasley to deliver me, hand me to Jerilyn, and then Jerilyn to hand me to mom ... Carol Ann. Loretta signed the papers in December 1967, months before I was born, for my mom and dad to adopt me. Your mom was the supporter of both Loretta and my mom. Your mom has a big heart, Chris."

He nodded. "That part, I know."

The bedroom door opened and Jerilyn entered the living room, taking a seat in the recliner. "Christine's in labor, and I think it's going to be a long night. She doesn't want to go to the hospital. She's been planning to have the baby at home with Dr. Gentry delivering. She asked if you'd mind, Chris, if she stayed here. She's just too tired to move."

"Not at all, Mom. Whatever is better for Christine."

Chapter Five

The Long Night

*"Lo, children are an heritage of the LORD: and
the fruit of the womb is his reward."*
Psalm 127:3

Sunday Evening - Monday Morning

Chris looked to his mom, whom he completely trusted in this situation. "Should we call Dr. Gentry?" asked Chris.

"You should tell him she's in labor, I'm with her, and the pains are presently seventeen minutes apart." With that said, Jerilyn returned to Christine and Brian.

Chris punched in the phone number. "Hello?" the lady on the other end of the line responded.

"Hi, Mrs. Gentry, this is Chris Wright. Is Dr. Gentry at home?"

"No, he's not, Chris. Dr. Evans is on call for him this weekend."

"Thank you, Mrs. Gentry."

When he tried Dr. Evans, he found he was at Vanderbilt Hospital delivering another baby.

He relayed the information to his mom. "Call Dr. Beasley, Chris, and see if he will come. Although he's retired, he's been a family friend for many years."

"Hi ... Mrs. Beasley?"

"Yes."

"This is Chris Wright. Is Dr. Beasley home?"

"No, Chris, he isn't. Is everything okay?"

"Well, Christine Demeter is presently in my spare bedroom, and apparently in labor. However, Mom is with her – and Brian, too. Dr. Gentry and Dr. Evans are both out of town."

"Do you know how far apart her pains are?"

"Mom said seventeen minutes."

"Well, Christine has quite a ways to go. No need to move her, so let her stay in your spare bedroom, if that's convenient. I'll try to reach Dr. Beasley on his car phone and let him know. He's out to dinner with colleagues, but he should be finished and back in his car within the hour. If not, I'll call the restaurant and ask for him. If Christine's pains get to be seven minutes apart, call here again. Or call if Jerilyn suspects any problem. Your mom has been a midwife or aid many times during births. No need to worry. And tell Brian to stay calm." She laughed, obviously knowing the fears of expectant fathers and especially first fathers. Dr. Beasley had probably delivered more babies than they all could count.

"Thanks, Mrs. Beasley."

"You're welcome, Chris."

They hung up, and Chris turned to Lori Anna, relaying the information. "It looks like it's going to be a long night. If you need to leave, I'll call you in the morning when the baby arrives."

"If you don't mind, I want to stay. This is exciting. A new life born here tonight. One of God's miracles."

"Good! And anyway I'd appreciate the company."

Chris's next call was to Mr. Hanover to trade shifts with him on Monday. Like Lori Anna, he wanted to be a part of this evening. After all, this would be his great-nephew or great-niece. "I suppose I'd better update Mom on the doctors." He knocked on the door and passed on the news.

"Thanks, Chris. Next, you need to call Lily and John. They're visiting John's family in Middletown, Ohio, but they'll still want to know their grandchild is on the way." She reached in her purse and handed him her booklet of phone numbers. "Also, call your father. Tell him to just stay home and hold down the fort in case any family members call for updates. Maybe you could suggest he make some calls to inform the out-of-town family."

"I'll take care of it, Mom."

Returning to the living room, he picked up the phone, called Lily, and explained the situation.

"Oh, Chris, please tell Brian and Christine that John and I will leave in the morning at first light, and we should be home by late morning. "We'll be grandparents!"

When he hung up from Lily, Lori Anna asked, "What about Christine's family? Don't you want to call them?"

Chris bit his lower lip and shook his head. "They died in a car crash three years ago, around the time she met Brian. She has no siblings. We're her only family."

"Oh," was Lori Anna's only response, but sadness appeared in her eyes along with a wrinkling of her forehead and a trembling of her lips.

If one really could peer into another's soul through the eyes, Chris knew what he would see in Lori Anna's soul. *She's beautiful inside and out.*

Throughout the night, Jerilyn walked Christine several times up and down the hall, and drawing her a warm bath on one occasion. Brian rarely left his wife's side. Chris brewed a pot of coffee, and kept their mugs full.

One of the times Lori Anna and Chris were alone, Lori Anna looked closely at him. "Tell me more about your home," she said, sweeping her hand around the room.

"What would you like to know about it?"

"Well …" and she looked toward the kitchen. "Most of your home is modern, although I haven't seen the bedrooms or the bathroom, but the kitchen … My goodness, I feel as if I'm in a time warp. I need to know the story behind this house ... especially why you've maintained the old-fashion look. I'm just curious."

He laughed. "There's a story behind this house. Events took place here before I was born."

Fritz woke up and lumbered toward him. He sat while Chris scratched him behind the ears.

"What kind of events?"

"Well, first of all, this house sat empty thirty or more years, before I bought it eight years ago. It was in pretty bad shape when I first looked at it, but I knew from the moment I saw it I wanted it, especially because of my sister Lydia Grace's fondness for this house."

Cocking her head, and drawing her eyebrows together in a puzzled expression, Lori Anna said, "Now I'm even more intrigued. Lydia Grace and her husband are famous concert pianists, known the world over. Why this particular house?"

"Okay, well, it appears we have plenty of time for me to tell you the story. I think this baby might wait at least a few more hours to appear. At least, that's what Mom says about first babies. Maybe we'd better let the dogs out first."

Bella had now awakened, too, and sat in front of Lori Anna, wagging her tail and barking once.

"I'll let them out, Chris, while you see if we need more coffee perked."

When Lori Anna returned, she said, "I need to visit

your bathroom. Which door?"

"First door on the left."

When she rejoined him, he handed her a fresh mug of coffee. "Okay ... old-fashioned bathroom, too. There are claw feet on the tub and a pull chain for the toilet."

Chris laughed. "Let's sit down. I'm sure the dogs will let us know when they want back in."

They settled back on the sofa. Lori Anna removed her shoes, tucking her legs underneath her.

"Lydia Grace was kidnapped at birth."

An audible gasp escaped from Lori Anna. "I never knew. That's one story that must not have circulated in our small town."

"It did for a while, and then died down. I won't go into all the details, but back to this house. Lydia Grace was only eight years old when an angel who protected her brought her to this house."

Her eyes rounded in surprise. "How do you know it was an angel?"

"Good question. Keep in mind this happened before I was born, so I'm only going on hearsay. Mysterious things happened around this angel. Such as, when he brought Lydia Grace to my parents at Christmas Hotel. Before my parents knew she was their long lost daughter, he drove a wagon pulled by a horse."

"That was probably in the early to mid-fifties ... right?"

"That's true."

"A horse and wagon wouldn't be so uncommon in a farm town back then."

"No, that's not what was mysterious. After he dropped her off at Christmas Hotel, my parents ran out the door to tell him something. But within less than a minute, he and the horse and wagon had vanished."

Her eyebrows shot up. "Oh."

"Yes. Also, before dropping her off at the hotel, he'd brought her to this house to feed her. Lydia Grace said the house was well-kept, and appeared to be lived in. When my parents, brother, and sisters came here to visit the man a few weeks later to thank him, the house was in a state of deterioration, and it gave the impression of being abandoned for years."

"My, what a story. What did Lydia Grace say when you bought this house?"

"She was thrilled. In fact, when she and Jacob, her husband, are in town, they often spend the night in the guest bedroom. I decided to repair the house and leave some of the interior, like the bathroom and kitchen, the way Lydia Grace saw it the first time. I'm used to it and comfortable here. Maybe because of room number seven at Christmas Hotel, I like old-fashioned décor."

"My parents told me about room number seven. It was in that room they signed the papers to adopt me. I'd love to see it sometime," she said, with a wide-eyed and obviously expectant look on her face.

"I think that can be arranged. I *am* the manager,

you know."

A scratching sound at the backdoor interrupted the conversation.

"I do believe our *kids* want in," said Lori Anna.

"I'll get them. You look far too comfortable to have to get up."

She glanced down at her stockinged feet. "You're right."

Three hours later, the dogs were asleep again in front of the fireplace, and Lori Anna was asleep with her head on Chris's shoulder. Chris was also asleep, with one arm around Lori Anna, and his head resting on her head when he became aware of a light knock at the front door. Brian opened it for Dr. Beasley. Lori Anna didn't move even when Chris gently removed his arm and laid her down on the sofa. He removed the afghan on the back of the sofa and covered her. The dogs raised their heads, but Chris quieted them with his hand in the stop position and told them to stay.

Brian was already walking Dr. Beasley back to the bedroom. Chris whispered to them, "Is there anything I can get?"

Dr. Beasley whispered back, "You can find something to bathe the baby in, and heat some warm water for his or her first bath. An old quilt will come in handy to cover the bed."

Two hours later, Lori Anna awakened to the baby's

cry. She sat up, rubbed her eyes, and smiled at Chris. "I hear the baby."

"Yes, sleepy head. Dr. Beasley has been here for two hours."

"I don't even remember falling asleep."

"Actually, I awakened when Dr. Beasley arrived. We were both asleep. We're both pitiful. We couldn't stay awake."

Brian entered the living room, all excited. "I've bathed my son for the first time!"

"Congratulations, Brian," said Chris, slapping him on the back.

"How's Christine?" asked Lori Anna.

"Tired, but very happy. I need pictures, Chris. As soon as Grandma finishes washing Christine and brushing her hair, would you do me the honor of taking some pictures?"

"I'd be happy to commemorate this blessed occasion for you and Christine. Does he have a name?"

"We said if he was a boy we'd call him Nicholas Adam Demeter."

Lori Anna nodded and hugged Brian. "Beautiful name, Brian." Dr. Beasley opened the door. "I think Jerilyn has Christine ready for visitors."

Brian shook his hand, "Thank you, Dr. Beasley. You're probably the only doctor in the country who would deliver a baby at home, while retired."

"It was my pleasure, Brian. Call and make an

appointment for Christine and your son at Dr. Gentry's office on Tuesday. He'll want to check Nicholas more thoroughly."

Chris and Lori Anna retrieved their cameras – Chris's in the hall closet and Lori Anna's in her carrying case by her purse – and then followed Brian into the bedroom. The baby was wrapped tightly in a blanket, but Christine opened it so Chris and Lori Anna could view him.

Lori Anna looked from Nicholas to his glowing mother. "He's so beautiful, Christine."

"Thank you," and Christine caressed her baby's cheek.

Jerilyn was still brushing Christine's hair. "There, Christine, I believe you're now presentable for pictures."

Lori Anna helped pose Christine, Brian, and Jerilyn for the pictures. Lori Anna snapped a few with Chris in the pictures.

"Now let's get a picture of you, too, Lori Anna, with Christine and the baby," said Brian.

"You want me in your family pictures?"

"Certainly. You were here for the occasion, so I want all of us in the pictures. We'll need to bring the dogs in too. They can sit on the floor on either side of the bed."

Between Chris and Lori Anna, plenty of pictures were captured. Lori Anna left at 8 a.m. to get ready for her first class at WKU and take Bella home.

Chris walked them to the car. "Thank you for dinner last night – and staying the night."

She chuckled, "Don't let *staying the night* get around. Remember we're from a small town."

He laughed. "You're right. I'll be very plain with the facts when I tell the story about the birth of Nicholas Adam Demeter. Have a great day at class. Maybe I'll see you in the Christmas Hotel gym in the morning?" He checked his watch. "Wait, it *is* morning! How about tomorrow morning ... which is Tuesday?" He ran his fingers nervously though his hair. He blushed when he saw she noticed his nervous habit.

"I wouldn't miss it." Then she called Bella to the passenger side of the car.

Chris was waiting at the driver's side to open her door. When she was seated, he closed it.

As she drove away, he prayed aloud. "What now, Lord? Where is this friendship going?"

Chapter Six

The Stranger in Franklin

"Trust in the LORD with all thine heart; and lean not unto thine own understanding. In all thy ways acknowledge him, and he shall direct thy paths."
Proverbs 3:5-6

Monday and Tuesday
December 07 and 08, 1987

Chris managed a few hours' sleep that morning, and the Demeter family remained in the guest room. Fritz slept on the rug in Chris's bedroom and whined around 10:00 a.m. "I'm sorry, Fritz. I guess our schedule was a bit thrown out of whack last night."

Pulling on some jeans and a sweatshirt, he let Fritz out the back door. Yawning and rubbing his eyes, Brian walked barefoot into the kitchen just as Chris finished brewing the coffee.

"You're a bit disheveled, nephew."

"No kidding. Becoming a father has worn me out," Brian said as he plopped down at the kitchen table.

Chris laughed. "Don't say that to Christine. She'll likely knock you over the head with a skillet."

"Nicholas has already awakened for two diaper changes and feedings. I handled each changing, but I couldn't handle the feeding. I'm really glad Christine wanted to nurse our baby. I'd hate to have had to run out for formula this morning. My efficient grandma thought of the disposable diapers and bought some on the way here."

"I agree my mom – your grandma – is a very special lady," Chris said and grabbed two mugs, poured the coffee, and joined Brian at the table. "When I awakened this morning, it hit me that Nicholas was born on Pearl Harbor Day. You know Mom's first husband was killed that day during the attack."

"I forgot. Maybe having her first great-grandson born on the same day will help ease more of the pain of the memory."

Chris checked his watch. "I need to get showered and head to work. Mr. Hanover will be getting off at one o'clock and I'll be relieving him. Mom and Dad are taking today off. I want you and Christine to stay as long as you like. Oh, and feel free to cook some breakfast."

"Cook on your wood-burning stove? I don't think so." He laughed. "But thanks for the offer. I'll just get Christine and Nicholas home as soon as they awaken again and cook something at home. Awakening again, probably won't be much longer for Nicholas."

Chris chuckled and slapped Brian on the back.

"Buck up … Dad."

Chris parked his pickup truck on the East Cedar Street side of Christmas Hotel. He jumped out on his side and walked around to the passenger side to let Fritz out. Rounding the corner of the hotel, he abruptly stopped, and Fritz sat at his feet.

Strolling across the square from East Cedar Street, Lori Anna held the hand of a young man around her age. Chris stared, knowing he was being rude, but he couldn't help himself. The well-dressed young man wore a dark trench coat, Fedora hat, leather gloves, and highly polished dress shoes that gleamed in the bright afternoon sun. They sat on a bench facing away from Christmas Hotel. Lori Anna threw her head back laughing at something the young man said, and he pushed her hair out of her face in a gesture of familiarity.

The conversation lasted about five minutes, before they walked back to a new model, deep blue Porsche. For a few minutes the man leaned against the hood of the car with one leg crossed in front of the other, and Lori Anna stood in front of him in conversation. Before getting into the car, he kissed her lightly on the lips, sat down in the driver's seat, and waved goodbye as he pulled away.

To avoid her seeing him, Chris hurried into Christmas Hotel with Fritz at his heels.

Later at lunch, Chris could not get the scene on the square out of his mind. He ordered a sandwich, fries, and a Coke from the dining room, and sat in his office munching and logging guest information on the hotel's computer. His office was directly in back of the front desk, so with the opened door he could see if a guest or someone on his staff needed him.

After feeding Fritz, the dog slept at his feet under the desk. Lori Anna and the young man were never far from his thoughts. "She's not mine. What's wrong with me?" he said aloud, and banged the side of his fist on the desk.

Fritz awakened and sat up, alert to his master. "It's okay, boy," and Chris patted Fritz's side.

*****

The next morning, Chris was in the gym at four o'clock lifting weights. He still had not gotten Lori Anna and the young man off his mind. He finished his weight routine, and jumped on his treadmill just as the footsteps sounded on the steps. Fritz barked once and wagged his tail.

"Good morning, Fritz," Lori Anna said, and knelt down petting him and scratching him behind the ears. Hanging her coat on one of the wall hooks, and setting her small suitcase on the floor, she hopped on the treadmill beside Chris. "Good morning, Chris," she said and flashed a huge smile on her beautiful face. She punched in her warm-up numbers, and began the brisk walk.

"Morning," was all he said in return, and looked down and punched in six miles per hour. Running that hard, he knew he would not be able to converse until he slowed again. That way, he'd finish his treadmill workout before she did.

Twenty minutes later, Chris slowed down, wiped the sweat with his towel, and took several long gulps of water. Lori Anna was still running. He saw from his peripheral vision that she glanced over at him, but he avoided returning the look. He knew he was being rude. *Lord, help me. This behavior is so unlike me.*

He shut down his treadmill, wiped it with disinfectant and clean towels, nodded to her, and headed to the shower. "Come on, Fritz." He saw her puzzled expression in the mirror, but he kept on walking.

When he finished his shower and dressed, she was no longer on the treadmill, her suitcase was gone, but her coat still hung on the hook. *She must be in the ladies' dressing room.* He took the steps two at a time with Fritz at his heels.

After work, Chris knew he needed to talk to someone. With Fritz at his side, he walked to the Wright family home at 210 South College Street. He could always have a heart-to-heart conversation with his dad, and that's what he needed, along with some sound advice.

As he entered the front door, he called out, "Mom, Dad, I'm here."

His mother walked out from the kitchen, wiping her hands on the towel thrown over her shoulder. "Hi, honey," and she raised herself on her toes to kiss him on the cheek. "I'm peeling vegetables to go with a roast for supper. Can you stay and eat with us?"

"That sounds great, Mom. I need to talk to Dad."

"He's out back in his workshop. I've invited Brian and Christine over with the baby."

"Wonderful." He kissed her on the cheek and headed to the back door to walk outside to the workshop, and Fritz followed along.

The building was a converted shed, approximately three hundred square feet not counting the loft. An antique kerosene oil stove heated the shed in the winter, and a window air conditioner cooled the building in the summer. Two extra-large symmetrical windows aligned on opposite walls allowed fresh outside air in during the spring and fall seasons.

Mom filled the window boxes with colorful flowers every spring. Dad had always wanted a woodworking shop, and five years ago he converted and added on to this shed. A huge workbench with shelves and cabinets occupied the space along the back wall. Dad had purchased every woodworking tool imaginable: hammer driver drills, compound miter saws, random orbit sanders, to name a few. Although he mostly made bird houses – not just simple birdhouses, but ones with intricate detail and real cedar planks – his hobby had turned into a small business. His birdhouses were purchased from people in Simpson County and six neighboring counties.

The years managing Christmas Hotel didn't afford much extra time for Dad's photography hobby, so a second hobby of woodworking had been out of the question. However, by his late sixties, Dad turned over more and more responsibility to Chris, so he could enjoy his senior years and spend more time with his wife.

When Chris entered the well-insulated building, Dad was using a circular saw to cut eight-foot cedar planks. Wearing goggles, with popular music from the forties playing from the corner speakers, he didn't see or hear his son. Chris cautiously walked to the other side of the workbench so as not to startle him.

Stopping the saw and pushing his goggles up on his head, Dad smiled. "Well, Chris, what a nice surprise. What brings you over today?"

"I thought I'd spend some time working with you this afternoon. Mom invited me to stay for supper, so we've got less than three hours before we're called to dinner."

During that time, Chris did most of the talking while he and his dad cut wood, drilled, sanded, clamped, screwed, glued, stained, and applied polyurethane to several birdhouses, all of which were in different stages of completion. Five years ago, father and son knew nothing of this process. The man from whom Christopher purchased most of his tools had Parkinson's disease, and he could no longer work with them. However, he was able to mentor Christopher, as Christopher had later done for Chris.

Chris sighed. He had realized long ago that life was one long apprenticeship. He smiled to himself as he thought back over his life so far. *We learn to walk, talk, go to school, begin a career, and if we're fortunate, we marry, and are blessed with children to mentor. Even in our senior years, like Dad at seventy-four, we're still growing through mentorship, and Mom, too. At sixty-six, she's been writing the last few years, mostly, inspirational novels set in Franklin. She's joined and is being mentored by several writers' groups in Warren and Logan Counties. We're never too old to learn.*

While they worked side by side, Chris told his father everything from the moment he saw Lori Anna photographing businesses on the square eight days ago, and about his rudeness toward her in the gym that morning.

"Well, son, I think it's no coincidence you've spent that much time with Lori Anna this past week. I've always maintained our Lord brings individuals into our lives for a reason. I only regret you felt you needed to be rude to her this morning, but I do understand jealousy. I was once jealous when some men flirted with your mom at the train depot's diner where she worked, even though we were not yet dating. It's normal, but rudeness is not. Why don't you ask Lori Anna about the man she met on the square? It may be something quite harmless."

"Dad, that's not the real issue. I have no right to be jealous. Good grief, she's thirteen years younger than me. My feelings for her are wrong."

Dad smiled, and his eyes twinkled in amusement. "If you came here to validate your concern over your ages, it's not going to happen. If you'll remember, your mom is eight years younger than me. Yes, I know the age difference is not as great, but she was twenty when we met and I was raising five-year-old Lily. When your mom and I married, she became a mother to a child just fifteen years younger. My point is, we don't know who we'll fall in love with. Only God knows.

"Your mom was a fragile and broken woman when she arrived in Franklin forty-six years ago. I knew I loved her almost immediately, but I had to wait until she was ready to respond to love again. I sincerely believe to this day that God brought us together. Chris, you have rarely dated over the years. Consider the possibility that God was waiting for Lori Anna to grow up just to become your wife. Trust in Him."

Chris laid his sander down and removed his gloves.

He sighed. "Thanks, Dad. You're right, as always. How did you get to be so wise?"

He chuckled. "Even though my dad died when I was a teenager, I felt the same about him. Your children will someday feel the same about you."

Chris checked his watch. "We'd better get washed up and to the house. Mom's going to have dinner ready, and I don't want to be late for her roast beef, veggies, and cornbread. Brian and Christine are coming with Nicholas. I'll need to take more pictures."

Dad shut off the heat, and he and Chris wiped down the tools, placing them exactly where they belonged. *Orderly, that's my dad ... and my mom. I can't think of two better parents for their five children. I certainly hope Dad's right, and someday I'll be married with children.*

The two men walked out of the workshop together. Christopher's hand rested affectionately on his son's shoulder. Fritz followed the men at a respectful distance, as if he sensed he shouldn't interrupt the comradery of father and son.

Chapter Seven

An Apology and a Date

"Make a joyful noise unto the LORD, all the earth:
make a loud noise, and rejoice, and sing praise."
Psalm 98:4

Wednesday and Thursday
December 09 and 10, 1987
On Wednesday morning, Lori Anna awakened at three, knelt by her bed, and began praying aloud. "Dear Lord, You and I both know there are developing feelings between Chris and me. I'm quite aware he thinks he's too old for me, but I don't feel the same way. After all, my father is eleven years older than my mother, and they've had a wonderful, loving relationship. Chris's own father is eight years older than his mother. Why is age so relevant to so many people? I don't believe that's the way love works. I might be wrong, but I believe You have placed Chris and me together for a reason – at least I hope so.

"If it isn't Your will for us to be more than friends, please let me know. However, if it's Your will for us to be more than friends, please let Chris know, so he'll quit fighting his feelings. Maybe that's why he was so cold to me yesterday. Thank You, Lord, for Your guidance, as always, amen."

Bella waited patiently beside her. "I hear your tail wagging, Bella. Okay, we'll go outside, but I'm not going to the gym this morning. You and I can go for a run outside." She reached up and turned on the end table lamp.

*****

Lori Anna did not show up Wednesday morning for the workout, so Chris was surprised when he heard her footsteps on the stairs Thursday morning. Fritz rose to greet her, wagging his tail.

"Good morning, Fritz. I missed you, too," she said while patting his head. She looked up at Chris, and he set down the weights he'd been lifting. Grabbing a towel, he wiped his face as she hung her coat on the wall hook and set down her suitcase. She turned to Chris. She greeted him in a bland voice. "Good morning, Chris."

Chris was aware she spoke without her normal warmth. Her eyes didn't light up and her dimples didn't do that dance when her smile spread across her face.

She started toward the treadmill, but Chris knew he needed to apologize. He lightly touched her arm. "Lori Anna, can we talk first?"

She checked her watch. "I have a class at eight

o'clock, and then I have an assignment for the paper."

"I just wanted to apologize for the other morning," he said, looking into her eyes and running his fingers through his hair.

"You have nothing for which to apologize," she said evenly, and turned toward the treadmill.

"Yes, I do. Please hear me out. I was jealous. There – I said it. It's not a pleasant subject to admit, but it's true."

She turned to face him. He now had her attention. "Lori Anna, I thought I was beyond jealousy. I didn't know it would rear its ugly head, but it did. I have no right to be jealous, and I realize I have no claim on our relationship." He took a deep breath and let it out slowly. "I saw you the other day in the square with a well-dressed man who drove a Porsche. You kissed him."

Pursing her lips, but looking him square in the eye, she said, "He was someone I knew and sometimes dated when I attended the University of Louisville. Collin Anderson is a spoiled immature young man who's been given everything by his daddy. He's in his last year at the university, and will go onto law school to become a lawyer, like his dad. There's nothing wrong with attorneys, but I think Collin is only striving to please his father. I knew that, after the first date. I should never have accepted other dates, and I think he only asked me out as a challenge because I didn't fall

all over him like other girls. We were definitely *not* an item. He's one of the reasons I transferred to Western."

Cocking her head and smiling that amazing dimpled smile, she cupped her palm on his cheek. "Chris, you have no reason to be jealous. Collin came here to try and win me back. He thought maybe I missed him. The kiss was a farewell, and for the record, *he* kissed me. I wished him all the best. I also told him there was a man in my life ... at least I hoped there was." She dropped her hand to her side. "Is there a man in my life, Chris? Only you can answer that."

A broad smile crossed Chris's face and he didn't hesitate. "Yes, there is."

Her eyes lit up and sparkled. "Good. That matter is settled. So let's get on with our workout. I need to get to class, and you need to get to your hotel management duties."

They stepped on their treadmills. "By the way, after class and after my photography assignment, I'd love for you to show me the famous room number seven at Christmas Hotel. Do you have time around one-thirty?"

"I do, and it's a date."

*****

Nine hours later, Lori Anna walked into Christmas Hotel and found Chris waiting for her.

"You're prompt, Lori Anna."

"I've been looking forward to this visit all day."

With key in hand, they climbed the cherry horseshoe-shaped stairway to the second floor. Lori Anna was used to seeing the elegant exterior of Christmas Hotel, but when she reached the top of the staircase she stopped to stare, as she had never seen the elegant lobby from this vantage point. The floors, checkered squares of black and white marble, were shined to perfection. In the middle of the horseshoe of the staircase stood a life-size model of the Nativity scene, with Mary, Joseph, and the shepherd men, all watching the small babe in the manger. Life-size barn animals surrounded the lovely scene.

The Christmas tree in the middle of the room nearly touched the ceiling to the second floor. As Lori Anna reveled in the magnificence of the tree and the beautiful ornaments, she lifted her chin and viewed the lovely angel atop the tree, smiling down on her in greeting.

Several sofas, high back chairs, and cherry end tables decorated the room, with beautiful oriental rugs in the middle of the furniture groupings. A fire roared in the stone fireplace. Along the fireplace mantel shelf hung at least twenty-five stockings, all embroidered with the Wright family names: Christopher, Jerilyn, their five children, the spouses, and all the grandchildren. The stocking for newborn great-grandchild Nicholas had already been added.

She noticed Chris turn, watching her. Finally he

said, "You're just like all the others, Lori Anna. The beauty of Christmas Hotel never ceases to amaze. That's why my parents will never completely retire from here. They are thrilled with the reactions of the new and repeat guests. So am I."

Lori Anna turned to him, with tears in her eyes. "My biological mother Loretta lived here in one of these rooms before I was born. Do you know which room, Chris?"

"Yes, I do. I was only twelve when she arrived here, along with two other young women, so you could say I knew you when you were in the womb. Would you like to see that room first?"

"Yes, I would," she said in surprise. "I didn't know if it would be empty, especially this close to Christmas."

"It is until tomorrow." He led her down the hall to room number ten and unlocked the door. Holding the door for her, she stepped over the threshold.

She walked around, picking up on the décor. The Christmas theme and colors carried into the room with a wallpaper border of the repeated pattern of the exterior of Christmas Hotel. A cherry queen-sized bed and two matching nightstands graced the space on one wall. Fresh poinsettias were placed in matching green cut glass vases on the nightstands. A roll top cherry desk, dresser, two lounge chairs, and end tables, along with an entertainment center holding a television, radio, and CD player rounded out the furniture.

Lori Anna took in the floor-to-ceiling windows, decorated with heavy gold drapes and a red valance. Another doorway led to a bathroom with an adjoining dressing room. In the modern bathroom, a towel rack held heated towels with CH embroidered on each one in green or red, and the same with the matching his and her robes.

"It's beautiful, Chris. Is this the way the room was decorated when Loretta stayed here?"

"All the furniture is the same. Of course the drapes, towels, robes, radio, and television have been updated. One wouldn't want a television from 1967 with rabbit ears. Also, there were no CD players back then. We did have radios and tape players in every room, though."

Chris walked to one of the night stands and opened the drawer. "A Bible was placed in every room back in 1850 when Christmas Hotel was built. That would have been long before the Gideons placed Bibles in hotel rooms in the early part of the twentieth century."

Taking one last view of the room, she said, "Thanks, Chris. This is special for me."

"You're welcome." He followed her out and locked the door. Placing his master key back in his pocket, he pulled out an antiquated key.

"I've never seen such a key, Chris. May I hold it?"

"Certainly."

She held the three inch long brass key in her hand,

turning it over and over. Finally, she said, "It's very heavy. The number seven has faded. I presume this is the original key to the room."

"It is indeed. You will think you're time traveling again, and even more so, like at my house when you view the room."

She returned the key to Chris and followed him into the room.

Opening the nightstand drawer, he retrieved some matches, and lit the kerosene lamp on the table by the door. Lori Anna surveyed the room by the yellow light. "Wow. This room *is* in a time warp! However, quite beautiful." she commented in awe.

She was aware of Chris smiling as she absorbed the beauty of the nineteenth century room in amazement. She touched the smooth wood of the high oak four-poster bed and the sheer curtain around it; and noted the beauty of the antique marble top oak dresser and attached matching mirror. Next to the dresser, a ladies vanity with a silver tray held a mother of pearl hairbrush, comb, and hand mirror.

"May I snap some pictures?"

"Of course. I knew that would be your next question. As a fellow photographer, we can't resist."

She was already removing the camera from its case. Walking toward the two brocade chairs in front of the window, Chris lit the other kerosene lamp on an occasional table between the chairs. Heavy deep green velvet drapes pooled on the floor from four floor-to-ceiling windows. Centered between the four windows, a set of french doors led to a small balcony. A writing desk with very small drawers and pigeon holes stood against another wall. Lori Anna snapped everything she viewed in the room ... including Chris.

"I've heard some of the history of Christmas Hotel, but would you tell me in your own words, please?"

"I can, but most of this is a canned speech I've heard a thousand times from my parents for the guests. Here goes. Christmas Hotel was built in 1850 by Thomas Hoy and his wife Lucy Goodnight Hoy. They were a prominent couple in Franklin at the time. They desired to build the hotel so people could come here and experience the birth of Jesus Christ every day. In 1883, Captain Jacob Barnabas Bazell and his wife Mary Eve Winters Bazell arrived here with the intent to purchase Christmas Hotel. They brought their twenty-year-old daughter, Carrie Emeline."

"That's the same name as one of your sisters."

"Yes, my sister was named for her. My mom always thought of Carrie Emeline Bazell as a sister from another century. Sometime I'll have to tell you how that connection came about, or I know Mom would enjoy telling you the story. Although she never met the nineteenth century Carrie Emeline, Mom loved her.

"This room was where Carrie Emeline Bazell stayed when the Bazells first arrived one hundred and four years ago. Captain and Mrs. Bazell stayed in room number eight. After their daughter died of pneumonia the following March, Mr. and Mrs. Bazell decided not to change the décor of this one particular room. It became the untouched room at Christmas Hotel – that is until my mother arrived in December of 1941. There was no room at the inn, you might say. The Bazells let her this room which had not been used since their daughter died."

"Amazing story."

After viewing the bathroom, Lori Anna walked out, chuckling.

"What's so funny?"

"It looks like *your* bathroom with the pull chain on the toilet, and the claw feet on the tub."

"Maybe I'm a bit old-fashioned, too."

"That's fine with me, Chris. I like old-fashioned."

They stepped into the hall. After Chris locked the door, she looked up and pointed to the mistletoe above this doorway and above all the others. A couple walked out of room number five and kissed under the mistletoe. Holding hands, they nodded to her and Chris and descended the staircase.

Lori Anna looked up again and back at Chris, offering a strong hint. Bending down to her, he cupped his hands around her cheeks and kissed her gently on the lips. Hand-in-hand and smiling, they descended the horseshoe staircase.

Chapter Eight

A Christmas Wish

"This is the day which the LORD hath made; we will rejoice and be glad in it."
Psalm 118:24

Friday
December 11, 1987
Friday morning, Lori Anna worked out with Chris in the Christmas Hotel gym, and at noon she ate lunch with her mom in the hotel's elegant dining room.

When she entered the lobby with her mother, Carol Ann Stanley, Chris was on duty at the front desk, checking in guests. Lori Anna smiled and waved, and continued to the dining room with her mom.

After they were seated and had ordered their meal, her mom clasped her hands under her chin, resting her elbows on the table, and confronted her daughter. "Okay, honey, out with it. I saw how you and Chris looked at each other just now. Your dad and I also know you've been leaving the house most mornings by four o'clock. I realize you've always been an early riser, but you never left *that* early in the past."

Lori Anna didn't even try to hide her smile. "You know me too well, Mom. Chris and I have been seeing each other casually since December first."

Explaining in detail the meeting in the park, the gym workouts, the joint love of photography, and the birth of Brian and Christine's baby, she saw the pleased expressions on her mother's face.

Their food arrived and she continued. "I've loved Chris since I was a little girl." She stopped a moment to take a bite of her sandwich, swallowed, blotted her mouth, and continued. In between bites, she told a story from years ago. "He probably doesn't remember this story ... but I remember it well. I was six years old and skipping home from school by the square. I was happy, and I remember thinking how much I liked my new first grade teacher, Mrs. Frank. She called me her little dumpling. I didn't know what that meant, but I thought it had something to do with the fact I was so short. I was aware I was the shortest girl in the class. Even the younger girls in Kindergarten were taller than me.

"Two third grade girls walked by me and deliberately bumped me. I was knocked off balance and dropped my 'Benji' lunch pail. I bent over to pick it up, and when I looked up at them they were laughing and taunting me. 'Hey, Midget Girl Lori Anna, the girl without a real Mama and Daddy. Did you know you were adopted? Your actual parents must not have wanted you.'"

Her mom placed her hand on Lori Anna's. "Oh, honey, I'm so sorry. You never told your dad and me that story."

"I know, and I couldn't understand why they were being so mean to me. I cried, and they kept laughing at me. Chris saw me. He was walking toward his truck, but stopped. He must have seen what happened. He yelled at them. 'Get away from her! What's wrong with you two?' They took off running. He placed his package on the seat and returned with a box of tissues. Kneeling down, he used a tissue to wipe my eyes and nose. I was crying so hard, but he hugged me and patted my back. When I finally stopped crying, I started hiccupping. When I was able, I asked, 'What's adopted, Chris? They said my real parents didn't want me. I don't understand. Mommy and Daddy love me.'

"He hung his head, and he didn't speak at first. When he looked back at me, I thought he was going to cry, too. His eyes were moist, and he kept blinking. 'Oh, sweetheart, they were cruel girls. They shouldn't have said that to you.'

"'Is *adopted* a dirty word?' I asked him.

"'No, Lori Anna, it's not. Far from it. It means your Mommy and Daddy wanted you a great deal. They probably love you more than most parents love their children. As far as what it means in your situation, I'm going to drive you home. I know your mommy and daddy are going to want to explain adoption to you. It's their place to do this, not mine.' Chris rescued me that day, and I loved him for it."

"I remember that day Chris brought you home, but all he said was you wanted to know what adoption meant. I didn't know you were being bullied. Why didn't you ever tell me the whole story?"

"I didn't need to, Mom. Chris took care of me. He was my knight in shining armor, and I savored those few moments with him."

"So, honey, where is this relationship leading?" Mom asked, and then took another bite of her sandwich.

"I don't know, Mom, but I do know I've never come close to these feelings with any other boy or man."

"You need to pray about this, dear."

"I have been, Mom."

"The age difference doesn't bother you?"

Lori Anna frowned. "You, of all people, should bite your tongue. Daddy's *eleven years* older than you."

Mom laughed. "I know that, Lori Anna. I just wanted to make certain it wouldn't trouble you down the road. I can see it doesn't. I approve of your choice, and I know your dad will. You have my blessing."

"Thanks, Mom. That means a lot."

They finished lunch just as Chris completed his shift. As they neared the front desk, Chris called out to Lori Anna, "I'm getting off work, and I owe you a dinner. So how about dinner in Bowling Green tonight at the Bistro?" Remembering his manners, "Uh ... hello, Mrs. Stanley. I didn't mean to be disrespectful."

She laughed. "It's quite all right, Chris. Mr. Stanley and I were young once."

Lori Anna leaned over the front desk. "I'd like that. What time?"

"I'll pick you up at six o'clock."

A few minutes before six o'clock, Chris arrived at Lori Anna Stanley's home where she lived with her parents on West Cedar Street, just two blocks from his own parents' historic home on South College Street. Christmas decorations lit up the exterior of the home, and a tall Christmas tree sparkled in the living room window. Seconds after ringing the bell, Mr. Stanley opened the door.

With a huge smile, and an offered handshake, Mr. Stanley greeted him warmly. "Good evening, Chris, and please come in."

Mrs. Stanley came out from the kitchen, smoothing her apron, and then wiped her hands on a towel. "Chris, we welcome you to our home, and please have a seat in the living room. Lori Anna will be down shortly."

They all three waited, making small talk. "How's that great-nephew of yours?" asked Mrs. Stanley. "I know your mother is ecstatic over her first great-grandchild."

"Nicholas is doing fine, but his parents are half-asleep each time I see them."

Mrs. Stanley glanced toward her husband, took his hand, and smiled. "We remember those days quite well. New parents just have to expect at least a couple of months of sleepless nights. You'll experience that someday, Chris."

He nodded. "I sincerely hope so."

They all turned toward the staircase as Lori Anna appeared. Chris stood, raking his eyes quickly over Lori Anna. She wore a long sleeved black dress with black lace at the wrists and hem. Her glorious black hair was swept up and held with her ruby ornamental clasp. A heart shaped ruby gem on her necklace and dangling ruby earrings finished her jewelry. *Of course, she was born in July. It's her birthstone.* Lastly, she stood about four inches taller in her black heels, and she carried a small black clutch purse.

"Hi, Chris."

Her smile took his breath away. "Lori Anna, you're beautiful."

"You look rather dashing yourself."

Removing her coat from the hall closet, she handed it to Chris. As he helped her into the sleeves, he noticed the glance between her parents. It appeared to be approval, which encouraged him. "I'll have your daughter home at a decent hour."

"I know you will, Chris. You two have a wonderful evening," said Mr. Stanley, as he placed his arm around his wife's plump waist.

After placing their order for the Mediterranean tilapia with roasted asparagus and wild rice, they each relaxed and enjoyed the ambience of the restaurant. Located in historic downtown Bowling Green and just two blocks from Fountain Square, the Bistro, a converted home circa 1890s, was a popular place to eat for their many guests from miles around. When not dining at Christmas Hotel, the Wright family spent many enjoyable evenings in this fine restaurant.

Tonight, Chris placed reservations for 6:45, and requested a table in view of the beautiful stone fireplace. Lori Anna's dark brown eyes sparkled in the firelight, and he found himself staring deeply into them. He noticed they contained tiny specks of yellow, but possibly it was reflection from the fire.

He jerked a bit startled when she said, "I hope I don't have a smudge on my face, Chris."

"I apologize, Lori Anna. You couldn't be more perfect. I was just thinking you have lovely eyes, and possess a natural beauty. I like the fact you don't wear much makeup. So many of the women today think they need gobs of makeup, heavy eyeliner, and big teased hair. You're content with what God gave you."

"Wow, you do have a way with making a lady feel

special. I hope you don't say that to all the women you've dated." However, there was softness in her voice and no condemnation.

He paused a moment before he answered. "No, Lori Anna. I've also not regularly dated anyone." He saw the one brow lift, and knew she was unsure of that statement. "Let me clarify. I've been to dinner with a few women, but only one time with each. I found them to be superficial; certainly not one I can see myself married and spending my golden years. I've not found a woman with whom I've been completely relaxed and comfortable ... until now." He stared back into her eyes. "Am I going too fast, Lori Anna?"

She placed her hand over his. "Not at all, Chris."

Following dinner, he suggested they walk over to Fountain Square. "It's such a beautiful evening, Lori Anna, and the fountain is restful to view, and so pretty at Christmastime."

Other couples meandered around the fountain or sat on the benches, holding hands.

"I love this fountain, too, Chris."

"Let's have a seat on that bench," and he steered her in the direction.

After they were settled, he asked, "Christmas is coming soon, so what would you want more than anything this year?"

Lori Anna stared into the fountain for a long time. He wondered what was on her mind. Her face was intense, and she worked her jaw back and forth. She finally turned to him. "I don't know Loretta – my biological mother. I do know she once told my parents she'd never interfere with my raising, and she never did. I've seen her from a distance a few times, when she and her husband – your brother – were at Christmas Hotel. I want to know her, but I don't want to hurt my parents. However, it's been on my mind since I've been spending time with you, Chris. I honestly don't know what to do."

He took her hand. "I know Loretta wants to know you, too. She doesn't speak of you a great deal. Just occasionally, and most likely at the times she's seen you, too. Would you like to know more about her?"

Lori Anna's eyes lit up. "Yes, and very much, Chris." She pulled her hand away, looked down at her lap, now wringing her hands together. "I just didn't want you to think I've been seeing you so I could get close to Loretta."

She looked back at Chris, staring into his eyes. Tears filled her eyes. "I wouldn't do that, Chris. Please believe me when I say I care about you." One of the tears spilled down her cheek.

He wiped it away with his thumb and again picked up one of her hands. "I know you do, Lori Anna, and I know something special is happening between us. Maybe I can satisfy some of your dreams by telling you something about Loretta. Loretta is a lovely lady, and a devoted wife to my brother Ken. They married nearly a year after you were born. They have three daughters. Jenna is the oldest, and she's sixteen. Rebecca is fourteen, and Emma is their youngest. Emma just turned eleven."

Lori Anna's eyes widened. "Wow, I have three sisters. I knew they had daughters when your mom mentioned it at dinner at Christmas Hotel, but I didn't know how many. *Three* sisters, huh. Do they know about *me*?"

"That particular question ... I can't answer. I don't know how much information about you, if anything at all, has been provided for their daughters. You said it yourself; Loretta told your parents she wouldn't interfere with your upbringing. I know Loretta didn't want you pulled in two directions. She wanted you to have everything she couldn't give you when she was single: mainly, two parents to love you. I think she chose well with James and Carol Ann Stanley. I've heard they were thrilled when Loretta asked them to adopt you. My mother said James and Carol Ann had tried many years to have their own child, but Carol Ann kept miscarrying. When they finally decided to adopt, they were blessed with you, Lori Anna."

"Thank you, Chris. I want to meet all of them if I can."

"Now that you and I are seeing each other, you'll meet Loretta, Ken, and their daughters. You'll also need to speak with your parents. I want you with me this Christmas, and not hidden away. Would you like us to talk to them together?"

"I certainly appreciate you asking, Chris, but I need to have this conversation alone with my parents."

"I understand. I just want you to know I'm there for you if you ever need my help."

He stopped speaking as her face changed to seriousness and she caressed him with her eyes. "Chris, I'm glad you didn't choose another woman years ago. I'm glad you waited for me."

"I'm glad, too." He cupped his palm around her cheek and kissed her, not caring as the other couples walked by and saw them.

Chapter Nine

A Mother's Wise Advice

*"He that handleth a matter wisely shall find good:
and whoso trusteth in the LORD, happy is he."*
Proverbs 16:20

Saturday Morning
December 12, 1987

The following morning, the temperature had turned much colder. Chris and Fritz hurried to the truck, drove away from his home on 31 W, and headed to Christmas Hotel. At least it wasn't snowing. Chris pulled into his usual spot on East Cedar Street by the hotel, and watched as Lori Anna and Bella ran up to the truck.

While jogging in place and Bella barking beside her, she waved at him and then motioned for him to follow her into the square. She was so cute in her short white furry coat over her sweatpants, wearing jogging shoes, mittens, and a knit hat with a pompom on top. Fritz was already barking and wagging his tail on his side of the pickup truck, so Chris hurried around to the passenger door, let Fritz out, and both of them took off running to join Lori Anna and Bella.

While running in place, Lori Anna asked, "Do you mind a run around the square a few times this morning instead of the treadmill? I hear it's supposed to start snowing this afternoon, and I want to spend some time outside jogging while I can."

"Not at all. I think our dogs are excited to spend time together, too."

Twinkling lights decorated the courthouse and the trees for Christmas. They passed light poles wrapped with holly and big red bows at the top. Most of the businesses kept their lights on all night. They passed two jewelry stores in obvious competition for Christmas: *Whitley Jewelers* on West Cedar and *Kennedy Jewelry Store* on North Main. Both jewelers' display windows were surrounded by twinkling lights, and filled with sparkling jewelry in locked glass cases. Mannequins of children in bright winter attire adorned the display windows of *Pistols 'n' Petticoats*.

On North College Street they stopped to view the Nativity scene at Franklin Presbyterian Church, and then the scene at the First Methodist Church of Franklin.

In a soft voice, Lori Anna said, "I like the fact some things don't change, Chris. I love these two old churches, and I appreciate the fact they each celebrate Christ's birth with their Nativity scenes each year. They aren't in competition; they each simply love the Savior."

Chris placed his arm around her. "I agree. That's what I love about Christmas Hotel, too. It's changed very little since Thomas and Lucy Goodnight Hoy built it."

Placing his hands on her shoulders, he turned her around to face Christmas Hotel. Together they gazed across the square toward the magnificent structure. With the leaves off the trees, they had a complete view.

"That old hotel is in my blood, Lori Anna. Ever since I was a child, I'd dreamed of managing it. My parents are getting older and can't spend as much time here. I never tire of viewing the outside. Sometimes I feel like a guest when I see the façade of Christmas Hotel. The Italianate style architecture is fitting for this regal hotel. The carving in the stone, where Jesus' birth is a daily celebration, tells the story. Christmas Hotel is a place to worship our Savior. It's never been *just* a hotel. I think of the people who found their Christmas miracle here ... including your biological mother. I'm so happy Loretta chose life for you." He turned Lori Anna back to face him. "I'm falling in love with you, Lori Anna."

Reaching up to touch each of Chris's cheeks, she rose up on tiptoes, pulled his face down to her, and lightly brushed his lips with hers. With their arms wrapped around each other she added, "I've loved you since I was a little girl. I must confess I saw you and Brian from my bedroom window toilet papering Mr. McKinley's tree on Halloween. I thought it was funny, and that's why I told my parents. I'm the one who got you in trouble. I felt sorry for you when you had to do all that work for Mr. McKinley. That's why I helped you clean up the mess. It's probably my earliest memory. I was just past three years old that Halloween, but I've never forgotten."

She laughed, and those soulful brown eyes twinkled, and he wanted to kiss each dimple in her cheeks. *She is so darn cute. It's a wife I'm missing in my life.*

She startled him out of his musing when she playfully slugged his arm. "However, I realized when I grew older your parents were right in disciplining you. I'd handle the situation for my children exactly how your father did with you. You've had good upbringing, and so have I. You've become quite a wonderful man, Chris."

He pulled her close to him, and gave into the urge. Kissing both dimples and then her lips, they both relished a long leisurely kiss, standing under one of the light posts in the dawn of the morning, with the two dogs waiting patiently beside them.

By two o'clock that afternoon, Chris had finished his shift at Christmas Hotel. He dropped Fritz at his home and then headed to his parents' home. He would not be able to see Lori Anna, because she had promised her parents she'd have dinner with them, and she needed to study for finals the following week.

"Hello, I'm here," he called out when he opened the front door, and savored the splendid cooking smells from the kitchen wafting by his nose.

"I'm in my office, Chris," answered his mom. "Come on in."

He found her sitting at her desk in front of her Brother Word Processor, writing another novel. In the past eight years, his mom had written six novels and all had been published. Her novels were fiction, but based on stories about select guests at Christmas Hotel over the years. She called herself the Grandma Moses of writing, as she began writing so late in life.

The people of Franklin loved her stories that now sold around the country, Canada, and the United Kingdom. Chris was proud of his parents for staying busy in their semi-retirement years. He knew several people who retired and just sat. They didn't seem to enjoy their retirement. His parents still traveled to Bellingham Bay in Washington to visit Carrie Emeline and Marcus, and their five children every year for a month in the summer, along with working shifts at Christmas Hotel the other eleven months.

She rose and hugged him. "Thanks for coming to dinner, Chris. It's nice to see you at least once a week. I realize you're busy at the hotel ... *and* with a certain young lady." She raised one eyebrow. It was the look Chris knew so well. She clearly hoped for more information. His mother wasn't nosy, but he knew she wanted all her children happily married. He was the only one who remained single. He knew she'd move heaven and earth to see him settled.

She sat back down, and he took a seat in the comfortable swivel chair beside her desk. She didn't say anything, but waited for him to speak. He stared back, and smiled. "Okay, Mom, Lori Anna and I are seeing each other."

She clapped her hands with glee. "Wonderful! Lori Anna is a lovely girl. Of course, you know how much I love her parents."

"I didn't say we were getting *married*."

"Yes, dear, I know that." She winked at him.

"Mom, let's not rush this relationship ... okay?"

She smiled and gave him that knowing look again and nodded. "I wouldn't dream of even thinking that, Chris. No one in this family would encourage the rushing of a relationship. We all take years before we marry the one we love," she said in jest, then laughed at her own joke.

"Right. How long did you and Dad wait to marry? I believe two weeks?"

"Actually, it was sixteen days." She changed to a sober expression. "Chris, go at your own pace. You'll know if Lori Anna is the right one to be your life-long friend and wife. You'll become friends first, before you fall in love. Attraction diminishes, but true friendship and love do not. Outer beauty fades, but inner beauty will not. Make certain the woman you choose has those qualities. Pray about it. The Lord knows with whom you belong. God bless you, Chris. I love you so much."

"Thanks, Mom. I love you, too."

With a sweep of her hand she said, "Okay, get out of here now and go do your woodworking with your father. I'm going to finish this chapter, and then add the side dishes to our dinner tonight. We're having rotisserie chicken with a baked medley of vegetables, brown rice, a salad, and apple pie for dessert."

"Sounds great, Mom. I could smell the chicken as soon as I opened the door." He stood, and then bent down to kiss her. "I'll leave you to your writing."

Chapter Ten

Hope and Joy

*"Therefore my heart is glad, and my glory
rejoiceth: my flesh also shall rest in hope."*
Psalm 16:9

Sunday
December 13, 1987
Sunday morning at six o'clock, Lori Anna and her
parents James and Carol Ann joined Christopher,
Jerilyn, and Chris at the family's table in the Christmas
Hotel dining room. Chris stood and seated Lori Anna,
while Mr. Stanley seated his wife. When Chris returned
to his seat, he saw that knowing look communicated
between his parents, and then between Lori Anna's
parents, also. *It appears both sets of parents approve
of my relationship with Lori Anna.*

After ordering the dining room's famous weekend
omelets, Christopher turned to James. "I've been
meaning to ask you, how's your brother Louis faring?"

"I suppose as well as expected. It turns out he has a

blockage in his carotid artery. He goes in for surgery Tuesday morning, so the three of us will be in Atlanta for the surgery. At least my brother finally had the tests done. Helen, his wife said he went kicking and screaming when they said he had to have the tests."

Jerilyn smiled and cupped Christopher's hand. "Well, James, that's just an on-going problem with you guys. I have to force Christopher to make doctor's appointments even for preventative care."

Carol Ann jumped in and added while laughing, "You men are just big babies."

James stared at his wife, and with his hand over his chest he feigned pain. "You wound me." Then he laughed, too, and added, "Maybe that's a *little* true. Could be why God didn't let men have babies. We can't stand the pain."

Christopher and Chris simply nodded in affirmation. Christopher sobered his expression. "All kidding aside, I'm sorry to hear about your brother, James. We'll be praying for him. Is he already on the prayer list at church?"

"Yes, I called Pastor Mason as soon as I received the news. He promised the congregation would be praying for him."

The omelets arrived and the conversation changed to a slow grind. "This is what I missed while living and attending school in Louisville," said Lori Anna while slowly savoring her last bite with eyes closed. "Hmmm

... no one makes omelets like the Christmas Hotel chefs."

Christopher leaned back rubbing his belly. "I'm glad I don't eat here every meal. If I did, I'd gain ten pounds a year. Jerilyn would divorce me."

The others just chuckled, and Jerilyn leaned over and kissed his cheek.

Chris loved watching the obvious affection between his parents. He closed his eyes. *I want what they have, Lord.* When he opened them, he saw Lori Anna watching him, and she squeezed his hand. He squeezed hers back, wishing it was proper to kiss her in the restaurant. Someday, maybe, he thought.

Following church, Chris pulled Lori Anna away from the congregation. "Would you and Bella like to spend the day with Fritz and me? I have a tree to cut down and decorate for my house."

"We'd love to ... *and* I need a break from my finals prep. My brain has been on overload. I'll go home, change into something more practical, and be at your house within two hours. Okay?"

"Sounds like a plan. Wear warm clothes and sturdy boots."

Lori Anna headed home and when she had finished changing her clothes, she found her parents relaxing in the living room, holding hands and listening to forties and fifties music on old record albums. She smiled. She loved her parents so much. *Maybe now is the time to have the discussion about Loretta.* "Do you mind if I join you?"

"Not at all, dear," her mom answered. "Sit down. We thought you were going to spend the day with Chris."

"I am, but I wanted to talk to you two first."

She saw the slight smile between her parents and the sly wink from her dad to her mom. "I know what you two are thinking, and you're wrong. Chris hasn't asked me to marry him, although I won't say no if he does." She received huge smiles from both her parents.

"What I want to discuss ... is my biological mother, Loretta." She paused for their reaction. They sat up a bit straighter, and placed their hands in their laps.

Her father nodded and sighed loudly. "Go on, honey, we knew this conversation would be brought up sooner or later. You can't date Chris without thinking about Loretta, and we understand. After all, Loretta is his brother's wife."

Lori Anna inhaled a big breath and released it. "I want to meet her. Chris told me she and Ken have three daughters. I have half-sisters who I want to meet, too."

Her mom took her dad's hand.

"I want you to know how much I love you both, and you'll always be my parents." She looked directly at her mother. "I would *never* call another woman Mom. I'm just curious."

Her father moved forward on the edge of the sofa. "You have a right to be curious, Lori Anna. Please know we would not be jealous of you having a relationship with Loretta and your half-sisters. Loretta is a lovely woman. She gave us the best Christmas present ever when she asked us to adopt her baby still in the womb ... you."

"We couldn't be more grateful to her," added Mom. "Loretta knew it wasn't in your best interest to try and raise a baby, especially under the circumstances by which you were conceived, but you already know about that. We couldn't have been happier when she asked us to be your parents."

Lori Anna rose and hugged her parents. A tear slipped from her eye and she wiped it with her finger. "Thank you so much for being my parents. I love you both so much."

"We love you too, Lori Anna," said her dad with undisguised hoarseness in his voice. His eyes glistened, and her mother removed two tissues from the pocket of her dress, dabbing at her eyes and handing one to Lori Anna.

"Thanks, Mom."

Dad cleared his throat, and in a pretend stern voice, he pointed his finger at her. "You let us know when the young man proposes."

"I will, Daddy."

Mom sniffed and dabbed her eyes again. "You have our blessings, with both Chris *and* Loretta."

Thirty minutes later, Lori Anna and Bella arrived at Chris's home. Chris was in the backyard throwing the Frisbee for Fritz. Bella ran and caught the next one, out-leaping Fritz. Lori Anna walked straight to Chris, hugged him, and stood on tiptoes to accept his offered kiss.

"You look happy."

"I am. I just had the *Loretta* talk with my parents. They were fine with it and had already anticipated the conversation. I have their blessing to meet her and my three half-sisters. Although, I *am* a bit nervous."

"How about I arrange a dinner for all of us at my parents' home, Saturday night? Ken, Loretta, and my nieces are going to stay here in Franklin through Christmas."

"I don't want to put your parents out. I'm sure they have Lily, Carrie Emeline, Lydia Grace, and their husbands and children to entertain, too."

"First of all, my parents love company. Second, my other siblings and their families won't arrive until Christmas Eve, or maybe the day before. We'll have your parents, my parents, Ken, Loretta, and your three half-sisters all to ourselves. It'll allow you time to meet them privately."

"But you said my sisters may not know about me."

"They will before you and your parents arrive on Saturday. Ken and Loretta are driving down from Lexington on Friday, and we'll talk it all out before my nieces meet you." He hugged her again and kissed her. "My only problem is spending Friday evening without you. I'll miss you."

She smiled back at him. "I'll miss you, too. I'm now so used to seeing you every day."

"Well, you'd better show up at the Christmas Hotel gym Friday morning or I'll come looking for you." He released her from the hug. "Let's get the saw and your camera, and go find the perfect Christmas tree."

Ten minutes later, the two of them along with the dogs running after them, traipsed into Chris's woods behind his house.

"How many acres do you own here?"

"Ninety-five. There's ten acres around the house that include the two barns, three large ponds, and the horse pasture; although I haven't owned a horse in the two years since Thunder died. I've been thinking about getting another, though. There's about ten acres of woods on the south side, and the rest is cleared farm land. I don't farm it, but I rent it out to several men who do."

"What crops do they grow?"

"Oh, the usual. Corn, wheat, barley, soybeans, oats, and alfalfa. In some years, they've grown Kentucky tobacco. As you know, Kentucky is known for tobacco,

bourbon, blue grass, and thoroughbred horse racing."
He noted her round-eyed expression, and added,
"Don't worry, I don't indulge in the first two. But I do
enjoy a thoroughbred horse race on occasion, and I
have Kentucky Blue Grass sown around the house."

This gave him another excuse to hug her and kiss
her for assurance ... which he did.

"Okay, let's find our perfect tree, and then I'll use
my trusty camera and capture you cutting it down,
Chris."

"Great. I can add that to my lifetime of photos
cutting down a Christmas tree."

"Oh, there's a pretty tree. It's tall and full."

"Yes, it's so tall it probably would need to bend over
a foot to prevent it from touching my ceiling. Can we
keep it less than seven feet tall?"

"Well, when you're barely five feet tall, it's hard to
judge. How about that one?" She pointed to a tree
about thirty feet away. "It looks so sad."

"Yeah, it looks like a scraggly tree Charlie Brown
from the Peanuts cartoon would choose."

She socked him in the arm and stuck her tongue
out at him. "Okay. So you don't like short and thin?"

"Only if it's you," he bantered back. "How about
that one? It looks around six feet tall and full. It should
fit nicely in my living room."

She was already photographing it.

"I take it you approve?"

"Yes, sir, I approve. Start sawing, Paul Bunyan."

"I think he wielded an ax and had a blue ox, not a saw and a German Shepherd."

"Technicalities. Saw away, so I can get pictures."

He saluted her. "At your service, miss."

Twenty minutes later, Lori Anna was sitting cross-legged on the ground and leaning back on her hands. Chris plopped down beside her, wiping his forehead with his handkerchief. He looked over at her and her pretense of being tired. "Lori Anna, are you comfortable?"

"Yessiree. Whew! You wore me out watching you."

"Excuse me. Are you too tired to help me drag this back to the house?" He playfully chucked his hand under her chin.

"Just give me a minute to put the camera back it its case." Jumping up she asked, "Are you ready, Mr. Lumberjack? Or would you like me to help you to your feet?"

He looked her up and down. "Yeah, right ... all ninety-five pounds of you?"

She flexed the muscle in her arm. "I'm very strong."

He struggled to his feet. "Okay, let's get this tree back to the house and in its stand. You ready?"

"If you're waiting on me, Mr. Woodcutter, you're backing up." She took off walking at a brisk pace, the dogs running and barking at her heels. Chris just shook his head and picked up the cut end of the tree.

*****

With the tree finally straightened in its stand in front of the large picture window, they both flopped down on the sofa with their arms splayed and breathing hard. "I didn't think we'd ever get that straight. Should we cook something, or order a pizza?" Chris asked.

"I want to cook. I'm intrigued by your old-fashioned kitchen, and I've never cooked on a wood stove. Will you teach me?"

"Certainly. Let's check out the pantry. We can decorate the tree after we eat."

She opened the pantry door. "I thought you said you didn't keep your kitchen well-stocked. This is pretty amazing, though it appears your mom has probably been helping. I can't imagine you canned all this fruit and these vegetables. You work too many hours at the hotel."

"Okay, I've been found out." He held up a jar. "This is special spaghetti sauce from the chefs at Christmas Hotel. How about some spaghetti? That's quick and easy."

"Sounds good to me. What can *I* do?"

He checked out the ice box and the vegetable bin. "I've got salad makings, so why don't you toss us a salad, and I'll load more wood in the stove's firebox."

While he loaded, he was explaining. "I also use this cook stove to do much of the heating of the house. I use oak for my wood, and I have plenty of oak trees in my woods. Oak offers a slow, clean burn, while southern pine cooks much too rapidly."

Using a metal tool with a no-burn handle, he moved a lever on the left side of the stove. "This damper controls the air to the firebox, so I can raise or lower the burn. I can also completely shut down the flow of air to stop the fire."

On the stovetop he adjusted another lever. "This lever can be opened, closed, or somewhere in between to send the gasses up the chimney and control the heat in the oven directly below the top of the stove."

He placed the huge pot of water on the stovetop to boil, and added salt and cooking oil. Opening the sauce, he poured it into a pot setting it on the back of the stove, stirring with a long handled wooden spoon.

"Do you bake, Chris?"

"Not much, but I have. I had to learn in the Christmas Hotel kitchen everything in the art of cooking, which included baking." He chuckled. "I decided early on I was not gifted in the art of baking. I left that to my mom and sisters. They're truly talented, and particularly at Christmastime. In fact, when you go to Mom's on Saturday, you'll probably be enticed with Christmas cookies and gingerbread men. My sister Lydia Grace even cooks and bakes in my fireplace. She said one day, when she retires, she's going to teach hearth cooking to anyone interested so they can experience how our ancestors cooked."

"So what you're telling me is I'd better workout double each day this week."

He chucked her lightly under the chin. "More time with me."

"That, I can certainly handle." She frowned. "However, tomorrow evening I leave for Atlanta with my parents. We want to be there with Aunt Helen for Uncle Louis's surgery Tuesday morning." A tear escaped down her cheek. "I worry about him, Chris, but even more for Aunt Helen. Uncle Louis is her rock. They are very close, like your parents and my parents."

Pulling her into his arms, he wiped her tear away. "We'll pray together."

While holding her, he prayed aloud. "Dear Heavenly Father, we thank You for the blessings You have poured out on our families, and the opportunity Uncle Louis is being given at the hospital in Atlanta to correct the blockage in his artery. We thank You that his personal doctor caught this blockage in time for surgery. Please guide the hands of the surgeons on Tuesday morning. We pray for Your strength in whatever outcome You decide. We pray this in the name of Your Son Jesus Christ the Great Healer. Amen."

"Amen, and thank you, Chris."

They both turned toward the sizzling sound. "Just in time, too. The pot's boiling over."

An hour later, they set their chairs back from the table contented. "That was wonderful, Chris. The sauce was perfect and the garlic bread you warmed in the oven perfectly complimented the meal. I definitely need to begin that double workout tomorrow."

"I'll join you in the morning. I end my shift at Christmas Hotel at one-thirty. Will you have time for a second workout around two o'clock?"

"My classes don't end until Thursday for the Christmas break, but I'll be finished tomorrow by then, so yes. However, since I'm missing two classes on Tuesday, I'll need to find time for make-up, especially with finals. Dad will drive us down tomorrow evening, so I can probably get some studying done in the back seat. I can always take a flashlight. Their home is about forty miles north-east of Atlanta in Cumming, Georgia. It'll take about five and a half hours to drive there from here. That should give me plenty of time to make up my Tuesday assignments and complete Wednesday's."

Together they cleaned the kitchen, let the dogs in, and Chris dragged the box of ornaments from the hall closet. Thirty minutes after untangling the lights and replacing burned-out bulbs, they strung the lights, and then Lori Anna snapped more pictures.

"Chris, do you want them to twinkle?"

"I like twinkle. What about you?"

"I do, too." She replaced the one white bulb in each string with a colored bulb, so the lights would twinkle.

Opening a box marked *Chris's ornaments*, she smiled. The one on top said *Chris 1955* on a bright red bulb, and then *Chris 1956* as a fifteen-month-old baby, on a bulb with his picture, laughing at the camera. She counted eighteen "Chris" ornaments, ending with a picture on a bulb with *Western Kentucky University*, dated 1973.

"Mom made all of us kids an ornament for our first eighteen years, until we went off to college. Every year we hung our own ornaments on the tree. When we moved into our own homes, our personal boxes of ornaments went with us. She's done the same for each of her grandchildren, and I imagine she's already created an ornament for her first great-grandchild Nicholas. Actually, most of the ornaments were handmade."

He held up the little stocking ornament that said *Chris 1959*. "This one she crocheted. All the bulbs that say Chris and the date are in Mom's handwriting." He looked through the box and held up a particular ornament. "I really like this ornament. It's a stuffed doll representing me. She sewed this doll, the tablet in the boy's hand, and the lunch bucket in the other. *Chris 1960*," he read. "I was off to kindergarten that year."

"Your mom is an amazing woman, Chris. All the women in Franklin claim her as a friend. She's so loving and kind. My mom has said many times how good she was to her and Loretta when Loretta was pregnant with me. I love your mom for many reasons."

"I agree, she is pretty special. I love her, too. I'll be right back. I need the stepladder to place the angel on top."

After positioning the ladder, Chris asked, "Would you like to do the honors, Lori Anna?"

"I'd love to, Chris." She climbed the ladder, and he handed the angel up to her. He held her waist as she backed down. Setting the ladder out of the way, they stood together to check their handiwork.

"You know, Lori Anna, this is always the best part of any job. I always like to stand back and appreciate the finished project."

She took his hand. "This *is* nice, Chris."

"Yes, it is, Lori Anna."

She tilted her head onto his shoulder, and they enjoyed the tender moment together.

Chris pointed. "Lori Anna Stanley, look up."

She saw the mistletoe dangling from the ceiling light, and she smiled.

Chapter Eleven

A Revelation

*"Thou wilt shew me the path of life: in thy
presence is fulness of joy; at thy right hand
there are pleasures for evermore."*
Psalm 16:11

Monday
December 14, 1987
At four o'clock, Chris was in the gym when he heard
Lori Anna hurrying down the steps. Giving Fritz a
quick rub behind the ears, she said, "I need to develop
these pictures before I work out this morning. I want to
deliver them to the paper before I head to class today."

"I'll help."

Following the workout, Lori Anna showered,
changed, and entered the darkroom to grab the dried
pictures. Chris glanced at one. "That's me, cutting
down the tree."

She smiled. "The editor wants a story about cutting
down a real Christmas tree and decorating it. All the
pictures are of you, Bella, and Fritz. This will be in this

week's *Franklin Favorite*, along with my first story."

"You're getting your own byline?"

"Yessiree, and the first time ever in conjunction with my photos."

"I want to read the article. Do you have it with you?"

"No, you'll have to wait until Thursday when the paper is delivered, just like everyone else."

"Wait a minute. We just did this yesterday. Unless you stayed up all night, it's not written yet."

"Right you are. It's in my head, though. As soon as I get the photos to the paper, I'll sit down and write the story, and then head to class. I won't be able to come back later today for that second work out we discussed."

Chris frowned, clearly disappointed. "Okay, but you can't leave until I get a proper goodbye." He bent down and kissed her. He pulled back reluctantly. "That'll have to do for now. I suppose I won't see you until Wednesday morning."

She placed the palm of her hand on his cheek. "I'll miss you too, Chris," she said softly. "I love you."

He smiled. "I love you, too. I'll be praying for your Uncle Louis."

"Thank you."

He watched her pet Fritz and then run up the steps and close the door.

*****

Following his shift, he again headed to his parents' home with Fritz, and a light snow was falling. "Knock, knock," he called as he opened the front door.

"Come in, Chris," his father called from inside.

He found his parents sitting together on the sofa in the living room, holding hands and drinking mugs of steaming chocolate.

"If you'd like a mug of chocolate, I have plenty on the stove," his mother said, while Fritz took up residence, sprawling across the hearth.

"I'd like hot chocolate, but don't get up, Mom. I'll get it."

When he returned with the mug of chocolate, he took a seat in the recliner across from them.

"Okay, we saw you Saturday evening and Sunday morning at Christmas Hotel, and later at church," said his mom. "This must be very important for us to see you again so soon. I'm not complaining, because I'm pleased."

"It *is* important." He took a sip of the chocolate and set it down on a coaster on the end table. Looking from one parent to the other, he said, "I plan to ask Lori Anna to marry me."

Both parents simultaneously set their mugs on the coffee table and stood. "Congratulations, son," said his father and shook his hand.

"I knew it, Chris." His mother beamed and hugged him. "When will you ask her?"

"She's leaving for Atlanta tonight, and her uncle's surgery is Tuesday morning. I'll see her at the gym on Wednesday morning, but she's going to need to make-up the finals that occurred on Tuesday, and of course she'll have exams on Wednesday and Thursday. I'd like to ask her parents for their blessing, so I'll talk to them Wednesday, while she's in class. I thought I'd ask her to dinner at Christmas Hotel on Thursday evening. That's when I'll propose. So many miracles occurred at Christmas Hotel, and *my* miracle will be Lori Anna saying 'yes', and God's blessing on our marriage."

He turned to his dad. "Of course, I'll also want you to perform the ceremony, Dad, in the Christmas Hotel chapel. After all, it's been a December tradition for all your children ... and you and Mom of course."

His dad chuckled. "December does appear to be *the* month for the Wrights to marry."

Chris turned to his mom and winked. "This family never has been famous for its long engagements, so why should we begin now with me?"

He caught his mom's eye, and she returned the wink. "Mom, would you come with me when I shop Wednesday for an engagement ring at *Whitley Jeweler's*? I want to wait until after I speak with Mr. and Mrs. Stanley. I don't want you choosing the ring. That's *my* job, but you might prevent me making a ghastly mistake. I'm sure you'll know what to avoid."

"I'd love to go with you, Chris."

"With that subject over, I have another request or announcement or whatever you'd like to call it. Lori Anna wants to meet and get to know Loretta and her half-sisters. She's already discussed it with her parents, and she has their blessing."

His dad responded first. "As you know, they'll all be here on Friday. We can discuss this privately with Ken and Loretta. They certainly need to be aware, especially *when* Lori Anna says 'yes' to your proposal. I'm not sure the three girls know about Lori Anna. Loretta and Ken need to deal with this."

"I agree, Dad. I thought Friday would be a good night for the discussion, and I'm hoping this can be decided on Friday, and then Lori Anna and I are hoping we can all have dinner here or at Christmas Hotel on Saturday evening, along with her parents. Kind of a way for all to get to know each other. Would that work for you two?" He looked from one parent to the other.

"It works for me," said his dad.

"And for me, too, Chris."

"Let's all pray now," said his dad. "It's going to be a week with several events that we will all need the Lord's blessing, strength, and guidance. We also need prayer for the Stanley family, as Louis Stanley endures his surgery tomorrow."

The family held hands and bowed their heads. "Dear Heavenly Father...."

Chapter Twelve

The Ring

"Shall not God search this out? for he knoweth the secrets of the heart."
Psalm 44:21

Wednesday
December 16, 1987
Wednesday morning, when Chris heard Lori Anna's footsteps on the staircase running toward him in the gym, he hurried and met her halfway. Hugging her close, he said, "It was so good to hear your voice on the phone yesterday. I'm so happy for you and your family that your Uncle Louis is doing well. I know how relieved you are."

"Oh, Chris, we're all so relieved. Thank you for the prayers."

"You're welcome, Lori Anna."

They both celebrated with a long, loving kiss, until the barking of Fritz interrupted them.

Lori Anna laughed. "I'm sorry, Fritz; I forgot you," and she broke away from Chris's arms to scratch Fritz behind the ears. He returned the affection with a lick on her cheek. Turning back to Chris, she said, "I've got to make this a quick workout. I have a busy day at school today and tomorrow. I won't be able to see you tonight, but I'll see you back here in the morning."

"I'll be here waiting for you."

After Chris's shift that day, he phoned Mr. and Mrs. Stanley and made arrangements to meet at their home in thirty minutes. He rang their doorbell, and they both greeted him. Mr. Stanley shook his hand and Mrs. Stanley welcomed him with a hug.

"It's good to see you, Chris," she said. "Please come in. I've made a fresh pot of coffee and a cheesecake. Would you like some refreshments?"

"Yes, ma'am, I would."

They settled in the living room, while Mrs. Stanley poured from the well-polished silver coffee serving set on her coffee table, and cut everyone a slice of cheesecake. Bella lumbered in from the kitchen, greeted Chris, and then settled on the hearth.

After getting the pleasantries, the thankfulness of Louis's successful surgery, and the discussion about whether they'd get more snow out of the way, Chris got down to the business at hand. He finished his last bite of cheesecake, took a sip of his coffee, and set the cup and the plate and fork on the table beside him. "That's excellent cheesecake and coffee, Mrs. Stanley. Thank you."

"You're welcome, Chris."

Chris cleared his throat and looked from Mr. Stanley to Mrs. Stanley. "I wanted to talk to you both while Lori Anna was in school. As you know, Lori Anna and I have been seeing each other. I realize it's only been a little over two weeks, but in that short time we've stayed up all night for the birth of my great-nephew, spent nearly every morning at the Christmas Hotel gym together, worshipped at church, played with our dogs, chopped down a Christmas tree, and had dinner together several times. In the meantime, we fell in love enjoying basic old-time courting, not much actual dating."

He stopped a moment when he saw the happiness on their faces, and the knowing looks between the two. He now had the encouragement he needed to continue.

"With your blessing, of course, I'd like to take Lori Anna to dinner at Christmas Hotel tomorrow evening and propose marriage."

Mr. Stanley joined hands with his wife. "We have been prepared for this announcement." He looked at his wife and she nodded and smiled. "You have our blessing, Chris."

They all three rose and the two men shook hands. Mrs. Stanley hurried around the coffee table to hug Chris. "I'm so happy you and Lori Anna will marry. I look forward to having you as a son-in-law, Chris, not to mention my best friend Jerilyn and I sharing grandchildren."

"She hasn't said 'yes', yet Mrs. Stanley."

She reached up and hugged him again, and then cupped his face in her palms. "She will, dear. She loves you, too. I've never seen her happier than she has been this month. You, Chris are the reason for her happiness."

An hour later, he met his mom out front of *Whitley Jeweler's* to view the engagement rings. "Do you know her ring size?" she asked.

He pulled a pearl ring from his pocket. "Her mom gave me one of Lori Anna's rings for Mr. Whitley to size."

They entered the store and browsed, while Mr. Whitley finished with another customer. He rang up her jewelry purchase and then turned to them. "Jerilyn and Chris. How nice to see you both. Normally, I only get to see you two in the Christmas Hotel dining room, while I enjoy the best dining in Simpson County. What can I do for you?"

"I'd like to look at engagement rings," answered Chris.

Mr. Whitley smiled at Chris. "Are congratulations in order, Chris?"

"Not yet, sir. I haven't asked the lady. But if she says 'yes', I'll invite you and Mrs. Whitley to the wedding."

"Good. My wife loves to attend weddings." He nudged Chris with his elbow. "I do too, but don't tell anyone." He chuckled softly. "Weddings are supposed to be for the women-folk," he whispered.

Mr. Whitley unlocked a display case and pulled out a tray filled with diamond rings in all shapes and sizes. "What'd you have in mind, and also pricewise?"

Chris examined the rings. "I really hadn't considered either." After a few moments, he said, "All of these rings are beautiful, but I wanted something more personal." He picked up his mom's left hand. "Mom's engagement ring is very old, unique, and also an antique. I always thought the sapphire and diamond setting very elegant. It was given to her and my dad by the Bazells, the second owners of Christmas Hotel. Knowing that my dad didn't have much money, and the Bazells had no living children, they provided Mrs. Bazell's pre-Civil War engagement ring. My dad never replaced it with another ring. Mom has loved this ring. We all love it, because it's special. It's unique. I suppose I want something exceptional for Lori Anna that says the two of us are a couple. I want something distinctive and special, too."

"I have an idea, Chris," his mother interjected. "Carrie Emeline's engagement ring from Andrew was quite extraordinary, with her birthstone and his joined. Lori Anna's birthstone is a ruby and your birthstone is a sapphire. What about the two gems surrounded by diamonds? I think the red and deep blue would look nice together."

Chris's eyes lit up. "That's sounds perfect, Mom."

Mr. Whitley looked at him and frowned. "When would you need the ring, Chris?"

Chris recognized the uneasy look on Mr. Whitley's face. "Uh ... tomorrow ... mid-afternoon."

"That's a tall order, Chris." Mr. Whitley thought a moment and snapped his fingers. "Wait a minute." He hurried to the office behind the store and returned with a jewelry case.

In the case were dozens of rings, but one in particular sparked Chris's interest. It was a ruby, with diamonds framing the gem. "This jewelry case belonged to the estate of the late Margaret Fitzgibbons. The auction of her estate was held last month, and I purchased most of her jewelry. This case holds her rings."

He removed the ruby and diamond ring, along with a star sapphire ring, and held them out to Chris.

While Chris studied the rings, Mr. Whitley continued. "I could change the setting by removing one of the diamonds, and adding the sapphire from this ring which is the same size as the ruby. I can center both gems together, and surround the two gems with the diamonds. What do you think, Chris?"

"I like it, Mr. Whitley, but ...."

His mom must have seen the grimace on his face, because she asked, "How much would it cost, Mr. Whitley?"

Mr. Whitley smiled. "A ring like this could easily sell for above $10,000. However, I received a very good price for all of Mrs. Fitzgibbons' jewelry at the auction." He turned to Chris, "I can change the setting and have it ready for you by mid-afternoon tomorrow. I'll sell it to you for $1,500, and I'll still make some profit."

Chris smiled and shook Mr. Whitley's hand. "It's a deal, sir, and I thank you very much."

"You're welcome, Chris. I hope the lady says 'yes'. And in the meantime, I'll keep your secret," he said with a wink. "Just don't forget the wedding invitation. Oh. I almost forgot. I'll need her ring size."

Chris fumbled in his pocket and retrieved the pearl ring and handed it to Mr. Whitley, who in turn slid it on the jeweler's ring mandrel to measure the size. "Five. She's a little lady," he commented.

Chris nodded in agreement. "Yes, she's petite."

Mr. Whitley handed the pearl ring back to Chris who returned it safely to his pocket.

Mr. Whitley looked up as the bell on his door jingled. When the door opened, in stomped portly Mrs. Huffington, the town's gossip. Whispering to Chris, he said "You'd better leave now if you want it to remain a secret."

Chris chuckled as he and his mom said hello to Mrs. Huffington, and hurried from the store.

Chapter Thirteen

The Proposal

"Beloved, let us love one another: for love is of God; and every one that loveth is born of God, and knoweth God."
1 John 4:7

Thursday
December 17, 1987
Following a quick early morning workout, Chris and Lori Anna headed to their dressing rooms. Chris sat petting Fritz when Lori Anna reappeared, twisting her slightly damp ponytail into a knot on the top of her head and securing it with her ruby clasp. Grabbing her coat, Chris helped her into it.

She turned to kiss him, and said, "I've got to run. Last day of finals, and I need to stop by the paper first."

She had her foot on the first step, when Chris yelled, "Wait! I want to take you to dinner at Christmas Hotel. We can celebrate the end of your finals. Pick you up at five-thirty?"

She looked back over her shoulder with a huge smile. "Yes, I'll be ready. Bye again," and up the steps she dashed.

Promptly at five-thirty, Chris straightened his tie in his reflection in the door glass, and rang the doorbell at her home. Mr. Stanley greeted him. "Come in, Chris."

"Thank you, Mr. Stanley." He unbuttoned his long black cashmere coat, exposing his neatly pressed suit. Reaching in his pocket, Chris withdrew the pearl ring. Returning it to Mr. Stanley, in a low voice he said, "I've the blessing of you, Mrs. Stanley, my parents, and God. I've prayed about this marriage proposal, and I feel peace. I know I love her – and she says she loves me," he added anxiously, running his fingers through his hair.

Mrs. Stanley approached them and smoothed Chris's hair back in place. "Don't be nervous, Chris. Lori Anna loves you, and we're very comfortable giving our daughter to you. I can speak for Mr. Stanley when I say we've prayed for her since she was in Loretta's womb. We have prayed she'd marry a Godly man. I thank Him for answering our prayers."

They turned as Lori Anna descended the staircase. As always, she looked breathtaking. Tonight she wore a strapless, floor-length red satin evening gown, a diamond necklace and matching, dangling earrings.

Chris's chin dropped. "Wow, Lori Anna. You're

drop-dead gorgeous."

"Wow to you, too, Chris. You're quite dashing to celebrate the end of my finals with me." She turned to her Mom. "Thank you for the loan of your necklace and earrings."

"You're welcome, dear. They were a gift from your dad when you were born. Although, I did not birth you, you were always close to my heart, and your dad wanted me to feel like any new mother who would receive a gift from the father of her child."

"Aw, Mom, I'm going to cry."

"Don't do that. You'll ruin your eye makeup, and you look perfect." Mrs. Stanley turned toward Chris, who hadn't taken his eyes off Lori Anna. She laughed and said, "I think Chris agrees."

Chris woke up from his stupor and shook out the cobwebs in his brain. "Yes, you're right, she *is* perfect."

Mrs. Stanley opened the hall closet and grabbed Lori Anna's floor-length black wool coat and handed it to Chris. He helped her into the coat and caught the tear in her mom's eye.

Mr. Stanley stopped them and cleared his throat. "I forgot. Your mom and I want a picture before you leave, to commemorate you two going out to dinner ... uh... in celebration of your finals finished." He removed Lori Anna's camera from the closet. "You'll just need to show me how to use it, dear. Both of you will need to remove your coats. I want to see you in that beautiful evening dress, Lori Anna, along beside Chris in his suit."

"Not a problem, Dad."

After a quick demonstration, her dad snapped four pictures: two without their dress coats, and two with. "Just to make sure I got a couple of good ones." He hugged Lori Anna. "I love you very much. Have a good evening with Chris."

After they were seated at the Wright family table in the Christmas Hotel dining room, Chris asked his waiter, "What's the special tonight, John?"

"Roast duck with a sour cherry glaze. As sides, I suggest roasted potatoes and creamed peas, sir."

Chris looked to Lori Anna who nodded in the affirmative. "Sounds perfect, John. That's what we'll have, and thank you."

He turned back to Lori Anna. "Okay, lovely lady, now that your finals are over, and you already had your Associates Degree, and you're one semester toward your Bachelor's Degree, what will you be when you grow up?"

She laughed. "I honestly don't know. I like journalism. Maybe I'll be one of those television reporters, the next Barbara Walters. Maybe I'll be the editor of a big newspaper in Nashville or Atlanta, or a small paper like the *Franklin Favorite* right here. I honestly don't know, Chris." She stared back at him and said, "I suppose it depends."

"Depends on what, Lori Anna?"

"I don't know. A certain situation, I suppose," and her big brown eyes twinkled in the low dining room lighting. A fire popped and crackled in the fireplace and reflected a rosy glow on Lori Anna's cheeks.

Their dinner arrived, and Chris lost the moment to ask about the certain situation. They updated each other through dinner. He told her about the pending arrival of Ken and Loretta and the girls the next day, and his mother's excitement to see them. She was already making sure the guest rooms were ready, and had been baking Christmas cookies and gingerbread men all day.

John, the waiter, asked them about dessert, trying to entice them with strawberry cheesecake or Southern Red Velvet Cake.

Lori Anna shook her head 'no' and patted her stomach.

Chris smiled at Lori Anna and addressed their waiter. "I think our meal is complete, John. Thank you." He placed a generous tip on the table, signed the check, and helped Lori Anna with her coat. "Are you warm enough to walk across the road to the square with me?"

"I am. Thank you for asking, Chris."

They took a seat on the bench facing Christmas Hotel. "Let me tell you about this bench. It has great significance for the Wright family. It was on this bench my father proposed marriage to my mother nearly five decades ago. Others in our family were engaged on this bench: two of my sisters, Lily and Carrie Emeline." He knelt in front of her, pulled the ring case from his pocket, and flipped it open. "Lori Anna, I love you. Will you do me the honor of becoming my wife?"

Her beautiful brown eyes glistened, and she didn't hesitate. "Oh, Chris, I love you so much, and I'd be honored to become your wife." She pulled off the leather glove from her left hand.

He slipped the engagement ring on her shaking finger, sat back beside her, pulled her face close to his, and stared into her eyes. "You are the one I've waited for all these years. I always wondered why the Lord didn't provide a wife for me. I've wanted to be married for many years. As my dad suggested, He was just waiting for you to grow up, so I could marry you. God knew all along you were the one." Chris stopped speaking, placed his arms around her, and kissed her.

When he released her, she looked at her ring, and wiped her teary eyes. "It's beautiful, Chris, and it fits perfectly. How did you know my size?"

"I guess you could say your parents were in cahoots with me. They gave me your pearl ring to size it at the jewelers."

"Now I know why Dad insisted on taking that picture of us tonight. He knew I'd appreciate the celebration of the evening, and it *wasn't* for the end of finals. I love my parents."

He told her about his mom going with him to *Whitley's Jewelers*, Margaret Fitzgibbons' estate sale, and the ring decided upon.

She looked up into the sky, and said, "Miz Maggie, I will always treasure your gems that created this ring." To Chris, she only offered a long, leisurely kiss.

Chapter Fourteen

Loretta

"And the LORD God said, It is not good that the man should be alone; I will make him an help meet for him."
Genesis 2:18

Friday
December 18, 1987
While Chris finished his shift change with Mr. Hanover, his mom phoned him. "Ken and Loretta and the girls are here. What time will you be home?"

"I'm just finishing my shift-change paperwork."

"Well, I thought maybe we could all visit Brian and Christine before dinner. The five of them haven't met Nicholas. I talked to Christine about the girls staying and cooking dinner with her and Brian. That way your father, you, and I can have our private talk with Ken and Loretta without the girls present. Will that work for you?"

"That's a great idea, Mom. Thank you."

When Chris arrived with Fritz, laughter and

excitement filled the house. Jenna, Rebecca, and Emma swarmed him first. "Uncle Chris!" Hugs and kisses followed, and to Chris the reaction seemed as if it had been years since he'd seen them, and not just since Thanksgiving.

Over the past year, Jenna, Rebecca, and Emma had blossomed into very lovely young women. Chris thought they appeared very mature, except when they greeted him and then Fritz.

"Fritz!" they yelled simultaneously.

Fritz allowed the girls to pet him, scratch his ears, and then he rolled over so they could rub his tummy. Chris smiled. They were three little girls again playing with Fritz.

"What a big baby you are, Fritz," Chris said to his beloved pet. He shook his head. Winding his way around his nieces, he was finally able to make contact with Ken and Loretta.

"How's my little brother?" asked Ken, as he hugged Chris and slapped him on the back.

"Couldn't be better." Chris turned to Loretta and bent down to hug her. "Has my big brother been treating you well?"

She looked up at Ken and smiled. "He's a good guy … when he's asleep," she said, playfully poking her husband in the ribs. Ken hugged her to his side and bent down to kiss her.

The love between the two of them was obvious.

Loretta remained an older version of Lori Anna. Chris realized for the first time how much they looked alike. Not only were they both beautiful and petite with black hair, dark brown and nearly black eyes, and dimples, but they both loved to have fun, and they had sweet personalities. *I suppose the nut really doesn't fall too far from the tree.*

"The dinner is in the oven and will cook while we're gone," said Mom. "I hate to break this up, but we need to get going over to Brian and Christine's."

Chris couldn't resist teasing her. "Okay, Mom, admit it. You look for excuses to see your great-grandson."

"Well, maybe ... just a little," and her eyes twinkled as she raised her hand, holding her thumb and forefinger an inch apart.

They spent an hour, taking turns holding and talking baby talk to Nicholas, and then they had to say their goodbyes.

"We'll pick you girls up around nine o'clock," said Ken.

"Have fun," added Loretta.

As soon as they returned to the house, the roast beef dinner beckoned to them. Chris inhaled the wonderful odors of his mom's cooking.

"I still have cornbread to make, but you can all join me in the kitchen," said Jerilyn. "You may as well start the conversation, Chris, about why we needed a private conversation without the girls."

They all sat around the kitchen table, and Chris began. "First, I'd like to say I'm engaged to be married."

His mom was the first to set down her mixing bowl, wipe her hands on her apron and hug him. "I'm so happy for you, Chris. So it's obvious she said 'yes'."

"Yes, Mom. It's now official."

His dad and brother shook his hand with their congratulations, and Loretta hugged him. "So who's the lucky girl to get my favorite brother-in-law?"

Chris stared at Loretta, smiled, and said evenly, "Do you say the same thing to Lily's husband John, Carrie Emeline's husband Marcus, and Lydia Grace's husband Jacob?"

"Sometimes. Oh such minor technicalities," she said, with a wink, a smile, and a slight wave of her hand.

Chris addressed Loretta. "My fiancée is Lori Anna," he said softly.

She stared back for several seconds. He could tell she was stunned. Finally she blinked and squeaked out, "Lori Anna ... *Stanley?*"

"Yes, Loretta."

Ken placed his arm around his wife. "Are you okay, honey?"

She looked up at her husband. "I'm fine. I just have so many thoughts shooting around my brain." She turned back to Chris. "Don't get me wrong, Chris; I'm happy for you both. You two have nothing but my best wishes. I suppose my main concern is Jenna, Rebecca, and Emma. Ken and I haven't told them about Lori Anna. Of course I've had updates and pictures from Carol Ann through the years. One can't carry a child for nine months and not have feelings for the child. I've just always thought it best to keep our families separate. I've seen her from a distance at times when we've been in Franklin. She looks more like me than my daughters with Ken. However, I've wanted to know Lori Anna for a long time."

Loretta paused a moment and then cocked her head in a thoughtful expression. "Chris, tell me Lori Anna's thoughts. I know Carol Ann and James have told her about me and how she was conceived."

He took a deep breath and exhaled. "Lori Anna loves her parents very much. Regarding her conception, she's of course pleased you chose to give her life, especially under the circumstances. However, her wish this Christmas has been, even before we became engaged, to meet you, Ken, and her three half-sisters. Now we're going to be married, I don't think this can remain a secret any longer. We're all going to be together for family events. We haven't set a date for the wedding, but I want all my family in attendance. I'm hoping we can marry while the family is gathered this Christmas. Loretta, I know I'm asking a lot, but we're going to be family."

Loretta looked up at Ken again. "We must tell our daughters ... and soon, or this will eventually leak out to the girls from some busybody. What are your thoughts?"

"I agree, honey. The only problem I see is that Jenna has always thought she was your first born, and she's going to find out differently." He turned to Chris. "Are you planning a meeting for all of us?"

"I spoke with Mom and Dad, and we thought a dinner here or at Christmas Hotel tomorrow, for all of us to get together along with Lori Anna's parents. My nieces need to be told tonight or tomorrow morning. We must do this before our sisters, their husbands, and all their children arrive for Christmas, and before Lori Anna and I marry." Chris let out a big sigh. "I know this is going to be difficult telling the girls after all these years, but now we have no choice. I want Lori Anna to feel welcome by *all* of the Wright family."

Ken addressed Chris. "She will, Chris. Loretta and I will handle this." He turned to his wife. "I suggest we sleep on this, Loretta, and tell the girls first thing in the morning."

"I just thought of something," said Loretta. "The girls are Lori Anna's half-sisters, but will also become her nieces. They're your nieces, Chris, but they'll also be your sisters-in-law. I'm your sister-in-law, but now I'll be your *other* mother-in-law. Biological, of course.

This is going to be quite confusing!"

This time Mom joined the conversation. "I suggest for the future, we just keep things as if Lori Anna was not your biological daughter, Loretta. After all, she has parents who raised her, and she loves them and they love her. It only becomes confusing if we allow it. However, your daughters may surprise you. This may be quite intriguing to them. After all, another sister for them! Also, I think we should have the meeting here tomorrow evening and not at Christmas Hotel. This is a private matter and should not be told in public."

Dad placed his arm around Mom. "I agree with you, Jerilyn. The Lord will work this out. Let's all pray now."

They held hands and bowed their heads, while Dad prayed. "Dear Heavenly Father, we come to Thee for Thy wisdom and strength. We are really pleased Chris has found the right woman to share his life. We all love Lori Anna, and we know she will make Chris a fine helpmeet. Please supply Ken and Loretta with Thy words when they speak with their daughters tomorrow. We pray this union between Chris and Lori Anna will be a blessing for them, for the Wright family, and for the Stanley family. In the name of Thy Son Jesus Christ we pray … amen."

The others added their amens.

"Let's eat," said Dad.

Chapter Fifteen

A Family United

"Behold, I will do a new thing; now it shall spring forth; shall ye not know it? I will even make a way in the wilderness, and rivers in the desert."
Isaiah 43:19

Saturday
December 19, 1987
Saturday morning, Chris and Lori Anna took their run around the square, along with Fritz and Bella. After forty-five minutes they were breathless, and flopped down on "their" bench, with the two dogs panting on the ground beside them.

Lori Anna removed her left mitten and held up her hand. "I love my ring, Chris. Thank you for putting so much thought into it. We are entwined forever in these gems and our love." She leaned against him for a kiss.

"How did it go with your parents Thursday night when you arrived home?" asked Chris.

"Oh, they were waiting up wanting to hear every detail of the evening. Mom cried, and Dad tried not to show it, but I saw the tear he quickly wiped away. Of course they were enthralled with how the ring came about. It turns out Mom's grandmother and Miz Maggie attended a Simpson County school together, beginning in first grade, back in 1895 at Barnes Elementary School. They graduated high school together, too, here in Franklin. So how did it go with *you* last night, with Ken and Loretta?"

"It went well. Loretta was clearly surprised my fiancée happened to be you. However, she did say she's wanted to get to know you for a long time. Ken and Loretta are going to tell my nieces this morning. We all prayed that the news would go well with the girls. It was also decided we'd meet at Mom and Dad's house tonight, instead of Christmas Hotel. We need the privacy."

"What time do you want my parents and me there?"

"We thought we'd all meet at five o'clock, and then Mom will have dinner catered from Christmas Hotel for us at six. That way, she won't be stuck in the kitchen during the meeting."

Chris paused for a moment, and held Lori Anna's hand tightly. "There's one more item for us to discuss. I'd really like us to marry while my family is in town for Christmas. If we wait too long, not all my family may be able to attend, especially Carrie Emeline, Marcus, and the children. They live so far away up in Bellingham, Washington. I'd hate to leave out any of my family."

"What date do you suggest?"

"How about next Saturday? It's the day after Christmas. We can get married in the Christmas Hotel chapel, and my dad will officiate. However, I have been the photographer for weddings throughout the years. I don't know any other photographers, but you."

"I can get Megan and Amy at the paper to help. My biggest concern is finding a dress on such short notice. I'll try *Jan's Bridal Boutique* on West Kentucky Street. However, it's going to need to be a dress that can be altered quickly. I'll ask Mom to go shopping with me today."

*****

The Wright family was all present when Lori Anna and her parents arrived. Jenna, Rebecca, and Emma approached Lori Anna, and Jenna spoke first. "We are so happy to meet you, Lori Anna. When Mom and Dad told us about you, we were ecstatic. Another sister! You look just like pictures of Mom at your age."

They hugged one-by-one with tears freely flowing.

Lori Anna wiped her eyes. "Thank you so much for the warm welcome. I've wanted to meet you, as soon as I knew about each of you." Over their shoulders, she gazed upon Loretta.

Loretta greeted Carol Ann and James, and then turned to Lori Anna. Hugging her, Loretta said, "I hear best wishes are in order, and I'm very happy for you and Chris. Welcome to the Wright family."

"Thank you, Loretta. I was so worried, so I can't begin to say how happy I am right now."

Ken came forward next to hug her. "Welcome to the family, Lori Anna. I'm glad a woman finally captured my little brother's heart. We were all fearing he'd remain a bachelor all his life." Turning to Chris he smiled and added, "Well done, little brother."

"Thanks, Ken." Chris beamed, and Chris hugged Lori Anna to his side. Lori Anna's parents and Chris's parents stood together, and Chris saw the happy smiles between the two couples.

The dinner arrived from the hotel caterers, and the family of eleven gathered around the festive table Jerilyn had set with the monogrammed crystal bearing the English Wright family coat of arms, the Wedgwood china belonging to Christopher's great-grandmother, along with the Christmas linens and silver candlesticks holding long red tapered candles.

The families held hands so Christopher could ask the blessing. "Dear Heavenly Father, I feel so blessed and honored to stand in Thy presence with my present and future family. As always, Thou knowest for what we will pray long before it happens. Thou knew all those years ago, Loretta and Ken would wed and give Jerilyn and me three beautiful granddaughters. Thou knew many years ago that Lori Anna would become a part of our family. We thank Thee for our friends

James and Carol Ann, who will be joined with our family through the union of Chris and Lori Anna. Thank Thee for loving us and continuing to meet our needs. Thank Thee for Christmas Hotel, where our Lord Jesus Christ continues as a daily celebration. Thank Thee for providing this lovely meal prepared by the amazing chefs at Christmas Hotel for the nourishment of our bodies. In the name of Thy Son Jesus Christ we pray ... amen."

The others answered in unison with their amens.

As they passed around the two steaming platters of honey baked ham, bowls of macaroni and cheese, green beans, mashed potatoes and gravy, buttered peas and carrots, and corn bread, Jerilyn began the conversation. "So, Chris and Lori Anna, do you have a wedding date for all of us?"

Chris took Lori Anna's hand and smiled at her and then his mother. "Yes, we do. If Dad is available to officiate, we would like to be married one week from today in the Christmas Hotel chapel."

He paused for the reaction around the table. All he saw were surprised, but happy faces and nods. "I happen to know the chapel will be available that afternoon, so we thought a four o'clock wedding would be nice, and afterwards we could have dinner in the hotel dining room to celebrate with the guests. We also thought, since it's the day after Christmas, all my family would still be in town. It just wouldn't be the same if any of my siblings, their spouses, or any of my nieces or nephews weren't present. Do you think the chapel will hold us all, Mom?"

"Well, when you add boyfriends of Teresa, Mary Beth, and Ellie, Lily and John will have eleven with Brian, Christine and Nicholas. Ken and Loretta will be a total of five. Carrie Emeline, Marcus, and their five children make seven. Carol Ann and James and you two of course are four, plus Christopher and me. That's a total of … twenty-nine. Then you need to add two more guests, because you invited Mr. and Mrs. Whitley when you purchased the ring. Lori Anna, your Uncle Louis and Aunt Helen will probably want to make the drive up North if they're able. The chapel will seat comfortably about seventy, so you have room for about thirty-five more guests. Are you planning on many more guests than that?"

Chris looked at Lori Anna and she shook her head 'no'. "We hadn't gotten that far, but probably not. I'd like to keep it simple. What about you, Lori Anna?"

"I agree. The guests at dinner afterwards can be our extras. Except – maybe the staff who won't be working that afternoon at the hotel. We could invite them, and some of my friends from the paper and the University of Louisville."

"Yes, I'd like that too. They should all celebrate with us, and the Christmas Hotel staff is like family."

"What about your dress, Lori Anna?" asked Jerilyn.

"I know you and your mom went to *Jan's Bridal Boutique* today. Did you find anything you like?"

"I found a *lot* of dresses I really like. The only problem is having them altered to my size in time. They don't stock size two petite. We can go to Nashville on Monday, but I think we'll just have the same problem," she said with a sad face. "I had hoped you might have a solution."

Jerilyn shook her head. "I'm a good seamstress, but I'm afraid I probably couldn't alter a dress in time."

All was quiet around the table, and then Loretta made a suggestion. "My wedding dress happens to be a size two petite. I know Jenna, Rebecca, or Emma would never be able to wear it, because they take after Ken. Even Emma at twelve is already taller than me. Lori Anna, if you would like to wear my dress, I would be delighted to loan it to you for your wedding. It's been dry cleaned, and it's folded in a box in the back of my closet at home. Ken and I can go pick it up in plenty of time for the wedding."

"Oh, Loretta, thank you. I'd be honored to wear your dress."

"If you'd like to see it, there's a picture on the mantel in the living room of me wearing it on our wedding day."

Jerilyn nodded toward the living room. "If everyone is finished, let's all gather in the living room and Lori Anna can view the beautiful dress Loretta wore."

Jerilyn took the picture down from the mantel and handed it to Lori Anna. "Oh, it's spectacular. It's actually much prettier than all the dresses Mom and I saw today. What do you think, Mom?" She handed the picture to Carol Ann.

"I think you'll look lovely, dear." She turned to her daughter. "You know, Lori Anna, your father, you, and I attended Ken and Loretta's wedding, but of course you were only eleven months old."

Lori Anna smiled. "Well, I suppose there's nothing left to do but ask Megan and Amy from the paper to be the photographers." To the delight of her guests, Jerilyn distributed her homemade Christmas cookies, gingerbread men, and mugs of hot chocolate.

Chapter Sixteen

Christmas Eve

*"Commit thy works unto the LORD, and thy
thoughts shall be established."*
Proverbs 16:3

Thursday
December 24, 1987
After a lovely day full of family events, such as Lydia
Grace's birthday, and the traditional Christmas Eve
sermon by Christopher at the Christmas Hotel chapel,
Chris and Lori Anna discreetly bundled up and exited
from the group at the hotel to head to "their" bench on
the square.

Chris pulled her close to him. "You know this is our
next-to-the-last evening as a single couple," he said,
and kissed her forehead. "Are you overwhelmed yet
with all of your newly acquired family?"

"Not at all, Chris. I love your big family, and soon to
be *my* big family, too. In fact, I asked Jenna to be my
maid of honor and Rebecca and Emma to be
attendants. They bought new dresses yesterday. Also,

Carrie Emeline and Marcus's five-year-old twins Elise and Erica are going to be my flower girls."

"I chose Ken as my best man. It was a hard decision, because my nephew Brian is very important to me, too. Brian told me not to worry, and I *should* choose my only brother. So now we just need ring-bearers, and we need to choose quickly, because the rehearsal dinner is tomorrow evening."

"Speaking of rings, I bought your wedding band today. I want all the girls in Simpson County to know that you're taken. Your mom provided your ring size from your Franklin-Simpson High School class ring. Oh, and regarding ring-bearers, I've got an idea, Chris. I know this is extremely untraditional, but how about Bella and Fritz? We could rig necklaces to hold the rings around their necks. After all, we might not even be together if it hadn't been for Bella and Fritz."

"I like that. Those two dogs belong at our wedding. They're both so well behaved. We'll include them in the pictures tomorrow evening at the rehearsal dinner. Of course, while we're having dinner they'll need to stay in my office at Christmas Hotel. Megan and Amy will come tomorrow and take the pictures for the rehearsal dinner ... right?"

"Megan and Amy both said they wouldn't miss it – or the wedding."

"We also have an invitation from my sister Carrie Emeline to honeymoon at their cabin on Bellingham

Bay in Washington. Actually, they now live in the large Taylor family home. They outgrew their three bedroom cabin on the lake years ago. They normally rent out the cabin, but no one has rented it for January. If we want it, it's ours. We can snow ski, snow mobile, and ice skate ... all sorts of winter sports around Bellingham Bay. What do you think?"

"I say it sounds wonderful. But what about Bella and Fritz? Whether we drive or fly, we probably shouldn't take them. That's a long trip."

"That's solved, too. I told you Lydia Grace loves to stay at my home when she's in town, and she and her husband Jacob, and their son Anthony will be here in Franklin all through January. They have no concerts scheduled until Valentine's Day. They said they'd take care of Fritz and Bella, too, unless your parents want to keep Bella."

Lori Anna was quiet for a moment.

"What's wrong, Lori Anna. Is all this too much?"

"Oh, Chris, not at all. I was just thinking how God worked everything out in such a short time. We reconnected with each other as grownups December first, and look what all has happened. I received my Christmas wish to know Loretta and my three half-sisters. I'm marrying the man I've loved since I was a little girl. I'm getting a second dog to love. I'm going to wear the dress my biological mother wore at her wedding, which *just* happens to be exactly my size, and my three half-sisters will be part of our wedding. Christmas Hotel is definitely a place where miracles happen."

They both turned to the old building at the same time. "Why is that, Chris?"

"I think it's because praying families have owned it since it was built. We all know it's not the building, just like a building doesn't make a church. It's the praying families. I was missing a wife to help me with the prayers over Christmas Hotel." He hugged her.

"As you know, I cancelled all of my classes for the next quarter. I don't know when I'll finish and get my degree, but I will someday. I received my grades in today's mail, and I did have all 'As' on my finals."

"That's wonderful, honey. I'm happy for you, and you must be very pleased."

"I am, but right now I just want to be the best wife possible for you, Chris, and I want to help you with Christmas Hotel."

"Good, because I just want to be the best husband for you I can be, Lori Anna. With that in common, what could possibly go wrong? As long as we have Jesus Christ at the center of our marriage, we can handle anything. I love you, Lori Anna."

"I love you, too, Chris. There's a song I listened to last spring, and whenever I heard it play I would look out my dorm window on the Louisville campus. It's titled 'Somewhere Out There'. There's a line in it that says, 'Somewhere out there someone's saying a prayer, that we'll find one another in that big somewhere out there'. We found each other, Chris."

"Yes, we did." They shared their last kiss on Christmas Eve on their bench, while other couples meandered around the square.

Chapter Seventeen

Wedding Day

*"Wherefore they are no more twain, but one
flesh. What therefore God hath joined together,
let not man put asunder."*
Matthew 19:6

Saturday
December 26, 1987
On Friday, Christmas morning, the two families, some townspeople, hotel guests and off-duty staff gathered for Christopher's Christmas sermon in the Christmas Hotel Chapel. The rehearsal dinner later that evening went as planned, and the two dogs charmed the guests as they made their entrance with the rings on chains around their necks. Brian, after all, was recruited to be part of the wedding, by leading the two dogs down the aisle and removing the rings from the chains to hand them to Christopher when he asked for them. Megan and Amy captured every moment of the rehearsal evening with their cameras, and promised to be back the next afternoon for the actual wedding.

Now on Saturday, two hours before the wedding,

the men gathered in the groom's rooms behind the altar, and the women gathered in the private family room at Christmas Hotel: room number seven. Lori Anna sat at the dressing table wrapped in a pre-warmed Christmas Hotel bath robe, undergarments, her stockings, and three-inch white satin heels, while family members helped her get ready.

She chuckled and commented, "I'm not used to such fuss, but I can't say I don't like the attention."

Chris's oldest sister Lily carefully applied the makeup, and Lori Anna kept reminding her, somewhat nervously, "Not too much. Chris doesn't like women who wear too much makeup or cologne."

"I know," Lily answered each time with patience. "I'll be careful. John's the same way."

Jerilyn filed and painted Lori Anna's nails with a clear, glossy finish. Carrie Emeline and Lydia Grace arranged Lori Anna's long black hair, twisting it up in a braided chignon with baby's breath and a string of pearls carefully intertwined. They left wisps of hair that they curled around her face for a softer look.

Loretta helped Lori Anna into the floor-length A-line strapless white satin dress and the matching lace bolero jacket. A three-inch wide white satin band surrounded the waistline, drawing the appearance of her waistline to appear even tinier than normal. When Loretta added the white satin train trimmed with white lace and white pearl beads, it perfectly reached the hem of the dress.

Loretta and Lori Anna turned to the full-length mirror and locked eyes in the mirror. Lori Anna mentally noted how much she resembled the older woman standing beside her.

Carol Ann gasped. "My beautiful Lori Anna. You are a sight to behold! The dress fits you perfectly." Carol Ann turned to Loretta. "Thank you, Loretta, for your kindness toward my daughter in loaning her the dress. You gave her to James and me all those Christmases ago, and now we are able to give her to Chris. Thank you so much. We are all family." Carol Ann hugged Loretta, and Lori Anna, and dabbed at her eyes with a tissue.

Jerilyn examined Lori Anna up and down. "Your dress is old and borrowed, your shoes are new, what do you have that's blue?"

"I'm afraid I'm missing the blue."

"Oh, no you're not," announced Lily, waving a blue lace garter. "I always bring a blue garter. Later on, my little brother will be taking that off you," she said with a wink and a grin. "Here you go."

"Thanks, Lily," said Lori Anna, blushing as she pulled it up her leg.

Lydia Grace checked her watch. "I've got to head down to the chapel to begin the music. Everyone ready?"

The adult women eyed all the girls in their wedding

finery: the maid of honor, Jenna in her deep green satin dress, and the two attendants, Rebecca and Emma in their slightly paler shade of green satin dresses. The five-year-old flower girls, Elise and Erica, wore dresses in a combination of the two shades of green with white patent leather shoes, and white baby's breath in their hair, too.

"This is going to be another beautiful Wright family Christmas wedding," Lydia Grace commented softly. "We need a journal to keep track of all of them. Remember your cue. When you hear the first line of 'Somewhere Out There', all of you will file down the staircase."

The women and children exited the room to wait in the hallway, and James entered. "All right, everybody in their places. I need a few minutes alone with my daughter."

When everyone was out the door, James sat down with Lori Anna on the two brocade chairs in front of the window. He held Lori Anna's hand and looked around the room. "I haven't been in this room since the Christmas before you were born, back in 1967, when Loretta asked if your mom and I would be your parents."

He paused a moment and then kissed her hand. "Your mom and I waited a long time trying to have a child, but it wasn't meant to be, until Loretta's offer." He paused again to take a deep breath and sniff. "I want you to know we could not have loved you more if you were our own flesh and blood daughter. You are the best gift we have ever received. Your mother and I love you so much."

Lori Anna blinked back the tears threatening to spill and sniffed. "Thank you, Daddy. I love you both very much, too."

He patted her hand. "You have chosen wisely with Chris. He'll make you a fine and upstanding husband, and he'll be a good father to any children with which you two are blessed. I pray for God's blessing on this union. I'm not losing a daughter, just gaining a son."

They stood, and she hugged her father, watching as he discreetly wiped a tear.

"Thank you so much for choosing me, Daddy, and being the best father a girl could have."

His eyes filled with tears.

"Don't start crying, Daddy, or I will, too."

He blinked back the tears and sniffed. In a hoarse voice he said, "I'll be waiting at the bottom of the steps to give you away. You're beautiful, honey," and he patted her hand again.

He opened the door and saw the maid of honor, attendants, and flower girls all lined in the hallway. "Are you all ready?" he asked.

"We are," they chimed in unison. James headed down the cherry staircase to await his daughter.

Lydia Grace sat at the piano, along with her

husband Jacob, and they played several Christmas hymns. Then the first line of "Somewhere Out There" began, and was also sung by Lydia Grace in her sweet soprano voice, and harmonized by Jacob in his baritone.

The cute and tiny flower girls, Elise and Erica, walked the aisle scattering red and white poinsettia petals on the floor. They took their seats on the front row with their parents, Carrie Emeline and Marcus, and their three older siblings: Drew, Angela, and Heather. The twins were followed by Jenna, the maid of honor, who took her place at the altar opposite Chris and Ken.

Only Lori Anna, her father, and her two attendants remained. As Lori Anna finished descending the Christmas Hotel staircase, her friends Megan and Amy were feverishly capturing each and every moment on film. Rebecca and Emma straightened Lori Anna's veil one last time, and then they walked down the aisle, as the last line of "Somewhere Out There" was sung: "Then we'll be together, somewhere out there, where dreams come true."

When Mendelssohn's "Wedding March" began, James embraced Lori Anna's arm in his. "Are you ready, honey?" He kissed her cheek and lowered the veil over her face.

"I'm ready, Daddy."

The two cameras rapidly flashed when Lori Anna

and her father appeared at the door of the chapel. The congregation stood in honor of the bride, and Lori Anna saw many handkerchiefs appear while women dabbed at their eyes. The moment was surreal, and she felt as though she was floating on air, as she lightly stepped to the music and up the aisle on her dad's arm, passing each red and white ribbon draped pew. At the front she stared up into Chris's eyes and softly whispered, "Thank You, God, for allowing my dreams to come true. I have loved this man many years."

She stepped up to the altar while her father placed her hand in Chris's, and James took his seat with his already weeping wife Carol Ann on the front row. Rebecca and Emma straightened Lori Anna's train and sat with Loretta.

Pastor Christopher Wright addressed the overflowing crowd. "Good afternoon, and welcome to this most important moment to date in the lives of Chris and Lori Anna. Chris, as you all know, is the last of my wife's and my children to marry, and I must add that Jerilyn and I are very pleased with his choice of a helpmeet." He paused a moment to smile at his son and then Lori Anna.

He then addressed the congregation. "We are gathered together to celebrate the love between Chris and Lori Anna, by joining them in marriage in the sight of God and you witnesses. This is an opportunity for us to share not only in the joy of Chris and Lori Anna's love, but also to reaffirm and appreciate the love and the friendships we experience in our own lives. Chris and Lori Anna have chosen the intimate chapel at Christmas Hotel in which to be married, because it provides an appropriate backdrop for the public affirmation of their love."

Addressing the couple directly he continued, "Chris and Lori Anna, you should view marriage as a coming together at all levels of being – mind, body, and spirit. A marital commitment includes the willingness to be open and vulnerable, and the courage to take risks. Marriage is a conscious act of will. To successfully remain in marriage you must continually renew your will to be married, and you will need strength, courage, patience – and a really good sense of humor."

He paused at this, as the witnesses smiled or chuckled. Then he continued. "Marriage consists of entrusting our deepest selves into the loving care of another. The spiritual aspect of marriage by placing the Lord first in your marriage must be embraced openly, seriously, and completely for the marriage to endure. Chris and Lori Anna, you must promise to embrace conflict as well as peace; to work as well as play; to struggle as well as coast; to give as well as receive; and to be with, stay with, and move toward one another. So, let your marriage be a time of waking each morning and falling in love with each other all over again."

He looked out toward the chapel entrance. "Brian,

Fritz, and Bella, I need the rings please."

Chuckles and smiles filled the chapel as Brian walked to the altar leading the two dogs. "Brian, you may hand the appropriate ring to the maid of honor and the best man."

Brian removed the rings from each chain and handed them to Jenna and Ken, and walked back up the aisle with the two dogs to sit beside his wife and son on the back pew. Fritz and Bella obediently sat beside them, and Megan and Amy captured pictures of the animals.

Turning to Chris, Pastor Christopher asked, "Do you, Christopher Joseph Wright, Jr., take Lori Anna Stanley to be your lawfully wedded wife, to have and to hold, in sickness and in health, in good times and in bad, for richer or poorer, keeping yourself solely unto her for as long as you both shall live?"

"I do."

Turning to Lori Anna, Pastor Christopher asked her the same question, and she answered, "I do."

"May I have the rings, please?"

Holding the rings for all to see, Pastor Christopher continued. "From the earliest times, the circle has been a symbol of unity, of an unbroken and never-ending commitment of love. Chris and Lori Anna, when you look at this symbol, always be reminded of your love for each other, and the promises you have made today before God and these witnesses."

Handing Lori Anna's ring to Chris, he said, "Chris, please repeat after me: 'With this ring, I thee wed you, Lori Anna. Please wear it as a symbol of our love and commitment.'"

Chris repeated the words and placed the ring on Lori Anna's finger. Lori Anna followed with her words of love and commitment, placing the gold band on Chris's finger.

Pastor Christopher finished with, "May these rings hold the Lord's blessings on this couple and they will continue in love until life's end. May the significance of this moment and the vows and rings you two have exchanged, forever remain in both of your hearts. God bless you both. I now pronounce you man and wife. Chris, you may kiss your bride."

Chris lifted Lori Anna's veil, folding it back over her head, and kissed her. "I love you, Lori Anna, my lovely wife."

"I love you, too, Chris, my beloved husband."

To the congregation, Pastor Christopher announced, "I give you Mr. and Mrs. Christopher Joseph Wright, Jr."

The applause was loud, the congregation threw rice, Brian whistled his enthusiasm, Fritz and Bella barked, the camera flashes from Megan and Amy's cameras were blinding while Chris and Lori Anna smiled, waved, and blew kisses as they hurried back down the aisle toward their future.

Chapter Eighteen

Bellingham Bay, Washington

*"Delight thyself also in the LORD: and he shall give
thee the desires of thine heart."*
Psalm 37:4

Saturday
January 02, 1988
The plane carrying Chris, Lori Anna, Carrie Emeline,
Marcus, and their five children, landed at the Seattle
airport exactly on time at ten o'clock Pacific Standard
Time. A light snow added more to what was already on
the ground. Chris and Lori Anna gathered their
suitcases from the terminal's luggage carousel, and
helped Carrie Emeline and Marcus retrieve the bags of
the five children. Their only son, Drew, at seventeen
was tall and strong, and pulled much of the heavy
luggage from the carousel.

Drew, who was now a high school senior, had plans
after graduation of following in the footsteps of his
father, Marcus, and his biological dad, Andrew, by

joining the United States Army. He dreamed of one day being selected for the Army Rangers. Their oldest daughter Angela, now fifteen, hurried off to bring back two rolling luggage carts, while twelve-year-old Heather held the hands of the five-year-old twins, Elise and Erica.

With the entire luggage loaded on the two carts, the nine of them headed to the vehicle claim area to retrieve the Taylor family's 1987 full-size Bronco. Chris and Lori Anna moved to the rental vehicles to pick out a similar four-wheel-drive vehicle for their personal use while on vacation. Marcus had suggested it, because the Washington roads in January were sometimes treacherous.

With the vehicle rented, Chris and Lori Anna followed behind his sister and her family on the ninety mile drive to Bellingham, Washington. "Chris, the scenery is breathtaking. The snow covered woods and mountains are spectacular. I've never been to the North-West."

"I haven't either, honey. Just think, we boarded the plane in Nashville this morning, flew for five hours, and here we are in Seattle and it's still morning. I thought I'd be exhausted by now, but I'm full of adrenaline. I can't wait to see my sister's home and meet Marcus's family ... and see our honeymoon cabin." He smiled as he squeezed her hand.

"Oh, Chris, I'm so happy we came here for our

honeymoon. I know we could have gone to an exotic island, but I love winter. It's such a wonderful way to spend time with Carrie Emeline, Marcus, and the children. I know you normally only see them at Christmas time in Kentucky. This must be really special for you, Chris."

"It is. All my siblings and I have been so close, even Lily, who's nineteen years older than I am. You'd think Lily and I had nothing in common, but we do, and I love her, and John and their four children. Of course you already know how close I am to their son Brian."

"Lydia Grace helped make this honeymoon possible, too. I'm so thankful she, Jacob, and Anthony could stay at your home and care for both dogs."

He chuckled. "Believe me, she's happy to be staying at *our* home now, taking care of the dogs. I've told you how much she loves that house, and what it means to her. It can't ever be sold. It must always remain in the Wright family, just like our family home on South College Street where my parents live, and my dad grew up. *Oh, look.*" He pointed off into the edge of the woods. "*Two moose and their calves.* I want a picture, but we can't stop. We need to keep following Marcus and Carrie Emeline."

As soon as he said it, Marcus pulled his vehicle over, and he and Carrie Emeline stepped out and closed the doors. Chris pulled over right behind them. Carrie Emeline walked up to him, smiling and shaking her head. "We saw them, too, Chris. We knew you two photographers would want pictures."

Both Chris and Lori Anna grabbed their cameras on the back seat. While Chris and Lori Anna snapped pictures, Marcus provided information. "I don't know how much you two know about moose, but their calves are born in June, and these females are probably pregnant now. The mating season was in October. When these females have their babies, they'll run off these calves. She won't have two different families competing for her attention."

Chris nodded. "We do have a large deer population in Kentucky, and it's a similar mating season, but the gestation period is a bit shorter. We don't have a moose population, though. Obviously your children are used to seeing them because they didn't get out of the truck."

"We told them to stay there," said Carrie Emeline, looking around. "Black bears, cougars, and wolves are the main predators of the moose, and they're prevalent in these rural areas of Washington."

Chris frowned. "But don't bears hibernate in the winter?"

"Most bears do," said Marcus. "However, many of our black bears this close to the coast don't. We should get the pictures and get back to our vehicles. On the way to Bellingham, we'll stop again, where it's safer, and you can snap more pictures."

"You're going to love this other scenic place Marcus will show you. He took me there the first time we came to Bellingham nearly sixteen years ago," added Carrie Emeline.

Just south of Bellingham, Marcus turned onto Chuckanut Drive and pulled over. This time the whole Taylor family exited the truck, and Chris and Lori Anna joined them with their cameras. Marcus used his hand to sweep around the picturesque area. "From this vantage point you can see the San Juan Islands, the Olympic Mountains, the hills and forests of the Chuckanut Mountains, and several bays along the edge of the Salish Sea." He pointed in the direction of each place as he named them.

"Wow, Marcus, this *is* beautiful," said Lori Anna as her eyes feasted on all the sites he pointed out. She and Chris rapidly snapped pictures, only stopping to gently wipe the occasional snowflake from the lens.

Carrie Emeline chuckled. "I did the same thing when Marcus brought me here when Drew was about fifteen months old. We both took pictures holding Drew with the different views in the backdrop. However, it was summer, so we weren't fighting snowflakes on the lens."

"I want to take pictures of all of us," said Lori Anna. She positioned the Taylor family in different areas, along with Chris, and then he did the same with Lori Anna and the family.

"If you'll trust me with your camera, little brother, I'd be happy to take some pictures of you and Lori Anna. You'll want them for your honeymoon scrapbook."

"Certainly, Carrie Emeline." He briefly showed his sister the details of his camera, and she snapped several pictures for them.

Upon arrival in Bellingham, they parked both vehicles in front of Marcus's grand and historic family home. "It's beautiful," said Lori Anna, as she stepped down and closed the truck's door.

The wood-frame house, painted a creamy yellow with white trim and moss green shutters, displayed ten steps that led up to the homey wraparound porch encompassing the home on three sides. Two long rectangular sidelight windows with beveled glass and an overhead transom enclosed the heavy brown wooden front door. Directly above the front door, a walk-out balcony with another wraparound porch adorned the second floor, with another smaller balcony leading out from the third floor.

The front porch held five white rockers on each side of the door, along with many hanging flower pots and several flower pots along the railing around the wraparound porch which was now void of flowers, waiting for the spring planting. Wooden swings painted a deep green hung from the ceiling of each of the side porches.

Chris turned to his sister. "Carrie Emeline, except for the wraparound porch, it somewhat reminds me of our parents' historic home in Franklin."

"That's exactly what I said the first time I saw it."

They climbed the steps, and Marcus kicked the snow off his boots and opened the front door. His parents met them at the door. "Welcome home, children," said his mom as she hugged Marcus, Carrie Emeline, and the five children. Sophie, their Cocker Spaniel jumped up and down greeting them.

"Mom and Dad, you met a much younger Chris at Carem's and my renewing our wedding vows ceremony at Christmas Hotel back in December, 1974. If you'll remember, he took all our wedding pictures. Now meet his new bride, Lori Anna."

"It's a pleasure to meet you, dear, *and* someone my height that I don't have to stand on my tippy toes." They all laughed and Mr. Taylor shook their hands. "Come into the parlor by the fire and get warm. Who wants hot chocolate?"

The twins were the first to yell "me".

"Okay, Elise and Erica can help me in the kitchen and tell me all about the wedding."

Carrie Emeline and Lori Anna joined them. The twins were not much help. They wanted to tell their grandma all about Christmas Hotel, throwing the flower petals in the aisle before the wedding, and their pretty dresses. "It sounds like you girls had a wonderful time in Kentucky."

Elise's eyes rounded, she clapped her hands, nodded, and hopped up on one of the kitchen stools. "Oh, yes, Grandma! We had a wonderful time!"

Not to be outdone, Erica hastened to agree, while climbing on another stool. "Yes, Grandma, Christmas Hotel is really, really beautiful."

"Well, girls, I have to agree. It's a pretty special place. I hope your grandpa and I can visit again one day."

With eleven hot mugs of chocolate loaded on two trays, Carrie Emeline and Lori Anna carried the trays into the parlor with the two little girls bouncing in front of them. Carrie Emeline seated her youngest daughters on a pillow at the coffee table so they wouldn't spill their mugs, placing napkins in each lap.

As soon as Carrie Emeline sat down, Sophie jumped upon her lap, licking her cheeks. "I think you missed me, girl." To Chris she said, "I don't know if you know this or not, but Sophie is a direct descendent of a Cocker Spaniel we had years ago when I was born. Her name was Daisy."

Chris smiled and nodded. "Lily has told me many times about Daisy. She said Dad gave her the dog when she was around three years old. How did you acquire Daisy's ancestor?"

"Do you remember when Mom and Dad drove

cross-country when you were in college?"

"Yes, but that was eleven years ago."

"That's correct. Mr. Tanner who owns that big farm near Gold City in Simpson County bought one of Daisy's puppies back in 1942. Since then, he has raised Cocker Spaniels, and in later years his children bred them. Mom and Dad bought a puppy, and brought Sophie with them on that trip to give her to me."

"This can't be the same dog? She's pretty frisky for a dog that old."

"Definitely the same dog. It must be the climate. I'm pretty frisky for my age, too," and she winked at Marcus, and he placed his arm around her. Drew, Angela, and Heather all groaned.

"Yes, Carem is still very young," said Marcus, and he returned the wink, along with a quick kiss.

Carrie Emeline and the other adults laughed. Carrie Emeline added, "So, just like Bullet's progeny is all over Simpson County, Kentucky, so is Daisy's progeny all around Simpson County; and now all over Whatcom County, Washington. Sophie has had four litters over the years.

"Not to change the subject, but by the way, Lori Anna, you may not remember, but Marcus and I met you thirteen years ago. You were about six and your parents brought you to our wedding at Christmas Hotel when we renewed our vows."

"Yes, I do remember the wedding. It was the first

time I ever attended a wedding, and you were so beautiful. You wore a deep blue dress. However, what I remember later was dancing in the lobby with Chris. I stood on his toes. He was so handsome in his black suit. That was the third time I fell in love with him."

Chris placed his left arm around Lori Anna, and palmed the left side of his chest with his right hand. With a wide-eyed look, and feigning surprise, he said, "Huh, only three times in love with me by age six? *Why, that's unheard of!*"

The adults and teenagers chuckled, and the twins each wrinkled their foreheads in bewilderment.

When they finished the hot chocolate, Mrs. Taylor and Carrie Emeline guided Chris and Lori Anna on a tour of the old home. Mrs. Taylor explained, "It was built in the mid-nineteenth century in the Victorian architecture. We have six bedrooms upstairs on the two upper floors. Mr. Taylor and I use the back bedroom overlooking the garden. Marcus and Carem have the front bedroom with the walkout balcony, and Drew has his own room. Angela and Heather share a room, and Elise and Erica share their room. We have a spare bedroom, but Marcus and Carem thought you two would prefer the cabin on the bay ... by yourselves," and her old eyes twinkled in merriment.

Lori Anna blushed, but Chris laughed and hugged his bride to his side. "My sister and brother-in-law are correct, Mrs. Taylor."

Looking out the window to the back yard, Mrs. Taylor pointed out the gardens. "As you can see, everything is now dormant, but you should view the flowers in the summer from this window. We have two acres, and the gardens are lovely, thanks to Mr. Cramer and his wife. They have been the caretakers for the past ten years after our former caretakers passed away. They also take care of the landscaping and maintenance at the family restaurant, which Marcus and our daughter Sally now jointly own. In fact, if you two would like to head to the cabin to rest and freshen up, Marcus's brothers and their wives and children are coming to dinner at the restaurant this evening. I know they would love to meet you."

Chris checked with Lori, and she nodded.

"We've already stocked the cabin with the basic groceries for you two. Unless you require something special, I think you'll find it adequately supplied."

"Thank you, Mrs. Taylor," said Lori Anna. "That was very thoughtful of you."

"You're welcome, dear. Mr. Taylor and I hope you'll enjoy your honeymoon on Bellingham Bay and come back in the future. We'd like to invite you to attend church with our family in the morning, too."

"We wouldn't miss it," said Chris.

Following the guided tour of the three-bedroom log cabin on the lake, Marcus and Carrie Emeline gave Chris the directions to the restaurant, then left the couple alone. Chris and Lori Anna collapsed on the sofa in front of the fireplace.

Gazing into the fire in the fireplace, Chris took his wife's hand. "They thought of everything, didn't they, darling?"

"They certainly did. What they didn't think of, the caretaker did. He's brought plenty of seasoned firewood into the house, and a load for the back porch. I don't think we'll freeze. This cabin is beautiful. It's much larger than I imagined. I suppose I was picturing a replica of Abe Lincoln's log cabin in Kentucky, not this elaborate, but rustic cabin."

"Marcus and Carrie Emeline lived here until Heather was born. They were outgrowing the cabin and Marcus's mom and dad were getting up in years. Mr. and Mrs. Taylor asked Marcus and Carrie Emeline to move into their home with them. However, they couldn't part with this cabin. It's kept in the family, like our home in Kentucky."

"I've got to get used to saying *our* home instead of *your* home."

"Yes, you do." He kissed his bride, then checked his watch and set it back three hours. "When in Rome, do as the Romans. It's now three o'clock and we don't have to be at dinner until six. We can unpack later tonight." He stood, pulled Lori Anna up off the sofa, kissed her, and led her to their bedroom.

******

That evening, Marcus, Carrie Emeline, and a beautiful, tall and slender brunette greeted them at the entrance of the upscale restaurant on the bay. Marcus made the introductions. "I'd like you to meet my sister, Sally."

Sally hugged Lori Anna and then Chris. "It's my pleasure to meet Carem's family. I hope this won't be too intimidating meeting all these people. Marcus and I have three brothers. They all have wives. My husband Bret is here, and there are many children. In fact, two of our brothers each have two grandchildren, and they're here, too. There are so many in the family wanting to meet you, we needed to gather in the large party room off from the main dining room."

Chris nodded and smiled. "Well, I certainly won't be intimidated by all the people, because I come from a huge family, too. However, my wife is an only child."

"I'll be fine, Chris. After marrying into the Wright family, I'm now quite used to large family gatherings."

As soon as they walked into the party room, the introductions began, with hugs, hand shaking, and laughter. "Please forgive us if we have trouble remembering all the names," said Chris.

Sally laughed. "I should have made them all wear nametags. They're a good bunch. You'll be okay. We saved a window table for you two. You'll appreciate the view overlooking the bay. The outdoor lighting and the snow gives the private dining room an exquisite ambiance. Fresh crabmeat is in season, but if you prefer chicken or beef, it's not a problem."

Chris smiled. "Oh, I'll definitely want all the crab I can eat while I'm here. I don't know about Lori Anna, though."

"I've never had crab, but I'd love to try it."

"Wonderful. I'll place your order the same as the rest of the family. Fresh crabs ... and would sides of grilled asparagus, rice pilaf, and house salads be okay with you?"

"Sounds great, Sally," said Chris, and they both nodded in the affirmative.

Questions were thrown at them by Marcus's brothers and their wives. "How long have you been married?" "Are you staying at the cabin?" "How long will you be in Bellingham?"

Then there were the things-to-do suggestions. "You must spend at least a week of trips over at Mount Baker. It'll be a little over an hour's drive each day, but well worth the trip. There's downhill skiing, cross country in the Salmon Ridge area, snowshoeing, snowmobiling, and sledding. Mount Baker has all the winter sports you can think of."

Carrie Emeline also suggested, "When you tire of all the outdoor recreation, there are several lovely museums in Bellingham Bay and around Whatcom County."

By the time Chris and Lori Anna returned to the cabin, they had their three weeks' stay planned. Well-fed and content, they tumbled into their bed. Unpacking could wait until the morning.

Chapter Nineteen

Home

"Forsake her not, and she shall preserve thee:
love her, and she shall keep thee."
Proverbs 4:6

Saturday
January 23, 1988
After three weeks, they had completed everything on the suggested honeymoon vacation list. It was now time to say goodbye, and return to Franklin, Kentucky, and begin their future together.

Carrie Emeline hugged her brother close. "Come back anytime, Chris." She then hugged Lori Anna. "I love you, Lori Anna. You two are a wonderful couple. We'll see you both at home in Franklin in December."

When their plane landed at the Nashville International Airport, Lydia Grace, Jacob, and Anthony were there with the two dogs to pick them up. Fritz and Bella jumped around for ten minutes in excitement before they were settled enough to get in Christopher's GMC Suburban. It was the only family vehicle large enough to accommodate five people, two dogs, and the luggage.

When they arrived at the Wright family home, and Jerilyn saw them again, she teared up. "I was afraid I might lose another child to Bellingham, Washington. I'm so happy you're home." Her tears overflowed when she hugged them both.

Chris returned the hug. "I'm not leaving you, or Dad, or Christmas Hotel. You have nothing to worry about, Mom. Speaking of the hotel, did everything go well?"

Christopher also hugged them both and nodded in answer to Chris's question. "You had nothing to be concerned about, Chris. All of your assistant managers: Mr. Thompson, Mr. Hanover, Mr. Adams, Mr. Clark, and your mother and I had everything covered. I hope you weren't anxious. I certainly wouldn't have wanted to spoil your honeymoon."

Chris hugged Lori Anna to his side, "I wasn't worried at all, Dad, and I didn't miss a minute having fun with my bride." He smiled down at his blushing wife, and kissed her on the top of her head.

Jerilyn smiled at Christopher before addressing Chris and Lori Anna. "I suppose you two are in a hurry to return home, so we won't keep you. Will we see you for omelets at Christmas Hotel, and later at church in the morning?"

"Most definitely. I won't be working tomorrow, but

I'll resume my morning shift on Monday morning. That will free you both from the hotel duties. Dad can work in his woodshop, and you, Mom, can finish the book you're writing."

She smiled. "Actually, I've finished the first draft, but I need to read through it several times before sending it to my publisher. Otherwise, my editor gets a bit testy. I should have everything completed by mid-February."

"Let me know if you'd like me to read it with a second pair of eyes," offered Lori Anna. "I've had three years of journalism courses, and lots of creative writing. I'd love to help."

"That's wonderful, Lori Anna, as long as the newspaper doesn't have you too busy with the photography and articles. I don't want to take up too much of your valuable time. After all, you two are newlyweds."

"No trouble at all, Mama Jerilyn. I'm always reading at least one book anyway. I do love to read."

"Yes, she does, Mom. Now we should transfer our luggage to my pickup truck and take off." He turned to Lydia Grace, Jacob, and Anthony. "Thank you so much for taking care of our home and the dogs."

Lydia Grace planted a big kiss on her brother's cheek. "You know I love that house, Chris. It brings back poignant, but happy memories for me. Fritz and Bella were no problem at all. We also took down the

Christmas decorations, and we packed them away for next Christmas. We wanted to save you two from as many things to do as possible. I think you'll find the house clean, and the beds made up with freshly washed and ironed sheets."

"It was great having the use of your truck while we were here," added Jacob. "However, we need to leave after church in the morning and fly back to New York. We both have concerts in three weeks, and we need to practice."

Chris nodded. "Lori Anna and I would be happy to drive you to the airport tomorrow."

Lydia Grace patted his arm. "Mom and Dad are going to do that. You two should enjoy your last day off together."

"Thanks again to you both," and Lori Anna added her thanks.

"We'll see you two in the morning, and we'll be back at Christmas time. Maybe there'll be a baby by then," Lydia Grace added, raising an eyebrow and grinning at Chris.

Chris grinned back, winked at Lori Anna, and said, "Lori Anna and I'll work on that just for you, sis."

When Chris pulled into their driveway, they let the dogs out of the truck first. Grabbing two suitcases each, they headed to the back door. Chris set his down and unlocked the door. The lovely warmth of the kitchen stove added to the cozy feeling every time he came home in the winter months. He swung the door wide so Lori Anna could get through with her suitcases.

"You warm yourself by the stove, Lori Anna, and I'll go get the last two suitcases."

The dogs were nowhere in sight when he went out again. He knew they'd probably be gone at least an hour after being cooped up in his dad's Suburban for over two hours.

When he reentered the kitchen, Lori Anna was still warming herself, but she was now seated in one of the chairs with her head leaned back and her eyes closed. He smiled at his beautiful wife. *Thank You, Lord, for blessing me with Lori Anna.* He set down the last two suitcases, closed the door, and walked to her. He pulled off her knit hat, helped her to her feet, and removed her coat.

Dropping both of their coats on the kitchen floor, he drew her close to him and ran his fingers through every inch of her lovely, long hair and kissed her. "Let's unpack later," he said in a husky voice. "The dogs will be gone an hour or more. I have nowhere I want to be, but with you."

"Sounds good to me, and I don't want to be anywhere but with you. I love you, Chris."

"I love you, too Lori Anna." They kissed again. He picked her up and carried her to their bedroom.

Chapter Twenty

The Best News Ever

*"Lo, children are an heritage of the Lord: and
the fruit of the womb is his reward."*
Psalm 127:3

February 08, 1988
Upon returning from their honeymoon, they revived
some of the old routines and also added plenty of new
routines. They took the dogs with them to Christmas
Hotel every morning. Chris maintained his morning
shift, and they both worked out every morning in the
Christmas Hotel gym or ran with the dogs in the
square or over at Greenlawn Cemetery. Many days,
Lori Anna joined Chris at his side, greeting the hotel
guests. She wanted to learn everything she could about
the workings of the hotel, and Jerilyn arrived a couple
days a week to teach her.

In return, Lori Anna was an excellent editor for
Jerilyn's latest novel. Along with her fellow
photographers, Megan and Amy, Lori Anna also
handled many of the photography assignments at the

Franklin Favorite, and was given at least two bylines a month.

On the second Monday in February, Lori Anna woke up at three o'clock to prepare for the gym with Chris, but rushed to the bathroom and vomited instead. Chris hurried in to help her. He wet a washcloth and placed it on her forehead, and held her hair back until she finished. She was weak when she tried to stand, and he steadied her. "Can you walk if I help you to the chair?"

"I think so."

He settled her in the chair and asked in a concerned voice, "Do you want me to fix you some breakfast, or bring you a cup of coffee?"

"No, but thank you. I just feel nauseous. I don't think I could eat anything right now. A glass of cold water would be nice though."

He returned with the water, and she sipped it. "Do you feel better?"

"I don't know yet. Maybe I've just been doing too much after being lazy for three weeks with you in Bellingham."

"I don't consider either of us lazy for three weeks. I never experienced so many outdoor sporting activities in my life in such a short time. Just for today, you should probably take off from your shift at the hotel."

"Your mom is going to work with me in the dining room and teach me about hosting. I want to be there."

"Okay, if you feel better, but we're skipping the gym today," he said in a firm voice.

"Okay."

"You sit for as long as needed. I'm going to let the dogs out and make some coffee."

When he returned, Lori Anna was in the bathroom vomiting again. When she finished, this time he insisted he was putting her back in bed. She didn't complain. "Get some rest, and I'll call Mom and tell her you're rescheduling for tomorrow."

He poured his coffee and returned to the bedroom to check on her. She was sound asleep. He wrote her a quick note saying he'd call later to check on her, but if her condition worsened, she should call him.

Before he left the house, he called his mom to cancel for Lori Anna, and he explained the situation.

"Vomiting, huh?"

"Yes. I put her back in bed, and she's asleep."

"You go on to work, Chris, and I'll be over to check on Lori Anna. Just leave the back door unlocked."

An hour later, Jerilyn quietly opened the back door and slipped into the kitchen. She didn't see the dogs, so she assumed they were still outdoors. Grabbing the tea kettle, she filled it with water and set it on the iron stove.

While she waited for the water to heat, she found some saltine crackers in the pantry. When the tea was ready, she poured two mugs, set them on a tray with cream and sugar, along with the crackers, and headed to the bedroom. The door was closed, so she lightly knocked.

"Come in, Chris," Lori Anna said in a sleepy voice.

"It's not, Chris, honey, it's your Mama Jerilyn."

Lori Anna sat up in bed and pushed her tangled hair away from her face. Jerilyn watched as Lori Anna's face turned ashen, and Lori Anna rushed to the bathroom. Jerilyn set the tray on the nightstand and did the same as Chris, holding Lori Anna's hair back and pressing a cold, damp wash cloth to Lori Anna's forehead.

When Lori Anna finished, Jerilyn helped her on her feet and back to bed. "How long has this been going on?" Jerilyn asked, and swept some stray strands of hair behind her daughter-in-law's ears.

"Once yesterday, once the day before, but several times this morning. Chris doesn't know about the other two days."

Jerilyn smiled. "I brought you some hot tea and soda crackers. I think this will help settle your stomach. It always helped me."

"What do you mean?"

"Well, dear, I'm not a doctor, but you may very well be pregnant."

Lori Anna's mouth dropped with a stunned expression. When she finally recovered, she stared at

Jerilyn. "I didn't think about that. I thought about a virus I may have picked up. But pregnant ...."

"Sip the tea and eat the crackers. Do you have a family doctor?"

Lori Anna finished one cracker and swallowed the sip of tea before answering. "Mom and Dad have gone to Dr. Gentry ever since Dr. Beasley retired."

"He's a good doctor. Christopher and I see him. It's too bad he doesn't make house calls like Dr. Beasley did. I suppose that's now a thing of the past. Would you like me to make you an appointment? Dr. Gentry might even have a cancellation for today. I'd be happy to drive you."

"Yes, please." Lori Anna finished three more crackers and her mug of tea.

"How are you feeling now?"

"Actually, much better. Thank you."

"Why don't you shower, get dressed, and I'll phone the office. Call out if you need me."

Lori Anna showered and dressed, and Jerilyn obtained a nine o'clock appointment. "They had a cancellation. Are you ready to go?"

"Yes, Mama Jerilyn. Thank you so much."

Jerilyn sat in the examination room with Lori Anna per the request of her daughter-in-law.

The examination didn't take long, nor did the questions. When Dr. Gentry finished, he removed his rubber gloves, smiled, and said, "Get dressed, Lori

Anna, and I'll be back in a few minutes."

When he returned, Lori Anna was dressed, sitting on the examination table with her legs dangling over, and Jerilyn standing beside her. "Well, the good news is that you don't have a virus."

Lori Anna frowned. "Is there bad news?"

"Only bad news if you don't want to be pregnant."

Her face broke into a huge smile, and the two women hugged. "How far along am I?"

"From the information you provided, along with my examination, I predict five weeks. I'm setting your due date for October first."

"A baby. Chris and I are going to have a baby. I can't wait to tell him!"

*****

Chris had to work until five that evening, so Lori Anna turned the dogs outside and made him a special candlelight dinner: a salad, roasted chicken, asparagus, and white rice, along with cherry pie for dessert. She wore a deep blue evening dress, set off with her ruby earrings and ruby hair clasp. He walked through the door as she was lighting the candles.

His eyes lit up when he saw her, and the table set with the best linens, china, crystal, and silverware, and a dinner that smelled scrumptious. "Wow, this is great, and evidently you feel better." He kissed her. "You're beautiful, as always. Mom called and said you'd be just fine."

"She's right. I'll be just fine ... in about eight more months."

She could see the thought process taking place on Chris's face. The little smile turned into a huge grin.

"Are you happy, Chris?"

He picked her up and twirled her around. "Happy? I'm ecstatic! I couldn't have been given better news. This is amazing. I was so worried about you. I thought you had been afflicted with something terrible like the swine flu. I didn't even consider a baby."

Following dinner, Chris brought in mugs of hot chamomile tea, and they snuggled on the sofa. Listening to the fire crackle in the fireplace and the dogs at their feet, Chris sighed. "This is the life, Lori Anna," he said in contentment.

She turned toward him, and they kissed. "It won't be so quiet and peaceful when the baby arrives," she said, stroking his cheek.

"We'll just have to spend as much time alone as possible in the meantime. It may not be as quiet, but a baby .... I was beginning to think I'd be a bachelor all my life. Since December first, I've become a husband with a baby on the way. I couldn't be happier, darling. God is good."

"That He is," she said, as she snuggled closer.

Chapter Twenty-One

Independence Day

*"The lines are fallen unto me in pleasant
places; yea, I have a goodly heritage."*
Psalm 16:6

Monday
July 04, 1988
Sitting at the kitchen table and eating the breakfast
Chris had prepared, Chris took Lori Anna's hand, and
kissed it. "Happy birthday, Lori Anna."

Lori Anna took a bite of bacon. "Thanks, Chris. You
know, when I was little, I thought people set off
firecrackers just for my birthday. Mom and Dad never
said anything different until I was seven; just letting
me think the fireworks were for me. When I learned
about Independence Day, and that I just happened to
be born on the day when all of America celebrated
independence from Great Britain, I must say I was
slightly disappointed to learn it wasn't about me. Mom
and Dad told me the abbreviated story about the
Declaration of Independence, and what Independence

Day meant to Americans. I suppose I was somewhat spoiled, being an only child."

"That's reason enough to have a large family, and you already know that twins run in my family." He cocked his head. "We haven't really discussed it, but do you want a large family?"

Taking a bite of toast, she thought for a few seconds. "I would enjoy twins, and I want as many children as God wants us to have. Why not leave that decision up to Him?"

"I couldn't agree more.

"Oh, and by the way, what do you think about asking your parents to go with us to watch the fireworks in Nashville tonight? My parents took us kids every year to see fireworks, and in my opinion the best have been at Riverfront Park along the banks of the Cumberland River. That park was just built a few years ago. Have you been there?"

"No, I haven't, and I think my parents would love to go."

"Then we'd better plan on at least two or maybe even three vehicles. Lily and John, their children still in the area, and Mom and Dad will want to go with us."

Later that evening, sitting on blankets in the park, along with the huge crowd, they waited for darkness. Lori Anna lay back against Chris, and he placed both his legs around her so she could lean against his chest and get comfortable. "Does your back hurt, honey?"

"A little bit ... but mostly I just feel fat and clumsy."

Chris knew the family overheard, because his mother chuckled and said, "It'll get better, Lori Anna ... in about three more months."

Christine bounced seven-month-old baby Nicholas on her lap and added, "It's definitely worth it."

Lily looked over at Lori Anna. "Yes, it's definitely worth it, but wait until the last month when you spend all your time in the bathroom."

Lori Anna groaned and replied to all of them, "Thank you all for making me feel better."

Chris laughed, rubbed her back, and winked fondly toward his family.

A hush fell over the crowd when the show began. All they now heard were the oohs and ahs of the people, along with their own. Baby Nicholas stared wide-eyed and open-mouthed at the bright sparkling colors, but he didn't cry.

At the grand finale, the crowd applauded and whistled. Chris helped Lori Anna to her feet. "That was the best fireworks display I've yet to see here."

"I agree," said Brian, taking the baby from Christine and helping his wife to her feet.

"Thank you for inviting us, Chris," said Mama Stanley.

"You're welcome, Mama Stanley."

Dad Stanley agreed. "Yes, I enjoyed that. When Lori

Anna was growing up, I was driving the cross-country truck runs, so I didn't always get home for Independence Day, aka Lori Anna's birthday. I think I'm enjoying my retirement."

Lori Anna hugged her dad. "Mom and I are glad you're home now, too, Daddy."

After battling the traffic from all the vehicles leaving downtown Nashville, and then dropping Lori Anna's parents at their home, Chris and Lori Anna arrived home well after one o'clock in the morning. The dogs greeted them, but were ready to go outside.

"I'm glad I scheduled Mr. Adams to work in my place tomorrow – I mean today," said Chris, when he checked his watch and hung his keys on the hook by the kitchen door.

Lori Anna headed off to their bedroom. "I'm going to get changed for bed, Chris."

Chris let the dogs back in, and returned to the bedroom where Lori Anna stood at the vanity in their private bathroom, washing her face and then brushing her teeth to prepare for bed. She was wearing the sheer, pale pink nightgown and matching robe he'd given her for her birthday. He knew she wasn't feeling very attractive, so he wanted her to have something that was pretty and feminine, and would allow her to still feel womanly. He watched her, and thought her the loveliest woman in the world.

He sat on the side of the bed, and she turned when

she heard his shoes drop on the floor. She had just finished rubbing the night cream on her face and hands. Turning out the bathroom light, she walked into the bedroom and into his arms.

He sat her on his lap and kissed her. Rubbing her protruding belly, he grinned when the baby kicked his hand.

"He or she is going to be very strong, Lori Anna. Are you sorry we didn't ask about the gender when the ultrasound was done?"

"No, I want to be surprised, like Brian and Christine were when Nicholas was born. Just think, within three months we'll be parents, although, at the moment I feel so unattractive. I'm so heavy and clumsy. I can't wait until the baby is born."

"I'm glad we're waiting for the surprise of our baby's gender, too, sweetheart. However, you're wrong about the unattractive part. You're beautiful in every way to me." He kissed her again and turned out the light. The discussion was over.

Chapter Twenty-Two

Another Diagnosis

*"And hope maketh not ashamed; because the
love of God is shed abroad in our hearts by the
Holy Ghost which is given unto us."*
Romans 5:5

Wednesday Morning
August 31, 1988

It was the third day in a row that Lori Anna awakened
with chills. She threw on her heaviest robe and entered
the bathroom feeling so tired she could hardly walk.
She knew the weight-gain might be the problem, but
today she thought she possibly had a fever. Even her
bones hurt.

Chris was already dressed, and had been in the
kitchen, but he followed her into the bathroom. "Cold
again?"

She sat down on the stool in front of her vanity and
felt her forehead. "Oh Chris, I hope I'm not getting a
summer cold less than five weeks before the baby is

due," she said, shivering and wrapping her robe tighter.

Chris felt her forehead and removed the thermometer from the medicine cabinet. They didn't speak while Chris timed the three minutes on his watch. When he checked the reading, she knew he was alarmed.

"What is it?"

"It's 101.6 degrees. We're going to Dr. Gentry's office. Let me help you get dressed."

"Chris, I just want to go back to bed. You know he's not in the office, yet. It's not even five o'clock."

"I'm calling him at home," he said, as he picked up the extension in the bedroom and pulled out the phonebook in the drawer.

"Hi, Mrs. Gentry. This is Chris Wright. I'm sorry to bother Dr. Gentry at home, but I need to speak with him."

"Chris, I'm sorry, but Dr. Gentry is out of state at a medical conference until Saturday. He left a number of another doctor in case of emergency, though."

Chris took down the information, and turning to Lori Anna he said, "We need a doctor who knows the family. I'm calling Dr. Beasley for his advice."

Forty minutes later, the old doctor, and a long-time friend of the Wright family, pulled into their driveway. Chris was watching for him and opened the front door. Apologizing again for asking the doctor's help in his retirement, Dr. Beasley put up his hand and stopped him. "It's okay, Chris. I don't mind, and there's nothing for which to apologize. I brought my medical bag." He held up the old, worn bag. "So lead me to the patient."

Following the examination, Dr. Beasley's face showed concern. "Lori Anna, I'm not your doctor, but if I was, I'd want to do some blood work on you."

With both hands, Chris gripped the chair arms. "What's wrong, Dr. Beasley?"

"I'm not certain, and I don't want to reveal my suspicions until the blood work is completed. Who's the doctor that Dr. Gentry has on-call?"

Chris handed him the name and number.

"I'm going to use the phone in the other room to get things moving with Dr. Evans. He's a good man, and he has an office here in Franklin. Like Dr. Gentry, he also works out of Vanderbilt Hospital."

Chris was tempted to pick up the bedroom extension to listen in on the conversation, but he stayed with Lori Anna, sitting on the edge of the bed and holding her hand.

Dr. Beasley returned. "I'm sorry, Lori Anna, but you need to go into the clinic. Dr. Evans will meet us there. The clinic is open now."

Chris helped his wife dress, and they followed Dr. Beasley in their truck. While Chris filled out the paperwork, Dr. Beasley met with Dr. Evans. "I'm leaving now, Chris, Lori Anna, but you two are in good hands with Dr. Evans. You can call me anytime. Chris, I've been friends with your parents too long to quit being a friend now."

"Thank you, Dr. Beasley," said Chris, and Lori Anna echoed her thanks.

"You may come back now," said Dr. Evans. "We're going to draw the blood, and I'm going to give you a thorough examination, too. Then I want to transfer you to a room with a bed where you'll be more comfortable while I run some tests."

Lori Anna's eyes rounded, and the fear on her face was apparent to Chris. "Dr. Evans, please tell us what you and Dr. Beasley suspect?"

Dr. Evans sighed and paused before speaking. "Chris and Lori Anna, I understand your concern. Please let me check the blood work before I make this evaluation." His face and demeanor displayed kindness, but his tone was firm.

With blood drawn and the examination completed, Dr. Evans entered their private room two hours later. Lori Anna shivered in the bed, even with several blankets wrapped around her. Chris sat beside her, holding her hand.

Dr. Evans pulled up the extra chair and sat down. He pursed his lips and exhaled. "I'm ready to discuss my suspicions and those of Dr. Beasley." He paused again to look both of them in the eye. Turning to Lori Anna he said, "Lori Anna, your blood count suggests leukemia."

"Oh Dear Heavenly Father, no, please no!" And she cried for the third time that morning. Chris still held her hand, teared up, and leaned over to hold his wife.

Chris finally turned back to Dr. Evans. "What's the next step, doctor?"

"I've contacted Dr. Gentry, and we're in agreement. I've called Vanderbilt Hospital, and Lori Anna will have a room waiting. I've already sent the blood I've drawn by courier, and there will be many more tests and more assessments."

"What about ... my baby, Dr. Evans?" asked Lori Anna, now clearly distraught.

Dr. Evans patted her hand. "Your baby will be just fine. He or she is now able to be born, and labor can safely be induced if the baby has moved into position. If the baby is not in position, the baby can be taken by Caesarean section. A thirty-five-week baby is only gaining weight and developing body fat these last few weeks. Your baby would of course need to spend time in an incubator at the hospital. Now then, all arrangements are made. You will need to go to the main check-in at Vanderbilt Hospital, and then you'll be transported first to oncology."

He stood and shook Chris's hand and patted Lori Anna's hand, and smiled weakly. "God bless you both. When Dr. Gentry gets back to town, he'll be down there to see you. We must hope and pray for the best."

As he exited the room, Chris and Lori Anna held each other and cried before getting her dressed for the drive to Vanderbilt.

Chapter Twenty-Three

Vanderbilt Hospital

"To every thing there is a season, and a time to every purpose under the heaven: A time to be born, and a time to die; a time to plant, and a time to pluck up that which is planted; A time to kill, and a time to heal; a time to break down, and a time to build up; A time to weep, and a time to laugh; a time to mourn, and a time to dance;"
Ecclesiastes 3:1-4

Wednesday and Thursday
August 31 and September 01, 1988
Before leaving for the hospital, Chris called his and Lori Anna's parents, requesting them to meet in the chapel at Christmas Hotel in thirty minutes.

Chris and Lori Anna were huddled together crying and praying at the altar when the two sets of parents rushed to their side. "What's wrong, Chris?" asked Jerilyn in a soft voice, as she knelt beside him, placing her arm on his shoulder. "Is it the baby?"

His father stood behind him with hands on Chris's shoulders. Carol Ann was already kneeling beside her daughter, and Lori Anna turned to her mom and cried in her arms.

After Chris explained what he knew, and that they were now headed to Vanderbilt Hospital to check in, both sets of parents immediately made the decision to go with them. Following a prayer led by Christopher, Chris informed Mr. Hanover at the front desk he'd be gone for an undetermined amount of time, and provided him with a brief explanation. Chris asked Mr. Hanover to schedule the other three managers for the next week, or until he knew more.

With tears glistening in his eyes, Mr. Hanover responded with, "I'll take care of everything, Chris. God go with you both."

Chris drove Lori Anna in the pickup, while his dad and the other three followed in his dad's Suburban. Forty-five minutes later, both vehicles parked in the Vanderbilt Hospital's garage. The check-in was easy, since Dr. Evans had paved the way. Lori Anna was seated in the wheelchair, and they were escorted to oncology where they were to meet Dr. Michael Rouse.

When they arrived at the oncology check-in, Dr. Rouse introduced himself as head of the oncology department. Christopher could not help but ask, "I knew a Dr. Michael Rouse in the early forties over at Baptist Hospital, which was then Protestant Hospital.

Are you related?"

Dr. Rouse smiled and nodded. "That's my dad. He's now retired, but doing well." Turning to Lori Anna, "Let's get you settled in a room for some extended tests. I have the blood that was drawn this morning by Dr. Evans. He was also kind enough to have Dr. Gentry's office fax your medical history. Excuse me while I make a few checks back in the office."

Dr. Rouse returned shortly. "Lori Anna, I need you to put on this hospital gown so I can check your liver and spleen, and I need to examine you for enlarged lymph nodes in your neck and underarm. We will then do a complete blood count and a bone marrow aspiration and biopsy. I can do all from this room. However, I will have a technician and a nurse with me, so I need all but one person to step out into the waiting room. I'll be back with the equipment."

The parents returned to the waiting room, while Chris stayed with his wife. As Chris watched them hook up the equipment, and although nervous, he was extremely impressed with the efficiency of the doctor and the technician and nurse.

When they finished, Dr. Rouse addressed Chris. "I've made arrangements for Lori Anna to stay in this room at least for tonight. There are still more tests needed, and the tests will take the better part of the evening. If you like, I can have a cot brought in for you, Chris, but your parents may want to check into a nearby hotel for the night. I won't have all the results anyway until morning."

"Thank you, Dr. Rouse, and I'll take that cot."

*****

The next morning, both sets of parents returned in time for Dr. Rouse's report.

Dr. Rouse had extra chairs brought in, and he sat with the family. "Lori Anna, your tests are back. I won't mince words, the prognosis is not good. You have acute lymphocytic leukemia, commonly known as ALL." He paused, so the information could sink in with all of them.

Chris closed his eyes and dropped his head. A few seconds later he looked back to Dr. Rouse. He wanted to remain strong for Lori Anna, but his heart was breaking. With a trembling voice he asked, "How do we begin treating this, Dr. Rouse?"

"We need to start Lori Anna on an intensive treatment plan in high dose chemotherapy and total body radiotherapy."

Lori Anna's eyes grew big and round. "Wha ... what ... about my baby?" she asked.

Dr. Rouse patted her hand in comfort. "Your baby will be fine. In fact, I've discussed this with Dr. Evans, and he's prepared to be here as soon as I say it's time to move forward and deliver your baby. If all goes to plan, we're preparing to send you to maternity. However, I do have a few more questions before we can move forward. After the baby is delivered, we need to begin your chemo and radiotherapy treatments as soon as possible. This treatment will kill off all your bone marrow cells. However, there's one dilemma. We can't begin the treatment without a match donor. I understand you are adopted. Do you know anything about your birth parents and possible siblings?"

Lori Anna turned to her parents, and looked back at the doctor. "Yes, I know my birth mother, and I have three half-siblings."

"Full-siblings are a one in four match, but we can test these three and the mother – that is, if they are willing."

This time Mrs. Stanley spoke up. "We'll contact her today, doctor. How soon do you need to test them for a match?"

"The sooner the better. Today, if possible. We can't begin Lori Anna's treatment without the match. It would kill her."

After calling and discussing the situation with Ken and Loretta, and they in turn talking with their daughters, five hours later the five of them arrived at Vanderbilt Hospital.

Dr. Rouse immediately set up their blood tests, and later asked them to join him in his office. Lori Anna, Chris, his parents, Ken, Loretta, their three daughters, and Mr. and Mrs. Stanley gathered in Dr. Rouse's office at Vanderbilt Hospital to hear the news.

The doctor cleared his throat and began. "The results from everyone in Lori Anna's biological family are now in." He looked down at the paper in his hand. "I'm so very sorry to inform you that none of you are a bone marrow match for Lori Anna." He stopped to allow the news to digest.

Chris spoke first. "I visited the Vanderbilt Library today, and I read about bone marrow data being collected all over the United States through the National Bone Marrow Donor Registry. There may be a match out there for Lori Anna."

"I'm sorry, Chris, but we've checked that database, too. The project is very new, and there just aren't many people who've signed up. It didn't become federally funded until two years ago. Prior to then, good-hearted people paid with their own money to have their blood registered."

After a long pause, Chris asked, "So what's the next step, doctor? We can't begin the chemo and radiotherapy without a match, and it seems we've exhausted every means for a bone marrow donor."

Dr. Rouse looked down and shuffled his papers.

Following the long pause, the three couples grew quiet and looked to Loretta. She now spoke up. With a catch in her quivering voice and tears in her eyes she said, "We've another possibly of a match." All eyes trained on her. "We've completely ignored one other possibility, and the elephant in the room. There's ... Barry," she said, barely above a whisper.

Chapter Twenty-Four

The Search

"For where two or three are gathered together in my name, there am I in the midst of them."
Matthew 18:20

September 01 – September 04, 1988
Loretta asked her daughters to step out into the waiting room. Now was not the time to enlighten her girls about the rape.

Ken stared at his wife. He briefly closed his eyes, sighed deeply, and then asked the rhetorical question, "How would we find him? You haven't seen him ... since that night. Are you really sure you can face him?" He shook his head and pursed his lips. "I don't know, Loretta."

Except for Dr. Rouse and the three daughters, the remainder of the family knew Loretta had been raped, and that's how Lori Anna was conceived. Dr. Rouse was clearly perplexed.

Ken placed his arm around his wife. Loretta squared her small shoulders, and explained to Dr. Rouse the situation. "Would he be a possible match, doctor?" she asked.

"Well, yes, a biological parent, or any children he may have, would bring some hope. However, like your children, they would be half-siblings. As I said before, even with full-siblings there's only a one in four chance of a match." Dr. Rouse turned back to Chris and Lori Anna. "I'm sorry. I must be frank with you, and I just don't want you to get your hopes up too high and then return the same news." He shook his head, "This is a tough situation. Lori Anna's biological father will need to be found quickly."

Chris shifted from one foot to the other. He chewed on his lips in thought and ran his fingers through his hair. He finally said, "We will all maintain hope, Dr. Rouse. My nephew Brian can find him. He's a private investigator, and his search-record is excellent."

"Okay, but I recommend Lori Anna stays here in the hospital in the meantime. We'll also forego inducing labor for now. The baby should remain with her until we can begin the aggressive treatment."

Less than three hours later, Chris appeared in Brian's Bowling Green, Kentucky office. "Chris. How did I rate a personal visit to my office?"

"I'm here to hire you."

Fifteen minutes later, Chris had relayed as much information as Loretta had provided for him. "So let me get this straight, Chris. Barry attended the

University of Cincinnati back in 1967, at least in the month of October. We don't know his last name, but he did live in a fraternity house; however, we don't know which one. He was approximately six feet tall, with dark hair."

"That's correct. That's all the info Loretta could remember." He looked down and shook his head. "I realize it's not much to go on."

Brian slapped him on the shoulder. "It's enough, Chris. I'll find him, and when I find him, do you want me to confront him ... or question him in any way?"

"No. Loretta was clear we should all go together. We need a praying army of two or more. Loretta, Ken, you, and I, and maybe my parents. So, you think you can find him?"

"I don't have a lot to go on, and that was twenty-one years ago. Barry was a common name then, but how many guys named Barry could possibly attend UC, *and* live in a frat house in October, 1967?"

"I guess we'll find out, won't we?" and Chris smiled for the first time in two days.

"I suppose we will, buddy."

An hour later, Chris walked in to Christmas Hotel, waved to Mr. Hanover at the desk, and headed straight into the chapel. On his knees at the altar, he prayed aloud and cried out to God. "Dear Heavenly Father ... I need You." He stopped to sniff and wipe his eyes. "Your Son Jesus is the great healer. I know that only You know how long we will live, and You have counted the very hairs on our heads. Dear Lord Jesus, You can heal my wife. I love Lori Anna so much, and our baby will need her mother."

He paused again and then he choked out, "I know I sound as if I'm begging, and I'm not too proud to say that I am. Please don't take her, Lord. She's so young. I'm scared. I'd give my life for her."

My Son gave His life for all of you.

Chris stopped and looked around. He was alone.

"Lord?"

He turned when he heard the light footsteps coming down the aisle. "Mom."

"I'm here, son," she said softly. "Brian called me. I was working in the hotel's office when you arrived. Mr. Hanover told me you were in the chapel. Lori Anna's parents are still with her. Your father and I stopped at your home, picked up Fritz and Bella, and brought them here." She knelt beside him, wrapped her arms around him, and held him while he cried. "It's okay, Chris. You *should* cry."

He used his handkerchief to wipe his eyes and blow his nose. "Mom, I'm worn out. I'm in here begging the Lord to heal Lori Anna. I don't know if I was hearing my own thoughts, or if God spoke to my heart. It was so clear."

"What did you hear, son?"

"I heard, *'My Son gave His life for all of you.'*"

She released him and rocked back on her heels and sighed. He watched as she looked around the chapel and then focused on the empty cross behind the altar. "I've spent a lot of time in this chapel, Chris. I don't think any other place on earth could make me feel closer to God. When I first came to Christmas Hotel, I felt pulled into this chapel, on my knees at this altar. I didn't know what to do. I was depressed, but I was also falling in love with your father. So my emotions were conflicted. The Lord worked it out for me.

"Loretta prayed here when she was pregnant with Lori Anna. She nearly terminated her pregnancy. And when Lily's biological mother died giving birth to her, your father prayed in here.

"Son, what I'm trying to say is the Lord has a plan for you, Lori Anna, your baby, and all of us. I believe you did hear Him speak to you in your heart. Jesus gave His life for us, so that we would live. The best advice I can give you is to stay close to Him. Trust in His love and mercy for you, for Lori Anna, and for your baby. Don't run away from Him, as I did many years ago. It won't do you any good, anyway. He will find you and bring you back home. Stay in prayer. Stay close to Him. He will answer your prayer in His time, which is always the best time."

"Thanks, Mom. Will you pray with me?"

"Of course, son. Dear Heavenly Father ...."

Chapter Twenty-Five

Found

"Judge not, that ye be not judged. For with what judgment ye judge, ye shall be judged: and with what measure ye mete, it shall be measured to you again."
Matthew 7:1-2

Sunday and Monday
September 04 and 05, 1988
Chris, his parents, and Lori Anna's parents had been taking turns staying with Lori Anna. This was only the second time he'd returned home to shower, check on the dogs, and rest. Thankfully, he had two good neighbors to come in twice a day to feed the dogs and let them out.

Two days later, on a Sunday evening, Brian knocked on Chris's front door. Both dogs greeted Brian, and Chris could sense good news.

"I found him, Chris."

Chris closed his eyes and softly exhaled. "Come in, Brian, and have a seat. Tell me about it." The two dogs resettled themselves by the warm fireplace hearth.

"I traveled to the University of Cincinnati first. In October of 1967, there were three students named Barry. However, only two lived in a fraternity. There were pictures of both men on file. Only one had dark hair. His name is Barry Spencer. His parents' address was still on file and their names are Howard and Doris. At the time, they lived in Florence, Kentucky, just over the state border."

Chris nodded to Brian to continue.

"A young couple now live in his parents' former home, and they had no information on the Spencer family. I checked the local obituaries, and Howard passed away seven years ago. It listed his son Barry, his wife Diana, and their four children Jessica, Julia, Jason, and Jeremy living in Hamilton, Ohio."

"And?" said Chris, trying to sound patient.

"I was off to Hamilton, Ohio. I checked the white pages of the Hamilton phone book and there were two Barry Spencer's listed. I wrote down each address, bought a local street map, and later waited outside each house. At the first residence, a man was mowing his lawn. He looked to be in his mid-fifties. A woman about his age opened the front door and called, 'Barry, your dinner is ready.' He responded with, 'I'll be right in, Martha.' I ruled out this Barry Spencer.

"At the next house I hit the jackpot. A man fitting the description Loretta gave, and the right age, opened his front door and picked up his evening newspaper. A woman pulled her car into the driveway, rolled down the window, and said to him, 'Barry, can you ask the kids to help me with these groceries?'

"'Sure, Diana,' he answered. He then called them by name, 'Jessica, Julia, Jason, and Jeremy, come help Mom with the groceries.' They all came running out the front door, and each grabbed a sack of groceries."

Chris had been sitting on the edge of his seat. He finally relaxed and leaned back in his chair. "What do we do now, Brian? He's a family man. We can't just barge in and tell them we need their bone marrow tested because he or one of his children may be a match."

Brian rose and handed Chris the report. "I know you'll want to discuss this with your parents and pray about it." He patted Chris on the shoulder. "God bless you, Chris. I'll see myself out."

The door closed, and Chris stared into the fire. As the tears rolled down his cheeks, he bowed his head. "Lord God, help me help my wife. Help me to do this right. Lord God, please help us all."

*****

The next morning, the Labor Day holiday, Chris loaded the two dogs into the truck and drove to his parents' home. He knew Mom and Dad Stanley were currently at the hospital with Lori Anna. As soon as he walked into the house he smelled the wonderful aroma from the kitchen. He pointed to the hearth and told the dogs to go lie down. He then followed the smell to the kitchen where his mother peeled potatoes for the noon meal.

"I have news."

"Did Brian find Barry?"

He nodded. "Yes, he did."

The swinging kitchen door opened and then closed. His father looked expectant. "I thought I heard you and the dogs come in, Chris. Did I just hear that Brian found Barry?"

"Yes. Brian stopped by last night when he drove home from Hamilton, Ohio. That's where he found Barry, his wife, and their four children."

He filled his parents in on the information from the report. "I need advice on how to handle this. We certainly can't knock on their door and ask them to have their bone marrow checked. His wife may not even know what her husband did all those years ago, and certainly not his children."

"No, we can't just blunder in," agreed his father.

"I had thought when Barry found him, that Brian, you two, Mom and Dad Stanley, and I could go and talk to him. Possibly even Loretta and Ken, although Loretta may not want to face him."

Dad nodded. "I say we begin by calling a family prayer meeting. Let's call James and Carol Ann and Brian to meet here at noon today. We can all eat your mom's wonderful fried chicken dinner, and call Loretta and Ken to get their thoughts about traveling to Hamilton, Ohio. If they agree, we can pick them up in Lexington, have prayer, and then head to Hamilton. Let's seize the day."

Chris felt a great sense of relief. *Dad always knows what to say to me.* "Mom and Dad Stanley are at the hospital, but I can contact them at the nurse's station. By the way, Ken called me last night after Brian left. He and Loretta talked to the girls wanting them to be prepared. They told them that a man named Barry was Lori Anna's biological father without providing all the details."

At noon, James, Carol Ann, and Brian arrived. The six of them gathered around the table and Christopher asked the blessing. "Dear Heavenly Father, we are gathered here today to enjoy this wonderful meal Thou hast provided for the nourishment of our bodies, but more importantly to ask for Thy help and guidance for the desperate situation regarding one of our family members: Lori Anna. We pray it will go well when we travel today to meet with the Spencer family. We beseech Thee to go ahead of us and soften their hearts to what we are about to ask of them. We pray one of them is a match for our Lori Anna. In the name of Thy Son Jesus we pray, amen."

The others echoed their amens.

An hour later, they were on the road in Christopher's Suburban. Since Ken and Loretta agreed to travel up North, Dad stopped in Lexington to pick them up. Ken and Loretta kissed Jenna, Rebecca, and Emma goodbye, and Loretta reminded her daughters, "Don't forget, the Kerrigans next door will be over to check on you. It's already four o'clock, so we're not certain how long we'll be gone. According to the map, it's about a two hour drive from Lexington. We don't even know if we'll be able to speak to Mr. and Mrs. Spencer."

"Don't worry, Mom," said Jenna. "We'll be fine. We'll be praying all goes well, and they agree to the bone marrow test."

"We also will pray one of them is a match for Lori Anna," added Rebecca.

*****

On the way north to Hamilton, the eight of them formed the plan. "Since it's Labor Day," began Brian, "the family may or may not be home. There's always the chance they took a little vacation. I don't think all eight of us should knock on their door. I suggest all of you wait in the truck, and I'll go to the door and speak to them first. Even then, I feel only Chris, Ken, and Loretta should go in with me. But only if I give the signal that we're welcome. Eight people would be overwhelming. You four can remain in the truck as prayer warriors."

"What will you say?" asked Chris.

"I don't know, yet. Let's pray for God to provide me with the right words to gain entrance."

When they arrived at the house, Brian rang the front door as planned. Chris saw Barry and his wife look past Brian to the Suburban, after Brian flashed his private investigator credentials. After a few minutes, Brian waved Chris, Loretta, and Ken to come on. The four of them entered the home and were invited to have a seat.

Loretta stared at Barry, and he did the same in return. Ken and Loretta sat on a small love seat, and Ken placed a protective and comforting arm around his wife. Brian and Chris each sat in chairs, and Barry and Diana sat together on the large sofa. There were no children in the house that he could see.

Chris thought the house homey, with family pictures displayed on the walls and the tables. The aroma of dinner wafted past his nose. He wondered if they'd interrupted the meal, or perhaps the couple had just finished.

Barry opened the conversation. He cleared his throat. "Brian said he was a private investigator in Bowling Green, Kentucky and had been hired to locate me. He said you'd explain." He turned to Loretta, "I suppose I have an inkling of what's going on. I remember you from college, Loretta. You haven't changed very much."

Chris didn't think Barry appeared hostile at all. It was just a matter-of-fact statement.

"Yes," she answered in a soft voice, "that is part of the reason we're here."

Brian picked up the conversation, "We want to make certain we have privacy. I know you have four children, and what we have to discuss will be up to you to tell them. Are they at home?"

"No, they're visiting Diana's parents and will be home at eight."

Brian continued, "This is a sensitive subject, and we're only here because someone's life is at stake. Loretta had no intention of ever seeing you again, Barry. Please know she isn't here to cause a disturbance in your family. I don't know how much your wife knows about your college days, but I need to be blunt. Should we speak privately first?" he glanced toward Diana.

Diana took her husband's hand. "I don't think there's anything you can say I don't already know. I met Barry two years after he was graduated from the University of Cincinnati. He joined my church where my father is the pastor. When the Lord saved him, we started dating. Before he asked me to marry him, he told me about what he most regretted in his life. He told me about Loretta."

Barry picked up the conversation and turned toward Loretta. "Loretta, even after it happened, I was sorry. I tried to find you when we returned from Christmas break, but you were gone. I'm not as good a detective as Brian here. I wanted to tell you how sorry I was for what I did to you." He looked down and then back to Loretta. "I'm very sorry, Loretta. I deeply regret it happened." Loretta said nothing, but her lip trembled and her eyes filled with tears. She swallowed and sniffed. Ken hugged her closer, and Brian continued the conversation. "As I said before, we wouldn't be here except for someone's life is at stake, and that's the daughter you fathered. Loretta was a virgin prior, and abstained from sex afterwards. So there is no doubt she became pregnant that night."

Barry's jaw dropped. He sat with a stunned expression on his face, seeming unable to speak. Finally, he turned to his wife. "Diana, I didn't know. Please believe me."

"I believe you, Barry," she said softly and patted his hand, but tears welled in her eyes, too.

Brian continued. "Loretta left UC before Christmas that year with her college roommate. The college roommate is the sister to Loretta's husband Ken, seated beside her now. Loretta carried the child, a girl, and gave her to her adoptive parents who are in the vehicle praying for all of us now. The girl, Lori Anna, grew up and married Chris, a brother to Ken." He nodded his head toward Chris in the other chair. "Chris and Ken's parents are also out there praying."

"What can *we* do?" asked Barry.

"Lori Anna is eight-months pregnant and has just found out she has leukemia. The baby is viable enough to be delivered. Lori Anna will then need to have an aggressive treatment of chemotherapy and radiotherapy. However, the treatment could take her life, because her bone marrow will be killed. She will need it replaced. Loretta and Ken have three daughters, and the daughters, Lori Anna's half-sisters, and Loretta were tested. Unfortunately, none of them were a match for Lori Anna."

"I read about a nationwide bone marrow match organization that can help with bone marrow matching," said Diana.

"That's true," said Chris, now joining the conversation. "However, it's so new that there was no match for Lori Anna." He cleared his throat and continued with hoarseness in his voice. "We've exhausted every means for my wife. We have no other hope, except the possibility that you, Barry, or one of your four children will match." Chris choked, and his eyes filled with tears. "Please know that my wife is a lovely person inside and out. I pray you'll be willing to help her ... help all of us."

The silence hung in the air until Loretta broke it. With a trembling in her voice she said, "I don't even know if you *are* her father, Barry. My parents had just died in a car wreck before I went to that party with you.

That was my first and only experience with alcohol." She paused to catch her breath. With a big sigh she continued, "The night it happened ... I remember seeing three other men come into your bedroom, and then I passed out. Outside of you, I don't know who else violated me." The tears in her eyes now spilled over, and Ken placed both of his arms around her.

Barry's eyes glistened, and Diana wiped tears. "Loretta, again, I'm so sorry. Please believe me when I say it was just me. I was sick following what I did, and I threw the other guys out of the room before they could touch you. I couldn't even face you, and that's why you woke up on a sofa downstairs. I carried you there, and I covered you with the quilt." He bowed his head, squeezed his eyes together twice, and rubbed his forehead.

When Barry looked up at Loretta again, a tear had spilled down his cheek. He wiped it away, sniffed, and in a husky voice he cleared his throat and continued. "Loretta, I beg you for your forgiveness. Jesus Christ forgave me for my sins when He saved me. I always hoped someday I could ask for *your* forgiveness."

Loretta sat up straight, wiped her tears, and looked Barry in the eyes. "I believe you are being truthful, Barry. Jesus Christ forgave me of my sins, so I can do no more than forgive you, too. I will not be your judge."

Barry turned to Chris. "I *will* help your wife. There's leukemia in my family. My youngest sister died from the disease when she was ten." He exhaled slowly and wiped another tear that trailed down his cheek. "I'm sorry. I still miss her." He choked out the words. "I know it can be passed through the generations. I suppose I passed it to Lori Anna."

He paused and took a deep breath. "Diana and I will talk to the children tonight. Jessica is seventeen, Julia is fifteen, and we have twin boys, Jason and Jeremy who are thirteen. How soon do you need us for the test?"

"As soon as possible," said Chris. "Lori Anna is at Vanderbilt Hospital in Nashville. If you could be there in the morning by eight o'clock, I can have her doctor arrange the tests."

Barry looked at his wife, and she nodded. "We'll be there. Nashville's about a five hour drive from here. We'll get some sleep and leave by two tomorrow morning, since the time in Nashville is one hour earlier. Tell Lori Anna's doctor to be ready at eight. Diana and I will pray one of the children or I will be a match for her."

Now Chris's eyes teared. "I don't know what to say, except thank you. I also thank God. I didn't know how this meeting would go, or that you'd even receive us. The Lord paved the way."

Barry and Diana walked them to the door. "We'll see you tomorrow morning by eight," said Barry, and he shook hands with the men. To Loretta he nodded.

Chapter Twenty-Six

The Tests

"Let us therefore come boldly unto the throne of grace, that we may obtain mercy, and find grace to help in time of need."
Hebrews 4:16

Tuesday Morning
September 06, 1988

The families arrived back in Franklin around midnight, after dropping off Loretta and Ken, who also promised to be at Vanderbilt the next morning. "There won't be any home-schooling tomorrow, so the girls can come, too," said Loretta. "After all, when Lori Anna receives her bone marrow match, a baby will be delivered. The girls, and Ken and I will want to be present."

Chris appreciated Loretta's positive outlook. He didn't go back to his home, but drove straight to Vanderbilt, leaving the dogs with his parents. He wanted to give Lori Anna the news, and also call Dr. Rouse to set up tests for five people at eight o'clock in the morning.

A cot was brought in for Chris, and he lay beside his wife and held her hand. "Chris, I feel hope. The Lord was definitely with all of you tonight. It's amazing to discover I actually have four more half-siblings. I pray I'll live to be close to all of them." She choked up, sniffed, and tears ran from her eyes down into her ears.

Chris rolled her onto her side toward him, and as close to him as possible. Wrapping his arms around her, he wiped her tears and said, "Let's pray, Lori Anna. Dear Heavenly Father, I know You receive requests for miracles every day, but we are asking for one more. We understand the best chance for a match is one in four from a full-sibling. Lori Anna has four more half-siblings for that miracle, and we are going to pray for that miracle in one of these half-siblings or in Barry. We pray for Your strength tomorrow when the tests are performed. We will hold out with faith and trust a match is found. You know where her match lives, even if it's not one of the siblings. Please give us peace in Your decision. We ask for Your love and mercy. In the name of Jesus we pray, amen."

Lori Anna whispered her amen.

*****

Lori Anna and Chris awakened at five o'clock. For a few moments they enjoyed being alone together, not thinking about the consequences of what the day might bring. Chris chuckled and said, "This is sleeping-in for us. Why, less than a year ago we were meeting in the

Christmas Hotel gym every day at four o'clock."

"You know, Chris, with all that's happened I can hardly believe we've only been a couple for a little over nine months." She paused and added, "I love you so much."

"I love you, Lori Anna," he said, and kissed her.

"You do realize if one of the Spencer family is a bone marrow match, our daughter or son will be born today, September sixth. Another sapphire gem like you, Chris."

"Last night, before we parted from Ken and Loretta, Loretta wouldn't say *if*. She said *when* one of them is a match. You and I need to think positive, too. They'll be here this morning. They want to be present for the news, *and* of course the birth of our baby."

"We haven't discussed baby names, Chris. If we have a boy, I'd certainly like another Christopher. Christopher James, for the two grandfathers."

"Don't you think that three guys named Christopher in one family could get a bit confusing?"

"Maybe. We'll think on that some more. What about a girl's name?"

"When my sister and her first husband Andrew were pregnant with Drew, they were going to name the baby Olivia if he'd been a girl. I've liked the name Olivia ever since. What do you think?"

"I like Olivia, too. It's sophisticated. Olivia Wright. I like the sound of it, and for a middle name how about

Ann for my mom? As you know, my name Lori Anna came from a combination of Loretta and Carol Ann, my two moms."

"I like that. Okay, so Olivia Ann if a girl, and we'll think more about a name for a boy, if need be."

Chris helped Lori Anna dress so she could look nice for all her guests. She hoped Barry, Diana, and the four children would want to meet her. Chris had relayed all the conversation to her in the Spencer home. She was pleased to know they were a Christian family. At seven o'clock their breakfast arrived, and Lori Anna and Chris ate heartily.

Following breakfast, Lori Anna asked Chris to buy her some stationery, matching envelopes, and a good quality pen. She intended to write some letters while the tests were conducted.

He frowned. "Letters? Why are you writing letters?"

"Just never you mind, husband," she admonished, but in a soft voice. "I feel the need to write some letters. They should have everything in the gift shop. That will give me something to do while the testing is being done, and while I wait for the results."

When Chris returned with the requested items, her room was now full with his parents, her parents, Ken, Loretta, and their three daughters. He handed the items to Lori Anna. "You all visit. I want to find Barry, Diana, and their four children. I don't want them to feel abandoned when they arrive. They should have me to greet them and make them feel welcome."

"Thank you, Chris. Now bend down to me so I can kiss you, and you can set this sack of stationery on my nightstand."

Chris met with Dr. Rouse a few minutes before eight o'clock. The Spencer family had not yet arrived. "I've got everything set up and ready to go, Chris."

"Thank you, doctor."

As Dr. Rouse spoke, in walked the Spencer family. Introductions were made, and Dr. Rouse told the family what to expect, and about tissue typing or HLA matching: human leukocyte antigen. He explained in layman terms how their proteins needed to match Lori Anna's for a match. Although Diana was not being tested, she requested to go back with her family.

While Chris waited, Ken and Loretta joined him in the waiting room. Ken hugged Chris and slapped his back. "We wanted to be here for you and to pray with you. Mom and Dad, Carol Ann and James, our three daughters, and Lori Anna are praying, too. Brian and Christine, Lily, Lydia Grace, and Carrie Emeline are praying from their homes with their families."

They took seats in the waiting room with Ken and Loretta on each side of Chris. Chris reached over and patted his brother and sister-in-law's hands. "Thank you both so much. I need you here. I'm trying not to be negative. I know even if we have a match, there can still be a risk Lori Anna's tissues may attack the donor's cells, as they're foreign to her body. So many thoughts are going through my head. I can't lose her." The tension overwhelmed Chris and he broke down and cried, his face in his hands.

Ken placed his arm on Chris's shoulder. "Okay, little brother, let's pray now."

The three of them were huddled in prayer when Dr. Rouse returned. Chris heard the footsteps. He looked up and stood ready for any information. "Dr. Rouse, do you have the results, yet?"

"We have tested the father, and he's not a match."

Chris felt his countenance drop.

"Don't give up hope, Chris. We didn't think he'd be a match. We'll have better chances with the children. I'll be back when I know more."

Thirty minutes later, Chris and Lori Anna's parents joined the three of them. "Lori Anna kicked us out," said Dad Stanley. "She mentioned something about writing letters, and asked us to join you, and to keep you away through lunch. She said she needed time alone." He turned to Ken and Loretta. "Your daughters went to the lower level cafeteria."

None of them wanted a full lunch, but at eleven o'clock Ken and Loretta joined their daughters. They returned later with sandwiches and coffee for the others. The family ate, drank, talked, and prayed, waiting for Dr. Rouse. The morning dragged on. At noon he appeared with a huge smile. "We have a match. It's Jessica."

Shouts of praise and thanks filled the waiting room, along with tears of happiness.

"Next step," said Dr. Rouse, "let's get that baby delivered. I'll make the arrangements to send Lori Anna to maternity, and ask Dr. Gentry or Dr. Evans to come for the delivery."

Chapter Twenty-Seven

Olivia Ann Wright

"And let the peace of God rule in your hearts,
to the which also ye are called in one body
and be ye thankful."
Colossians 3:15

Tuesday evening
September 06, 1988
Dr. Gentry arrived mid-afternoon for the delivery, and since the baby was in position, he supervised the inducement of labor. At seven minutes past eight that evening – Chris checked his watch for the official time – Olivia Ann Wright arrived into the world.

After Olivia was washed and evaluated, Lori Anna and Chris each held her briefly, and then their five pounds and six ounce baby girl was placed into a portable incubator and whisked off to the nursery. Chris never left his wife's side. After stepping in to congratulate the parents, the remainder of the family followed the baby to the nursery.

Dr. Gentry sat in a chair beside Lori Anna. "Olivia's

very healthy, Lori Anna. Keep in mind that she's only a little more than three weeks premature. She's going to be just fine, so you can concentrate on getting well," and he patted Lori Anna's arm. "Because of your leukemia, and the possibility of this happening to a future child of yours, we have frozen Olivia's umbilical cord. There is new research attributing the cord blood of one child for saving the life of other siblings."

"Thank you, Dr. Gentry. Hopefully, this won't happen to Olivia or any future children God gives Chris and me."

After shaking hands with Chris, he made his exit and returned to Franklin.

"We're parents, Chris."

He grinned. "If you're up to it, there are some people who want to meet you just outside this room."

"I want to meet them, too, Chris. Oh, would you comb my hair first and hand me a tube of lipstick from my purse, please?"

Ten minutes later, Barry, Diana, Jessica, Julia, Jason, and Jeremy entered her room. "Congratulations," they all said nearly in unison.

"Thank you," responded Lori Anna and Chris. Lori Anna added, "Thank you, Jessica, for agreeing to be my bone marrow donor."

"I'm really glad I've been able to help. We were so surprised to find out we had another sister, but pleased."

"Well, I thank you again. You're only seventeen, and I want you to know you're doing a wonderful thing for me. I'm sure the doctor has explained what's involved – and it won't be pain-free."

"Yes, I do understand, but I also know you'll die if I don't donate my bone marrow. I don't want that to happen. I want to get to know you ... and my new niece ... or is she my cousin? I haven't figured it out yet. This is really exciting, but a bit confusing, too."

Lori Anna laughed, and agreed that the family was certainly mixed up.

Lori Anna looked closely at the man who had fathered her. Because of the conversation with the Spencer family that Chris had relayed to her, she couldn't hate him for what he did to Loretta twenty-one years earlier: only the violent sin. He had a kind face, and Diana was a lovely woman. At least he'd changed after that night, and asked Jesus to save his soul. If Jesus could forgive him, then like Loretta she could not judge him, only forgive him. Therefore, she smiled and said, "It's nice to meet all of you," but directed her eyes on Barry.

"You look like your mother ... or I mean Loretta. I realize she didn't raise you, and Mr. and Mrs. Stanley are your parents."

"That's true. I pray Jessica and I will be completely compatible in this bone marrow procedure, because I want to live for my husband and daughter." She smiled. "I also pray all of us can get to know each other."

This time Diana stepped forward. "Lori Anna, I think that can be arranged. We all want to know you and your family. "

Barry added, "We understand your high doses of chemotherapy and radiotherapy begin in the morning, and we were told to bring Jessica back in one week so the doctor can collect her stem cells and bone marrow. If allowed, we'll see you then."

Jessica stepped forward. "I want to visit Olivia. I hope you don't mind if we all stop by the nursery before we leave."

Lori Anna smiled. "I'd be disappointed if you didn't. After all this is over, and my isolation period is over, I hope you'll be back to visit me."

"I'll bring them down here at that time, too," said Barry, and he patted Lori Anna's hand and shook Chris's hand on the way out.

Chapter Twenty-Eight

The Treatments

"Wherefore comfort yourselves together, and edify one another, even as also ye do."
1 Thessalonians 5:11

September 07 – 12, 1988
The next morning, before the chemo and radiotherapy began, Chris helped Lori Anna into a wheelchair and wheeled her to the nursery to visit their baby. After moving over to a rocker, the nurse handed her Olivia.

"Oh, Chris, I know every mother says this, but she's beautiful. She has your firm jaw line *and* your forehead."

"Yes, but she has your enchanting dimples, high cheek bones, glorious black hair, and eye shape. I suppose we won't know the eye color for a while."

Lori Anna grew sober with her next statement. "Chris, I know you understand I may be infertile after this aggressive treatment. Olivia may be our only child."

"If that's what happens, then I'm sure the Lord will have some children waiting for us to adopt. Your

227

parents adopted you, and I know they love you just as much as my parents love me. We'll cross that bridge when we come to it," he said, while patting her shoulder.

"I visited Vanderbilt's library, and I read up on other side effects. It's likely I'll lose my hair, and very soon, because of the aggressive treatments." Tears glistened in her eyes.

Chris knelt down beside the rocker and held his wife's hand. "Lori Anna, you know I love your beautiful hair, and that was one of the reasons I was initially attracted to you. However, your hair didn't cause my love for you. I fell in love with your inner beauty. Your hair will grow back. I've read the side effects, too, and I know your hair may not have the same texture or even the same color. Don't worry about the side effects. We'll address them as they happen. I just want you to get well," and he kissed her and then kissed his daughter. "We have to go back to your room now, so they can prepare you for your first treatment."

"When I go into isolation, I won't be able to hold her ... or you either," and the tears spilled over and ran down her cheeks.

He kissed his wife, and then his daughter again. "It won't be forever, darling."

*****

As the week wore on, Lori Anna grew more fatigued. The nausea, vomiting, and diarrhea were horrific. At times she was unable to hold her head up. Chris stayed with her the whole week, and only left her side to use the hospital's guest shower or visit Olivia. After three days, Lori Anna could no longer maintain solid foods. She was given fluids and nutrition intravenously. Her stomach hurt from all the vomiting. Her mouth was dry and developed sores.

Her parents and Chris's parents visited daily. That first week, each time Chris brushed Lori Anna's hair, she lost more hair than normal. After one week of the intense treatments, her remaining hair completely fell out in clumps. Lori Anna was now anxious and stressed. Jerilyn and Carol Ann were prepared. They purchased a short haired black wig for Lori Anna and some head wraps, so she could use whichever she preferred.

Unbeknownst to Lori Anna, Chris saved as much of her hair as possible, tying ribbons around each clump. He hoped to salvage enough for a wig, but didn't want to raise Lori Anna's hopes.

On Monday evening, and the night before Jessica was due to donate the bone marrow, Lori Anna looked at Chris. "Please help me into the wheelchair so I can visit Olivia. When the bone marrow is administered to me tomorrow, I'll be in isolation for several weeks."

"Are you sure you're strong enough to sit up? I can always get a gurney."

"I can lean back in the chair. Just don't drive too

fast," and she smiled.

Although her face was much thinner, Chris thought her as beautiful as ever. It was the first smile he'd received from her in the past week. "I promise not to treat your chair like a race car."

"Please put my new wig on me first. I don't want to scare our daughter."

With the wig in place, and Lori Anna situated in the wheelchair, a nurse helped with the portable IV. When they reached the nursery they found their daughter being held and fed by one of the nurses. When the nurse saw them, she motioned for them to come in.

Chris took his daughter from the nurse and knelt in front of his wife's chair. Handing Olivia to Lori Anna, she then leaned down and kissed the baby's downy cheek. The nurse pulled up a chair for Chris and handed him the bottle. He in turn helped Lori Anna hold the bottle for Olivia. After a moment, a tear fell from Lori Anna's eye onto the baby's blanket.

"I had hoped to nurse her, Chris."

"I know, honey."

"If I'm barren, I'll never nurse a baby."

The nurse discreetly walked away while Chris wrapped his arms around his wife and daughter.

Chapter Twenty-Nine

Jessica Returns

"Take therefore no thought for the morrow: for the morrow shall take thought for the things of itself. Sufficient unto the day is the evil thereof."
Matthew 6:34

Tuesday Morning
September 13, 1988

Chris excused himself from Lori Anna's room. "I want to be present when Jessica and her parents arrive."

"Oh, yes, please go, Chris. I pray it's not too painful for Jessica when the bone marrow is harvested."

"We were assured she'd have anesthesia in the operating room, and pain killers when she goes home."

"I know, but she's my new sister. I'm so grateful to her, and I don't want her to be in pain."

"The procedure is supposed to take up to two hours, and then Jessica goes to recovery for about an hour."

"Will there be time for me to see her before they start my new drip from her bone marrow? They'll probably have me isolated right after."

"I don't know how soon they'll have the bone marrow ready for you, but I'll find out."

Within thirty minutes, Chris was in the OR waiting room with Barry and Diana. When he entered, they were holding hands and praying. They finished, and he sat in the chair beside Barry.

"I didn't want to interrupt."

Diana wiped a tear from her eye and said, "We were praying for Jessica's bone marrow to be accepted into Lori Anna's body with no complications. *And* we were praying for no rejection from Lori Anna's body."

"Thank you. That's my prayer, too."

An hour and a half later, the parents of Jessica Spencer were called to the front desk by the beeper they were given. Chris walked up with them.

"She's in recovery and doing fine," the spokesperson said. "Her blood pressure and pulse are steady. The red blood cells that were separated from the marrow are currently being returned to her through her IV. She may still be a little weak and groggy, but you may go back now, but just the parents."

"I guess this is where we part today," said Chris. "At some point in the next couple of hours, Lori Anna will go into isolation and receive the harvested bone marrow. God bless you for allowing Jessica to do this."

Barry smiled. "I don't think we could have stopped her once she made up her mind. Jessica is only seventeen, but she's a very determined young lady.

Please let us know when Lori Anna is out of isolation. We'll be back with all four children. Also, call us with updates."

"I will."

Two hours later, Chris said a temporary goodbye to his wife as she was moved to an isolation room where the bone marrow drip would be added to her IV. Lori Anna would not be able to visit Jessica beforehand.

"Chris, I want you to go home while I'm in isolation. I know you'll want to see Olivia daily until she's released, and I would imagine that will be soon. She's gaining weight. She'll probably be out of the incubator in a few days. You can phone the nurses' station to check on me. They may even allow a phone in my room."

Alarm bells rang in Chris's head. *What is she thinking, Lord?* "I'm not going to abandon you, Lori Anna."

"I know that, Chris, but we can't be in the same room together. I'll be in danger of infection. You need to spend time with Olivia. She needs to be held and loved when she goes home, and by you. I don't want you leaving her to visit me. Just call ... and please do this for me. Right now I have to think about today, and I'll leave tomorrow in the Lord's hands."

Four days later, Olivia was released from the hospital into Chris's care. She was eleven days old.

Chapter Thirty

The Visit

*"Be strong and of a good courage, fear not, nor be
afraid of them: for the LORD thy God, he it is that doth
go with thee; he will not fail thee, nor forsake thee."*
Deuteronomy 31:6

Saturday
October 01, 1988
Lori Anna had now been in isolation for eighteen days
and no sign of rejection, but Dr. Rouse's concern was
that her blood cell counts were still extremely low.
During this period she had received anti-viral and
antibiotic treatments, along with anti-fungal
treatments. Chris called several times a day, because
she was permitted phone calls. He wanted to visit her
every day, but he honored Lori Anna's wishes, except
for a few times.

When he called, her first question was always,
"How's Olivia doing?" Chris gave her each update, how
much formula Olivia was drinking, and who had
visited. In the past week he had returned to work.

Sometimes Lily drove in from Russellville, stayed in the family's room number seven at Christmas Hotel, and cared for her niece.

"It's no bother," Lily would always say. "I love caring for Olivia. You take care of Christmas Hotel, and I'll help with Olivia. She's such a good baby, Chris."

Sometimes he kept Olivia in the office while he did paperwork, with the dogs close by. Other times his mom, or Christine, or Mom Stanley asked him to leave Olivia with one of them for the day. Chris started calling them all "baby stealers" because they all loved having her around. Chris was relieved that Olivia was a good baby. She was not demanding, and she whimpered her needs with a soft cry. She was a pleasure to be around.

Today, Chris took the dogs to Dr. Crocker, their vet, for an annual checkup, while Jerilyn watched Olivia. During the checkup Dr. Crocker discovered Bella's pregnancy. "I'd say she's about four weeks along, and gestation is roughly sixty-three days," he informed Chris. "Keep a close watch on her around November first, give or take several days. You don't want her to have the puppies outside if the weather gets below freezing at night. You might want to get a box, and make Bella a bed in the kitchen so she can get used to it now."

Chris picked up Olivia, and hurried home with her and the dogs so he could call Lori Anna with the news.

She wasn't feeling any better; in fact she sounded worse. "What's changed?" asked Chris.

"I just don't want to worry you, Chris. You've got so much on your plate with Olivia, the dogs, Christmas Hotel – just let the doctors worry about me."

He paused, took a deep breath, and ran his fingers through his hair. "Lori Anna, I love you. How can I not consider your feelings? I want to know everything going on with you. You can either tell me right now, or I'm getting in the truck and driving down there this instant."

"Chris, please ... I'm just tired is all. I'm tired of being in the hospital, being sick all the time, not being able to hold Olivia and you." Chris could hear her softly crying. "I miss you so much. I don't think I'm getting better. I thought I would be out of isolation by now. It's painful, even with the medication, and now I feel like a bigger baby than Olivia. I'm sorry, Chris. I don't want to burden you."

"Honey, it's been eighteen days. They warned us it could be several weeks ... or more." Then he added as gently as possible, "You could *never* burden me."

Her sigh was audible to his ears. "I know, but I still feel like a whiny child."

"You're not a whiny child. You're my beautiful wife, and you're sick."

"I don't feel so beautiful right now."

He heard the depression in her voice. She needed

her spirits lifted. "Get some rest, honey. Please know I love you, and you're beautiful to me, always."

He hung up and called the nurses' station. After filling them in on the conversation, he made a special request. They called the doctor, and then called Chris back. "Dr. Rouse gave his permission. By the time you get here, we'll have the arrangements ready."

He changed Olivia's diaper and dressed her in her prettiest dress. He wrapped her in a baby blanket Lily had made for her niece, grabbed the diaper bag, and looked for the dogs. They were nowhere in sight, so he headed to the truck and strapped Olivia in her car seat.

Within the hour, he was at the nurses' station outside Lori Anna's room. A phone cord had been strung and taped down across the floor, and they had placed a chair for him beside the phone on a portable table. The curtain was still closed to Lori Anna's room, at his request. He had visited Lori Anna three times in the eighteen days, and as it turned out he could be in the same room with her as long as he wore an isolation suit, but children were definitely not allowed. Lori Anna had not seen her baby since the night before she began the aggressive chemotherapy and radiotherapy treatments.

He situated himself with Olivia on his lap so he could talk to Lori Anna, and she could see the two of them. "Is my wife awake?" he asked her nurse.

"Yes. She doesn't know you two are out here. She

questioned why her bed had been moved by the window. I told her so the cleaning crew could dust and mop one side of her room, and then the other. I'll go in and you can just give me five minutes to put on my isolation suit, wash my hands, and then you can dial her phone."

Five minutes later he dialed Lori Anna's room and the nurse picked up the phone, opened the curtain, and handed the phone to Lori Anna.

The surprise and happiness on Lori Anna's face said it all. "Chris ... Olivia ...." Her beautiful eyes welled up with tears, and her chin quivered.

"Hi, sweetheart. Olivia needed to see her mommy," he said into the phone. He moved his chair closer to the window, so Lori Anna could see her daughter better. He placed his hand with his palm to the glass and asked Lori Anna to do the same.

He heard the nurse say, "Wait, I'll put some latex gloves on you, Lori Anna."

Lori Anna then placed her gloved hand on the window with his. They couldn't touch, but it was comforting with each other's hands on the glass. He then placed Olivia's little hand on the window so Mommy and daughter could connect, too.

"Chris, she's grown so much. How much does she weigh now?"

"She's up to six pounds and four ounces. She has no problem drinking the proper amounts of formula ...

and keeping it down."

Olivia stared at her mom, and obviously, no recognition. Lori Anna's face changed from surprise and happiness to a distinct sadness. His heart broke, realizing Olivia didn't know her mom. He hoped he hadn't done wrong by bringing Olivia to the hospital.

"She doesn't know me, Chris," Lori Anna said as she slowly removed her hand from the window.

"I can change that, honey. I'll start bringing her every day."

"No, you can't do that. She needs a structured schedule. By the time you drive here, get parked, and walk up to this room, over an hour has gone by, and then there's the return home. No, Chris, this has been special for me, but I can already see she's tired."

"Hopefully, you'll be home in a week or two and then you two can make up for lost time."

"We'll see. I'm tired now, so I think I'll rest."

He realized Lori Anna had retreated into a shell. He saw the depression on her face, and heard the melancholy resonating in her voice.

"I love you, Lori Anna."

"I love you, too, Chris. Thank you for bringing Olivia."

"Be strong, Lori Anna. Have courage."

He saw the tears fall on her cheeks before she rolled over with her back to them.

Chapter Thirty-One

GVHD

*"Blessed be God, even the Father of our Lord
Jesus Christ, the Father of mercies, and the God
of all comfort; Who comforteth us in all our
tribulation, that we may be able to comfort them
which are in any trouble, by the comfort
wherewith we ourselves are comforted of God."*
2 Corinthians 1:3-4

Saturday morning
October 22, 1988

Two weeks later, Chris was at his home when he
received the call he had dreaded. Dr. Rouse reported
Lori Anna's temperature had risen and she was
experiencing abdominal pain. She'd also developed a
rash. These were signs of graft versus host disease, or
GVHD.

"Chris, there are two kinds of GVHD: acute and
chronic, and either can range from mild to severe.
We're taking her to the OR now to do a biopsy of the

mucous membranes in her mouth. This will determine the severity, and which type of GVHD Lori Anna is experiencing. We'll hope for acute and mild."

"I'll leave for the hospital now, Dr. Rouse."

He called his mother, dropped off Olivia with her, and drove straight to Vanderbilt. When he entered the waiting room, he was told Lori Anna was already in the OR.

"Please have a seat, and I'll notify Dr. Rouse you've arrived."

Forty minutes later, Dr. Rouse met Chris in the waiting room. "Lori Anna is in a special isolation room for recovery. She hasn't awakened yet."

"May I use an isolation suit to sit with her?"

Dr. Rouse stared into his eyes for a few seconds. "I'll make the arrangements, Chris."

Within thirty minutes, Chris was suited up and sitting beside his wife. He examined her face and head. She had no hair on her head, and her long, thick eyelashes and arched eyebrows were gone, too. Even the velvety hairs on her cheeks and arms had vanished. Her cheeks were sunken, her skin pasty in color, her breathing irregular. He lowered his head, and the tears filled his eyes while he prayed silently. *Dear Heavenly Father, words can't express how I feel right now.*

He stopped a moment to catch his breath and sniff. *You know how much I love this woman. I despise what has happened to her. She's so young, and she was so vibrant. We were so happy. We have a baby ... a baby who needs two parents. I have no right to ask, but please don't take her. I know I've asked this before, and here I go being selfish again, but I waited so long for the right woman. Please, Lord, please, make her whole again.*

What if making her whole would be taking her home to Me? Will you still follow Me?

He sniffed again. He couldn't wipe the tears in his isolation suit. They freely ran down his face. He looked at her face. She was so pale. He thought of what she'd been through. He couldn't bare her pain and anguish. *Thy will be done, Lord. Thy will be done. Amen.*

Her eyes slowly fluttered open. "Chris," she said barely above a whisper, and her voice hoarse.

"Yes, darling, I'm here," and he took her hand in his gloved hand.

"I'm really sick."

"I know you are." With his other gloved hand he touched her cheek. "Nothing that the Lord can't take care of."

She closed her eyes. When she opened them, she said in a whisper, "I'm really tired, Chris. I thought I was strong, but my strength has been sorely tested, and ... cancer is painful, even with the pain meds."

"I love you, Lori Anna. Please keep fighting ... for me ... for Olivia ... for yourself. Please don't give up."

She fell back asleep, but she was calmer, and her

breathing was not so irregular.

The nurse came over to check her vitals. "She's stabilized enough to return to her room, Mr. Wright," she said in a soft voice. "You can remove the suit where you put it on, and Dr. Rouse will meet you back in the waiting area."

Twenty minutes later Dr. Rouse joined him in the waiting room. "I should have the results in about an hour. You may as well head to the nurses' station outside her regular room. Lori Anna will be returned there shortly."

Lori Anna was enclosed in an isolation tent and on a gurney when she arrived back to her room. A nurse stepped around from behind her desk. "Mr. Wright, I have something for you."

Chris looked down at the stack of envelopes in her hands. "Lori Anna asked me to give these to you the next time you came," she said as she handed him the bundle.

He shuffled through the envelopes and realized they came from the stationery and matching envelopes he purchased for her when Olivia was born. That seemed like years ago, and not just seven short weeks. He'd hoped she'd be out of the hospital by now and on the mend, at home with him ... and Olivia. He bowed his head and momentarily closed his eyes.

When he looked up, they'd opened the curtain to her room. A chair appeared on his side of the window, and he sat. Although she was still asleep, he couldn't take his eyes off her face. She appeared at peace. *That's what people always like to say about the body in the coffin. "He looks peaceful" or "She looks sweet."* He shook his head. *I can't think like that, Lord. I need to be strong for her. Please give me strength.*

He heard the footsteps behind him. He turned his head to see his parents with Mom and Dad Stanley. His dad placed an arm on his shoulder and his mom hugged him. "Who's watching Olivia?" Chris asked.

His mom kissed his cheek. "She's fine, dear. She's with Christine. Nicholas was ecstatic to have another baby in the house. I left him jabbering away to her, and Olivia was so excited. They are so sweet together. He crawled to her and handed her his favorite toy."

His dad patted his shoulder. "We're here for you and Lori Anna. We've talked to the nurses and they're going to provide isolation suits for all of us. The five of us will be Lori Anna's prayer warriors. We can all gather around her and pray for her."

Chris stood to hug his dad, and the letters slid from his lap.

Dad Stanley bent over and picked them up. The one on top was addressed to Mom and Dad. "What's all this, Chris?"

"After Lori Anna birthed Olivia, and before her treatments began, she asked me to get her some stationery with matching envelopes and a pen. It appears she wanted to write some letters to select individuals. Her nurse just gave these to me. I suppose she wants me to give them out. You may as well keep your letter."

Dad Stanley handed the remaining envelopes back to Chris, and Chris called out the names on the envelopes. "The others are addressed to Jessica, Loretta, Olivia, me, and the man who wants to marry my daughter." His throat tightened on the last one. "She must be thinking she won't be around to meet that man," he said, blinking back tears, but failing. His mom placed her arms around him and held him while he cried.

A moment later he heard the nurse say, "We're ready, Mr. Wright. The suits are in the room that adjoins Lori Anna's room."

Chris had been in there many times over the past weeks. Although Lori Anna asked him not to bring Olivia anymore and upset her schedule, he'd been here on his own, ever so quietly, standing over her and watching her sleep. Sometimes he was only there less than a half hour, but he just wanted to hear her breathe. Yes, they could talk on the phone, but being here, and seeing her, provided him comfort. He lived for the moments she'd awaken and smile at him. However, lately, he was not blessed with those moments.

The five of them held hands around her bed. It was

so quiet and they did not want to awaken her. They decided Christopher would pray aloud softly for his daughter-in-law, and the others would pray in their hearts for her.

"Dear Heavenly Father, we are gathered here with heavy hearts. Our loved one is gravely ill, and we ask Thee for Thy healing touch upon her. Please help the doctors administer the proper treatment to aid in Lori Anna's complete recovery. We pray Lori Anna will have the opportunity to continue her role as Chris's wife and that she will have the chance to be the mother she so desperately wants to be for Olivia. We pray that Thou would give this family the strength to accept whatever Thy decision is for her healing. We are forever in Thy debt, and we pray this in the name of Thy Son Jesus Christ the Great Healer and the Great Savior, amen."

The others responded with their amens.

When Chris opened his eyes and looked at Lori Anna. She still slept, but he witnessed a slight smile on her face. Outside the room, Chris noticed the heads of all the nurses and Dr. Rouse were bowed in prayer.

"Thank You, Jesus," Chris said softly and gently touched his wife's cheek with his gloved hand. All of them did the same before they filed out of her room.

Dr. Rouse waited on them to change out of their suits. He was smiling when they approached him. "It's not chronic GVHD. It's acute and very mild. There has been success treating this with steroids. I'm starting her treatment immediately. The steroids have been ordered and we will begin in the hour. We all pray with you that Lori Anna will have a complete turnaround and His healing powers start now. God bless Lori Anna and you, her devoted family."

"Thank you, doctor, and God bless you, and this wonderful staff," said Chris.

Christopher placed his arm around Chris's shoulder. "Come to Christmas Hotel tonight at seven o'clock, Chris. Pastor Mason and the town are holding a candlelight prayer vigil for Lori Anna on the square. Meet us directly in front of Christmas Hotel."

Chris brought Olivia and the dogs. The evening was perfect: around sixty-five degrees, no wind, no clouds, the stars and the moon were clearly visible, and one particular star shined brightly overhead, as if the Lord had planned it. Hundreds of people were everywhere around the square and in front of the businesses surrounding the square, holding candles. In the center of the square, a stage with a microphone had been set up, and a young woman and a man came forward to sing. The only instrument was the strumming of his guitar.

As her beautiful voice filled the evening with "Amazing Grace" and "How Great Thou Art", Chris joined his family in front of Christmas Hotel.

Pastor Mason appeared next at the microphone and

cleared his throat. "I thank you all for coming to this prayer service for Lori Anna Stanley Wright. Let's pray. Dear Heavenly Father, we have all gathered here for Your child, Lori Anna. She is a beautiful young daughter, wife, and mother, whom we here in Franklin have had the privilege to watch grow up. We all have a heart for her, as she has a heart for Franklin and Simpson County, Kentucky. We lift her up to You tonight."

He paused here for a moment, to wipe a tear. Then he continued, his voice broken. "Together, we're asking You for a miracle; a miracle to stop the disease that's attacking Lori Anna's blood. Help her body fight back, Lord, and don't allow Lori Anna to quit fighting. Be with her now, Lord, and let her feel the peace and love these people have shown for her. We trust in Your love and mercy for Lori Anna. We all know life is but a fleeting moment. Please enable us all to appreciate our moment. Help us spread this love to a broken world. Help us return the love to others that our sweet Lori Anna has freely given all her life. In the precious name of Jesus Christ we pray, amen."

Amens were heard all around the square. Four people came forward to release helium balloons with Lori Anna Stanley Wright written on each one.

As the balloons flew higher into the sky, the singer and guitarist returned to sing "Lord, I Need Thee Every Hour".

"I need Thee every hour, most gracious Lord;
No tender voice like Thine can peace afford.
I need Thee, oh, I need Thee;
Every hour I need Thee;
Oh, bless me now, my Savior,
I come to Thee.

I need Thee every hour, in joy or pain;
Come quickly and abide, or life is vain."

The tears now flowed from Chris's eyes. *Lord, I do need Thee every hour.* He held his bundled daughter to his chest and wept.

Chapter Thirty-Two

The New Arrivals

"And he said unto me, My grace is sufficient for thee: for my strength is made perfect in weakness. Most gladly therefore will I rather glory in my infirmities, that the power of Christ may rest upon me."
2 Corinthians 12:9

Saturday Morning
October 29, 1988
Over the next week Chris visited his wife daily, although she was only aware once that he was there. She slept the other times. However, her skin was clearer, and her bouts with vomiting and diarrhea had lessened.

On Saturday morning it wasn't Olivia who awakened Chris, but Fritz whimpering at his bedroom door. As soon as he opened the door, Fritz jumped a few times then headed to the warm kitchen. Bella half-sat in the box he had prepared for her, and she was giving birth. Currently she was cleaning three puppies, and then labored with the next puppy. Over the next hour Bella whelped four more pups, for a total of seven. She nudged all of them toward her teats and lay down to rest.

Chris stroked her head. "Good job, Bella," and then he laughed when Fritz prodded his hand and whined. He patted Fritz's head. "Oh, and a good job to you, too, Fritz!"

Chris studied the pups. Four were short haired like Fritz, and the other three were long haired like Bella. "Well, Fritz, old boy. When we find homes for these pups, your ancestors Bullet and Gabe will have even more DNA spread around Simpson County."

After changing Olivia and feeding both of them and Fritz and Bella breakfast, he called Dr. Crocker's office. The receptionist made him an appointment to bring in Bella and her pups at one o'clock. In the meantime, he called Lori Anna.

"Seven puppies? How exciting. How's Bella?"

"She seems to be doing fine, and she did eat some breakfast and drink a lot of water. I've got an appointment to take her and her puppies to Dr. Crocker's office today. I'll call Mom and see if she can stay with Olivia. By the way, you sound chipper this morning, Lori Anna."

"Chris, I feel better than I have in days. I won't give all the credit to the new medicines. I do know you, your parents, and my parents were in here praying for me. I was too tired to open my eyes and speak to you, but I was aware of your presence. I only awakened for a few seconds, and I must have gone right back to sleep because I don't remember anything else."

He told her everything about that morning, and that Dr. Rouse and the nurses prayed for her, too.

"Well, Chris, as the saying goes, I don't know what the future holds, but I know Who holds my hand."

"I love you, Lori Anna."

"I love you, too, Chris."

Later that evening, Chris called Lori Anna's room again. She didn't answer. Next he called the nurses' station.

"She was feeling better earlier, Mr. Wright, but now she's fatigued again, along with more vomiting and diarrhea issues. Mr. Wright, she'll have her ups and downs, so please stay hopeful."

"Thank you. I appreciate the care you and the other nurses provide."

"You're welcome, Mr. Wright, and thank you."

He checked on Bella and the puppies, changed the bedding, and added a low-setting heating pad Dr. Crocker had suggested at the earlier appointment. Tired, he sat in his recliner and watched Olivia bounce happily in her swing. When she started fussing, Chris picked her up, and placed her face down across his lap and rubbed her back. He had noticed his mother doing this for Olivia, and it seemed to quiet her.

By his side on the end table sat his unopened letter from Lori Anna, propped up against his Bible. He picked up both of them. This past week he had mailed the letters to Jessica and Loretta. The other two letters: one for Olivia and one for "the man who wants to marry my daughter" were secured in the lockbox in his home office.

He prayed before opening his letter. What Lori Anna said earlier rang in his ears. "I don't know what the future holds, but I know Who holds my hand." Had she resigned her fate in the Lord's hand? Was she telling me it would be okay with her if she lived, or went home to her Heavenly Father? Was she asking me to make peace with whatever the Lord decided?

While Olivia slept on his lap, he sighed loudly and opened the letter.

My beloved husband Chris,

I can't describe how blessed I am to have you love me. You are every woman's dream for a husband, lover, and a friend. You are compassionate, and you know the right words to say when I hurt. You are loving and kind, and you bring me great joy and happiness. You have all of these fruits of the Spirit, along with peace, goodness, faithfulness, gentleness, and self-control.

You know I've loved you all my life. He chose me to be your wife, and I thank Him for that. I believe in soulmates, and I know that's exactly what we are.

However, I need to be realistic. I want what's best for you and Olivia. If the Lord takes me home, you will someday desire to love again, and Olivia should have a mother. Please don't be afraid to give in to your feelings, if that happens. I thank God Loretta was my biological mother, because she chose life for me. I've thanked her for that in her letter, and that she was wise enough to choose my adoptive parents, because my parents could not have been better parents if I had been born to them.

When your sister Lily's mother died following her birth, God later provided Jerilyn for Christopher's wife and Lily's mother. In turn, when Jerilyn's husband was killed at Pearl Harbor, God provided Christopher for her husband and the father for Ken and Carrie Emeline.

What I'm trying to say is that should He take me home, He will send the right woman for you and Olivia. Please don't think you are being disloyal to me to choose another love. You are too wonderful a man to live in sorrow and regret. That is my wish for you and Olivia.

With all my love,
Lori Anna

Chris folded the letter, bowed his head, and let the tears fall onto his daughter.

Chapter Thirty-Three

Thanksgiving and Adversity

*"In every thing give thanks: for this is the will
of God in Christ Jesus concerning you."*
1 Thessalonians 5:18

November 24, 1988
Over the past three weeks, Chris visited Lori Anna a couple days a week, or called two or three times each day. Some days she seemed happy and with energy, but other days she was tired and haggard looking. She had lost a great deal of weight over the past two months, and her gaunt face and body scared him. He did his best to act normal on the visits, but he could tell she knew it was an act. Understandably, she missed her baby. However, she was eating small meals now and no longer completely depended on the IV feedings.

On Thursday, after his family celebrated Thanksgiving, and with Dr. Rouse's permission, Chris took her some of the family special dishes: asparagus casserole, oyster cornbread dressing, corn casserole, and sweet potato casserole to add to the hospital's turkey dinner.

They said their prayer together, and Lori Anna added the verse from 1 Thessalonians 5:18, to give thanks in all things. She stared into his eyes and said with firmness but in a soft tone, "I meant that, Chris. I've been reading my Bible several times a day again, and I came across that verse this morning. I do give thanks to Him in all things, even my leukemia. I've learned so much about myself. I've been happy, like when I married you, and when Olivia was born, and I've been despondent. However, sometimes I feel so close to Him I can feel His arms around me, holding me. It's in those moments I feel such peace, and sometimes it's overwhelming. I've grown so close to the Lord, and I know I'll never take His love for granted ever again. If not for the leukemia, I may not have experienced this closeness with Him. Sometimes I wonder if He's preparing me to meet Him. What I do know is that He will heal me one way or another; whether in my earthly body or in Heaven with Him."

Although he was covered in his isolation suit, Chris took her in his arms and held her. Finally, he released her and changed the subject. "Okay, eat up while it's still warm, or my mom will never forgive me."

When she finished eating what she was able, she said, "Oh, Chris, please tell your mom that the food was amazing. I'm so full, and I've not eaten this much food since I was carrying Olivia."

He laughed and said, "I'm just going to have to

bring you food every day. Maybe we can fatten you up."

"How is Olivia?"

"Our daughter is as incredible as her mother. She now eats as much as you!"

Lori Anna smiled and it warmed his heart. He hadn't received that many smiles from her in the past two months, but he knew, at times, the pain was excruciating. "She giggles when I play peek-a-boo with her, and she points to the dogs and puppies and laughs."

"How are the puppies?"

"They wrestle with each other and bite and chew each other's ears to the point that I think one of them will be injured. I've never raised a litter, but to me, Fritz and Bella's offspring are overly rambunctious. I said that to Mr. Hanover and he just roared with laughter. His dogs whelped several litters over the years, and to quote him, 'It's quite normal.' Two of them crawled out of the box yesterday, but Bella kept an eye on them, not letting them travel out of her view. When the one rounded the corner, she picked it up by the scruff of the neck and put it back in the box, and the other runaway, too. I guess I'd better get a fence for the kitchen area to contain them."

He saw her eyes droop and knew she was tired. "You get some rest, Lori Anna, and I'll be back tomorrow."

They hugged, and she said, "I love you, Chris, and

tell Olivia I love her."

"I will and I love you, too."

When he returned to the family home to pick up his daughter, his mother was in her office working on a new novel, and his father sat in the living room reading his Bible. Near the feet of his dad, Olivia lay sound asleep in the cradle he and his four siblings had slept in as babies.

Chris took a seat on the sofa. "How was Olivia while I was gone, Dad?"

Setting his Bible on the end table and removing his reading glasses, his father said, "She was wonderful, Chris. She drank all her formula at her evening meal. How's Lori Anna?"

"If I could use one phrase, I'd say content with her situation." He relayed to his father what Lori Anna had said to him. "Lori Anna maintains her faith in Him and I feel as though I'm losing mine."

His father sat up straighter in his chair and rubbed his chin in thought. "I see Lori Anna's disease as adversity, but adversity is what defines us, son. I sometimes think about all the adversity your mother and I went through over the years, especially when Lydia Grace was kidnapped, and the two miscarriages of your mother. It's hard to think in the present how much stronger adversity makes one, but when looking back, it made your mother and me stronger."

Christopher sighed and shook his head. "When

adversity strikes, we sometimes forget to rely on God. It's important to recall past answers to prayer, guidance provided by the Holy Spirit, and what we learned in prior crises. Don't let your distressed emotions impede clear thinking. Whatever happens, you two will be fine, son. Know that God is *always* with you."

"Thanks, Dad. It's hard. I watch Lori Anna feeling and looking better one day, and the next day she's back at the starting point." He exhaled and rubbed his temples. "I wish I knew how and when this will all end."

He told his dad about Lori Anna's letter.

"It sounds to me as though Lori Anna is ready to accept whatever fate the Lord hands her. You must be strong, son. You must let her know you'll be okay. I think that's what she needs to hear from you. It's not giving up, Chris, it's letting go and letting God do what's needed for Lori Anna ... and you ... and Olivia."

Chris hung his head. "I don't know if I'm ready, Dad." He stood. "Tell Mom I love her, and I'll call tomorrow." He picked up his sleeping daughter and left for home.

Chapter Thirty-Four

In The Chapel at Christmas Hotel

*"This is the day which the Lord hath made; we
will rejoice and be glad in it."*
Psalm 118:24

Thursday
December 01, 1988
Chris tiptoed into the bedroom to check on Olivia. She lay on her back, sleeping with a slight smile on her sweet face. She had kicked off the covers, so he straightened the quilt and tucked her in. His mother had made this quilt over a period of eight months. With a chuckle and the inevitable hug, Mom had explained, "It's my first quilt. I want you to have it. You're my youngest and my last, so you get my practice quilt."

The phone rang, interrupting his reminiscing and jolting him back to the present. He stepped out of the room, quietly closing the door. "Hello," he said into the receiver. "Yes, Mom, she's asleep. Yes, I'm okay. I'll probably take off a few days from Christmas Hotel. I think Mr. Hanover, Mr. Adams, Mr. Thompson, Mr. Clark, and of course you and Dad can make certain all shifts are covered. I just need to be here *and* at the hospital."

"I understand, son. Please let me help you more. You're wearing yourself thin."

"I'm fine, Mom. I love you."

"I love you, too. Never forget that."

Chris let the dogs out for the morning romp, along with the puppies, knowing Bella would keep them in line. He fixed himself some coffee and toast and sat in his recliner to feed Olivia her formula. He watched as she suckled the nipple on the bottle. She stopped a moment, stared at him, and smiled. Formula trickled from the corner of her mouth. He held her closer and hugged her. "I love you so very much, Olivia. You're as cute as your mommy."

His well-worn Bible lay on the table, so he picked it up for his morning devotions. He bowed his head and prayed first. When he finished, he had an overwhelming urge to pray in the Christmas Hotel chapel.

Olivia was finished eating, so he changed her and dressed her in something warmer. He let the dogs in, making certain they had plenty of food and water, bundled up Olivia in her one-piece snowsuit, and set out for Christmas Hotel. He entered the chapel and knelt at the altar with Olivia in her car seat beside him.

"Dear Heavenly Father, I felt Your pull, drawing me into this chapel. I always feel closeness to You in this chapel more than any other place I know. I'm doing my best to accept the possibilities that can happen. You know how much I love my wife, my daughter, and all my family. However, I love You more. I will abide in Your decision and Your love. I give You my life and future completely. Whatever You decide I will honor."

I want you to preach.

"What?" Chris looked around, and he was alone. "Was that You, Lord?"

I want you to preach.

"Lord, that's twice I've heard you speak to my heart, while in this chapel. You're calling me to preach?"

Yes, I am.

A peace filled Chris's soul like none other. He thought about his dad, the preacher for the Christmas Hotel chapel, and the many years his dad spent as the chaplain on duty at Protestant Hospital, now renamed Baptist Hospital.

Olivia stirred and Chris picked her up. Hugging his daughter close to his chest, he looked up at the empty cross. "Thy will be done, Lord."

When Chris returned home, the phone was ringing. He reached the phone before the caller hung up. "Hello?"

"This is Dr. Rouse. Am I speaking to Chris?"

"Yes, sir."

"I have wonderful news. Lori Anna's most recent blood work came back an hour ago. I can say she's in complete remission."

An hour ago I was praying in the Christmas Hotel chapel. "What does complete remission mean exactly, Dr. Rouse?"

"It means her tests, physical exam, scans, and blood work show no sign of cancer."

"Is she cured?"

"No doctor will say a cancer patient is cured until at least five years have passed, and even then with reservation. I won't lie to you, Chris. Cancer cells can return. Let's pray Lori Anna will remain in remission, and thank God for today."

"Oh, I do Dr. Rouse. How long will she need to remain in the hospital?"

"Let's see about helping her get some strength back and fatten her up a little. We're moving her out of isolation as we speak. However, she will remain in a private room. When we do release her, we don't want her to overdo, and not lift anything heavier than her daughter. She won't be allowed physical exercise for a while."

"May I bring my daughter to the hospital – and our parents?"

"As long as no one has a cold. Lori Anna is still weak, and we don't want her to fight another ailment at this time. I think we can bend the rules a bit. I know there's a two-visitors-at-a-time rule. I'll have that worked out by the time you get here."

"Thank you, Dr. Rouse, for everything."

When Christopher, Jerilyn, James, Carol Ann, Chris, and Olivia entered Lori Anna's room, she was propped up in bed, wearing her own nighty, with the Bible spread open across her lap. She wore pale pink lipstick, the short wig Jerilyn and Carol Ann had bought her, and she had some blush applied on her thin cheeks. Chris's heart swelled in love for his wife. The parents stood back, allowing him to go to her first.

Mama Stanley took Olivia and removed her snowsuit while Chris hugged and kissed his wife, the tears flowing from the both of them. When he released her, he saw the others dabbing at their eyes. Lori Anna held her arms open for Olivia, and her mom sat on the other side of the bed, handed Olivia to her daughter, and then she hugged them both. Lori Anna wrapped Olivia in her arms, holding her close to her breast and kissed the velvety head. Olivia's eyes widened in wonder, and she placed her tiny hand on her mother's face. Lori Anna kissed the little hand, and Olivia laughed.

Dad Stanley was next to hug Lori Anna. Christopher and Jerilyn followed. The nurses had provided five chairs in anticipation of the visit. Dr.

Rouse's orders were that the visitors were to stay no more than one hour, so as not to tire his patient. They made the most of every moment.

For the final ten minutes the parents rose and left the little family with some time alone. Chris and Lori Anna prayed together for the first time while holding their daughter.

In a hoarse voice, Chris began, "Dear Heavenly Father, I am so overwhelmed with joy and love. Your decision to return my wife to Olivia and me is of course what I prayed would happen." He stopped a moment to squeeze his wife's hand and wipe a tear with the other. "You have given Lori Anna and me the opportunity to spend our lives together and raise our daughter, and we will not waste a single moment. We look forward to our future and we thank You for this blessed day. 'This is the day which the Lord hath made; we will rejoice and be glad in it.' I thank You for this day, Lord, and in the name of Your Son Jesus we pray."

Together they said, "Amen."

Chapter Thirty-Five

Homecoming

"Trust in the LORD with all thine heart; and lean not unto thine own understanding. In all thy ways acknowledge him, and he shall direct thy paths."
Proverbs 3:5-6

December 07, 1988
Chris awakened early that morning, showered, shaved, and dressed. Lori Anna was being released today. He hurried to the kitchen, put on the coffee pot, and let Fritz and Bella out, along with the seven pups. The five-week-old puppies were so lively and cute. A light snow fell and they played and wrestled in it. *Lori Anna will get to meet them today, too. She'll be so excited.*

He headed to Olivia's room where the east sun streamed into her room. She was awake, laughing, and batting her chubby little arms at the Noah's Ark mobile above her crib. The room had no baby decorations on the walls. That was something he knew Lori Anna would delight in planning after she returned home. His hope for his wife coming home was always in the back of his mind, even on those days when he had bad news, when he was losing faith. *Thank You, Lord, for the umpteenth time!*

He changed Olivia and chose her prettiest dress with matching leggings and hair ribbons. Lastly, he placed hand-crocheted booties on her feet made by Grandma Stanley.

"Oh, Olivia, you are so pretty," he cooed to his daughter as he tickled her belly. "It's hard to believe you're three months old, and Mommy's coming home today, sweetheart. You'll finally get to *really* appreciate her. You're going to love her, Olivia. She's the kindest and most loving person you'll ever know." He picked her up and hugged her close. "Let's go have breakfast."

Olivia could now sit propped up in her highchair with pillows all around her. He belted her in, and tied a large bib around her neck. She grabbed the cooled teething ring he set on her highchair tray. After he poured his mug of coffee, and set out Bella and Fritz's breakfast along with fresh water, he prepared and fed Olivia her baby cereal and mashed fruit, while drinking his mug of coffee.

By the time Olivia finished breakfast, the dogs were at the door waiting to come in. He helped the puppies back into the box and set their softened puppy chow and water in the box, while Fritz and Bella ate the bowls of their breakfast near the back door.

Olivia was ready for her bottle and a morning nap.

He sat down in his recliner to feed Olivia her formula and read his morning devotions and Bible, while nibbling on a blueberry muffin. He opened to the Book of Proverbs and read aloud. "'Trust in the LORD with all thine heart; and lean not unto thine own understanding. In all thy ways acknowledge him, and he shall direct thy paths'. That's me, Lord. I had not been placing my complete trust in You. I fretted, worried, questioned You, at times I grew angry instead of letting go and letting You handle everything. Don't get me wrong, Lord, I'm pleased you chose remission for Lori Anna, but I will no longer sit and beg You to do things my way. It's not my way that matters, it's Your way. If I've learned anything from this whole ordeal, it's that all decisions are made by You."

He looked down at his daughter, smiled, and she faintly smiled back at him, her eye lids drooping. "Direct my path, Lord. I feel Your call for me to preach stronger than ever. I'd still like to manage Christmas Hotel, too, but I will not step out of Your will. You'll have to let me know if I'll remain the manager or if You have someone else in mind. After all, it's still owned by my parents. I know they'll want to be part of Christmas Hotel until the day they die, just like the Captain and Mrs. Bazell."

At the ringing of the phone, he laid the now sleeping Olivia in her cradle and hurried to the kitchen to answer it, stepping over the fenced area.

"Hello, Mr. Wright, I'm your wife's nurse today, Nurse Hansen. I'm preparing your wife for check-out. Her papers are currently being processed. She should be ready to go home in about two hours."

"Thank you so much, Nurse Hansen, for calling. I'll be leaving for the hospital shortly."

He called her parents and his parents, asking if they'd like to ride along or just be at his home for a surprise for Lori Anna. Both sets of parents decided to surprise her at the house.

Lori Anna's discharge papers were complete, and she was in a wheelchair and ready to leave when he and Olivia arrived. She kissed and hugged Chris, and then she asked him to hand her Olivia. Olivia stared at her, but when her mommy kissed her she smiled and nestled against Lori Anna's breast. A tear escaped Lori Anna's eye, and Chris wiped it. "I've missed her first three months, Chris."

"Don't worry, honey, I took plenty of pictures and videos. They're waiting for you. You'll have ample make-up time with her."

When they pulled into the driveway, Lori Anna said in surprise, "Your parents and my parents are here."

"They wanted to welcome you home. I hope you're not too tired for a little visit."

"Not at all. I'm just so happy to be home."

He leaned over and kissed her. "I'll get Olivia out of

her car seat."

They entered the house, and she was greeted first by Bella, tail wagging furiously, and then hugged by the two mothers. Jerilyn said, "Today was a sad day for me and all of America forty-seven years ago: Pearl Harbor Day. I never thought then I could ever be happy again on this particular date. However, last year we welcomed the birth of Nicholas on this date, and now this year with your return home. I thank God today for smiling down on you and our family, Lori Anna."

"Thank you, Mama Jerilyn."

Her father and Chris's dad hugged her next, and then Fritz sat at her feet, wagging his tail and whining. She bent down to him, "Fritz, I haven't forgotten you," she said, while scratching him behind the ears.

The puppies jumped up the sides of the fence barrier, trying to get out. "Oh, the puppies are so cute." She stepped over the fence, sat on the kitchen floor, and picked up each pup, one at a time. Bella and Fritz sat beside her, tails wagging, as she admired the pups. After setting the last pup down, she hugged Bella and Fritz. "I'm so happy for you two. You have a beautiful family."

Chris handed Olivia to his mom and helped Lori Anna up from the floor, removed her coat, and led her to the sofa. Chris's dad had built a fire in the fireplace, creating a warm and cozy atmosphere for the homecoming. Removing Olivia's snowsuit, Chris then handed their daughter to Lori Anna, and sat down beside her on the sofa. Olivia cuddled in her mother's arms and promptly fell asleep. All three women wiped tears of happiness. It appeared Olivia was already bonding with Lori Anna.

Mom and Mama Stanley picked up the brightly wrapped package from where they had set it on the coffee table in front of Lori Anna. "We had this specially made for you, dear," said Mama Stanley.

"I don't want to disturb Olivia, so would you open it for me, Chris?"

Taped to the package was a card. "Lori Anna, we hope you will know that much love and thought went into this gift. Love, Mom and Mama Jerilyn," he read. Chris picked up the package, tore off the bow and the ribbon, and then tore into the wrapping. He removed the box top, opened the tissue paper, and removed a black wig, at least two feet in length.

Her mom watched her face. "It's your own hair, dear," she said softly. "Chris saved as much as he could, and then Jerilyn and I took it to a wig maker in Nashville. Now you can wear the short wig we gave you, or this one with your own hair until your own hair regrows."

Lori Anna's eyes glistened with tears. Chris placed his arm around her and hugged her close. "Thank you all so much," she choked out.

Her mom and Jerilyn bent down and hugged her.

"We're all going to leave now so you can rest," said her mom. "We've left a chicken casserole in the ice box for when you two have dinner tonight. There are also some fresh biscuits in the bread box."

"Your dad and I brought in more wood for the fireplace and the wood stove," added Christopher. "There should be plenty for tonight and tomorrow morning."

"Call us if you need anything," offered Jerilyn.

After they left, Chris wrapped his arms around his wife and daughter.

"We certainly are blessed with wonderful parents, Chris."

"I couldn't agree more," he said as he held his family.

Chapter Thirty-Six

Into the Woods and Nursery Decorations

*"My soul waiteth for the LORD more than they
that watch for the morning: I say, more than
they that watch for the morning."*
Psalm 130:6

Friday and Saturday
December 09 and 10, 1988
Lori Anna awakened even earlier than Chris and Olivia that morning, made the coffee, let the two dogs and seven puppies outside, and settled in the recliner for devotions and a mug of steaming hot coffee. She opened the Bible to the Psalms, which always brought her comfort. She read aloud, "My soul waiteth for the Lord more than they that watch for the morning: I say, more than they that watch for the morning."

She thought about that. *My soul has been waiting on You throughout this illness, Lord. Even when my mind thought You had abandoned me, my heart and soul knew differently. Sometimes, I thought the morning might never come for me again, and that the sun had set on my earthly life. I can't help from wondering why all this occurred. However, I knew Your love and mercy prevailed. I know You do nothing unnecessarily.*

Out of this ordeal, I met my biological father, his wife, and I now have four more siblings. After all these years, Barry was finally able to ask for Loretta's forgiveness. Loretta was able to find closure by forgiving Barry. Was that Your plan, Lord? Were You using me to bring all of these people together this Christmas? If that was Your plan, it worked. I must ask Chris about having a Christmas get-together with all my siblings.

She smiled when Chris entered the room. Sitting on the arm of the recliner, he kissed her, and then he gently ran his fingers through the long hair of her wig. "You look more like your old self every day. Your cheeks are filling out."

"I feel more like my old self every day."

"You were deep in thought when I walked in here."

"I suppose I was," and she explained her thoughts.

"That's heavy. Maybe He *was* bringing all of you together. After all, Barry is not the man he was all those years ago."

"I agree. I'd like to invite all of my siblings here before Christmas. Maybe they'd like to skate on our largest pond. That way they can get to know each other, too. I'd also like to offer Jessica the pick of the litter. Without her bone marrow, I would never have survived. In fact, Dr. Rouse told me that because of the GVHD, Jessica's healthy cells probably attacked the remaining cancer cells. As you heard from Dr. Rouse, he wouldn't say I've been cured, but I know he feels I have ... and so do I."

Chris patted her arm, "I do too, honey. How about we all have breakfast, and take Olivia into the woods for her first Christmas tree? Do you feel strong enough to carry her in the baby backpack while I chop down the tree?"

"Definitely. I'll also bring my camera and get lots of pictures to add to another album. We've already filled one album of pictures from our first year together."

Following breakfast, the family bundled up, ready for the trek into the woods. Fritz, Bella, and the seven puppies followed them.

"Just look at us, Chris. Last year we traipsed off to the woods with just the two of us, Bella and Fritz. This year we're married, we've added Olivia, and we have seven rowdy pups at our heels. What a difference a year makes."

Shortly, Lori Anna pointed to a beautiful and full tree. "How about that one, Mr. Bunyan?"

He stared at her and laughed, "So, I'm Paul Bunyan again?"

"Only when you cut down trees."

He held up his saw, "Remember I have no ax, just a saw."

"Is this a repeat of last year?"

"Only if you really think I can cut down this ten-foot tree and drag it back to the house."

She stood beside it, placed her hands on her hips, looking way up to check it out. "It *may* be a bit too tall. How about that one?"

He looked at the scraggly tree. "Are we returning to a Charlie Brown Christmas tree?"

"We could set it in Olivia's room on her dresser. She'll be fascinated with the lights. Speaking of Olivia's room, Mom and your mom are coming tomorrow to take me shopping in Nashville to purchase decorations for Olivia's room."

"Are you sure you're not overdoing it?"

"I'll be fine. If I get tired, we can always leave."

"Are you taking Olivia?"

"I think three women can take care of one little girl. We'll take the fold-up stroller."

He stopped and stared at a tree. "How about *that* one? It's full, and it's the right height for our living room."

"Perfect." She sat on a log and removed the backpack holding Olivia. Spreading a thick blanket on the ground, she pulled the legs tucked up in the backpack, turning it into a portable baby seat and sat it on the blanket with Olivia in it. With Olivia secure, Lori

Anna snapped pictures. The dogs and puppies ran around her and Olivia and Chris, playing in the light snow on the ground. Olivia raised her face to the snow and laughed when snowflakes fell on her face. Chris sawed on the tree, while the curious puppies jumped at his heels. Bella ran interference, steering her pups away from Chris.

Twenty minutes later, Chris plopped down on the log beside his wife and daughter. Removing a sweat rag from his back pocket, he wiped his face, removed his cap, and wiped his head. Olivia bounced in her makeshift chair. Chris looked from the dogs to his daughter, and turned to his wife. She smiled at him, displaying those dimples that delighted him. She kissed his cheek and snuggled against him.

He turned her face to him and kissed her. "Lori Anna, can life get any better than this? I love you and Olivia so much. I'm a blessed man."

"I'm a blessed woman."

They watched their daughter, both laughing as she batted at the snowflakes. "I think we'd better head back home, Chris or Olivia will be as wet in the face as you."

Less than an hour later they were back, wiping the paws of the two dogs and seven pups, ready to set the tree in the stand. The doorbell rang and Chris opened the door to his parents. "Just in time, Dad. You can help me get the tree straight in the stand, while Lori Anna rests with Olivia."

"Sounds like a plan, son. Your mom brought all of us a tuna casserole for lunch, and we'd be happy to help you decorate this tree."

While the men righted the tree, Lori Anna sat on the sofa feeding Olivia her bottle, and Jerilyn joined her. The puppies no longer stayed in the box, but they were behind the temporary wall fencing them in the kitchen. Jerilyn eyed the lively pups. "It appears they're big enough to go to new homes." She looked toward her son and Lori Anna. "I hope you two haven't grown so attached to them that you won't find them homes."

"Not to worry, Mom," said Chris, taking a break from decorating the tree that now stood proudly in the room. "They're six weeks old tomorrow, and we've already been talking about homes. In fact, we were planning on asking Jessica if she'd like to choose the first puppy. After all, she's the one that went through the pain to save Lori Anna's life."

"Splendid idea," said Jerilyn. "What about the others?"

"Well, I thought Loretta and Ken's three daughters might want a puppy," said Lori Anna. "They were in our wedding."

Christopher added, "Brian and Christine might want a puppy for Nicholas, and Lily and John currently have no dog. Their dog died last year. They're probably ready for another."

"That's a possible four," said Jerilyn. "Lydia Grace

will be home at Christmas. She and Jacob might want to take one back to New York for Anthony. In fact, they're driving in this year instead of flying, so they'd be able to take a puppy with them."

"Carrie Emeline has a Cocker Spaniel, so I don't think she'd want a German Shepherd and Golden Retriever mix," said Chris. He eyed his mom and rounded his eyes. "You and Dad haven't had a dog in a while."

His parents stared at each other, and his mother raised that one eyebrow in question to her husband.

"That's something we'd need to discuss," said Dad. "We mostly kept dogs for our children, but as you can see, you've all left the nest. I'm not sure we want to take on training a pup at our ages – do we, Jerilyn?"

"Well, Christopher, I don't know ... maybe. I kind of miss having a dog around."

"Well, that's a possible six," noted Chris. "Lori Anna has Bella, and I have Fritz, so I think Olivia should have a puppy to grow up with. What do you think, Lori Anna?"

"I completely agree. We'll keep the last pup for Olivia."

Olivia fell asleep after drinking her formula, so Lori Anna placed her in the cradle in the living room so she could be near them.

Chris hung the last ornament on the tree. "Voila," he said, "All done."

"Not quite," said his mom. She reached in her purse and pulled out a gift-wrapped box. "This is for Olivia. So who would like to unwrap it?"

Chris smiled and nodded toward his wife. "Give it to Lori Anna, Mom. I think she can do the honors this year. If it's what I suspect, Olivia can do the future honors."

Lori Anna tore into the wrapping. The box held a large round red ornament with *Olivia Ann Wright* written in gold script, and *First Christmas* in green script. "Aww, thank you, Mama Jerilyn. It's beautiful. Chris told me all about each of his ornaments you made, when we were hanging them on the tree last year." She held it up for her husband, "Chris, since I opened it, you find a prominent spot on the tree for Olivia's first Christmas ornament."

Chris took the ornament from her and hung it in a spot so it could be seen from anywhere in the room.

"And now, let's eat," said Dad. "Our next stop is to visit Brian and Christine, and deliver our great-grandson Nicholas's second Christmas ornament from your mom."

*****

The next morning, Jerilyn, Carol Ann, along with Christine and Nicholas arrived in the Suburban with Jerilyn driving. "Look who we picked up on the way," said Jerilyn, as she opened the door to the back seat for Lori Anna to strap Olivia in her car seat. Jerilyn knew that the company of Christine and baby Nicholas would be appreciated by her daughter-in-law.

"Christine, I'm thrilled you could come!" she squealed. "I wish I'd thought of inviting you myself!"

"Yesterday, when Grandma and Grampa Wright brought Nicholas's second year Christmas ornament, she invited me for a girls' day out with the babies. This will be so much fun, and we can get some Christmas shopping done, too."

"Mama Jerilyn, where are we heading?" asked Lori Anna.

"I thought we'd exit the interstate in Nashville and drive to *Castner Knott's*. They'll have everything we need, but I do miss shopping at *Harveys Department Store*. I'd been shopping there every year since I first arrived in Franklin, and now the building is demolished and the space is just another parking lot. I hope that doesn't happen to *Castner Knott's*. This particular store on Church Street has been around since the end of the last century. It's sad our historic old buildings are being torn down. Progress, I suppose."

"I agree, it *is* sad, Jerilyn," said Carol Ann, and she turned around in her seat to see her daughter. "What do you have in mind for Olivia's room, dear?"

"I want everything to do with nature. Chris and I enjoy the outdoors at home, and we've been known to sit outside even in the winter. I thought I'd like to find wallpaper with trees, birds, deer, squirrels, rabbits, and of course wild flowers. I want crib bedding with the same, and plenty of stuffed animals of God's little creatures. I already have the white crib, dresser, changing table, and a white rocker, thanks to my two moms helping Chris when Olivia was born." She paused and patted Carol Ann on the shoulder and smiled at Jerilyn in the rear view mirror. "I don't know what Chris would have done without *all* of his family and my mom. You three and Lily really came to his rescue when I was in the hospital."

Christine was the closest to Lori Anna, "We were happy to help, Lori Anna. We're family, and that's what families do for each other. We're just happy you're home now with Olivia and Chris, and we can have this shopping day together."

They arrived at the store, parked, and removed the two strollers from the rear of the Suburban.

Jerilyn again cautioned her daughter-in-law. "Lori Anna, if you get the least bit tired, please *do not* hesitate to tell us. We don't want you to wear yourself out. We have plenty of times we can come back."

"I promise, Mama Jerilyn."

Jerilyn was the first to see the "Pictures with Santa" sign. "Oh, look, let's get a picture of Nicholas and Olivia together with Santa."

"We'd better see how long the line is," said Carol Ann. "We don't want to get tired standing there, and not be able to shop."

Christine walked to the end of the short line and returned. "It looks perfect right now. I only see four ahead of us. Let's do it. The first Christmas we have both babies."

When it was their turn, at first Nicholas did not want any part of Santa. "I guess he's at that age of wariness," said Christine.

However, the children's photographer was excellent. She played with and teased Nicholas, encouraged a smile, and then from Olivia, too. The mommies and grandmothers wanted to have their own copies of the two babies together, and they wouldn't have to wait. The pictures would be ready by the time they finished shopping.

Lori Anna spoke to the photographer. "That was amazing. I'm a photographer for a newspaper, but I've never before seen a children's photographer in action. I didn't think you were going to capture a picture of the two babies both smiling, but you did, and you made it look so easy."

"It's not always easy," said the young woman. "Sometimes I get lucky."

She moved on to the next child, and the same thing happened as she turned the crying child into a smiling child.

Lori Anna walked away with the other women and commented, "I think the young lady photographer is very good at her job and extremely modest."

Next stop: the baby department. Now the real excitement began as each woman found something that might interest Lori Anna and held it up. About a dozen times, the three women said to Lori Anna, "What about this?"

The sales lady became enthusiastically involved after she was told the theme. By the time they left the baby department, Lori Anna had all she came for, except the wallpaper. The sales lady was on it. She called her friend in that department.

When she hung up the in-store phone, she turned to Lori Anna, and said with a big grin, "My friend Shirley in wallpaper and drapes says she thinks she has exactly what you want, and quite fitting for a baby's room."

After telling them which floor they would find their wallpaper, she wished them well, and they thanked her for all her assistance.

The sales lady in wallpaper and drapes was just as helpful. The wallpaper was perfect and not too busy with a whimsical repeating scene of trees, squirrels, rabbits, and even a deer drinking at a pond. They found bed sheets that Jerilyn offered to sew into curtains.

Jerilyn noticed Lori Anna appeared to be getting tired. There wasn't as much pep in her step. "How about we rest and have lunch in the *Castner Knott* dining room?"

"I agree," said Carol Ann.

The tired women settled at a large corner booth overlooking Nashville. Olivia and Nicholas had fallen asleep in their strollers, but awakened at the smell of food arriving. Lori Anna held Olivia and fed her a bottle, while Nicholas enjoyed his peanut butter and jelly sandwich, and his milk in his own personal sippy cup with his name on it – a gift from Grandma Lily for his first birthday.

Lori Anna asked Christine, "What are you giving Brian for Christmas."

"Well, I thought I'd get some ideas walking through this store today. I suppose I'm clueless."

"I'm the same about Chris."

"I have a suggestion," said Jerilyn. "They both love to fish and hunt, so we could stop in the fishing and hunting department before leaving."

"That's a great idea, Grandma Wright. Are you up to a bit more shopping, Lori Anna?"

"Yes, I'm refreshed, and I think our babies are, too. However, they'll both probably sleep on the way home." Lori Anna laughed and added, "I may join them."

They decided on new hunting jackets for their men. "Good gifts," said Jerilyn. "They both received their jackets from their dads around ages fourteen or fifteen. Neither one of those boys will admit that they've outgrown them."

Before leaving the store, they picked up the Santa pictures and headed home. True to her word, Lori Anna and the two babies slept all the way.

Chapter Thirty-Seven

Ice Skating with Seven Siblings

*"Thou wilt shew me the path of life: in thy
presence is fulness of joy; at thy right hand
there are pleasures for evermore."*
Psalm 16:11

Friday, December 23, 1988

Chris and Lori Anna lingered over their breakfast in discussion. The dogs and pups were outside for a morning romp, and Olivia slept in her cradle, following her morning cereal and formula.

"Well, Lori Anna, last year your Christmas wish was to meet Loretta. Out of that Christmas wish you also met three siblings. This year, we both received our wish, for a healthy baby and that you would get well." His eyes misted over, he sniffed, and blinked back the tears building.

Lori Anna looked around their cozy kitchen and into the living room where the tree twinkled and the gifts under it had piled up over the past two weeks. "No doubt about it, Chris. We've been blessed. How could anyone think what happened throughout this past year was a coincidence, because I certainly don't."

"Neither do I."

"God knew what He was doing. We just needed to be patient and wait. Out of this ordeal I've found four more siblings, of which one saved my life. I'm also getting my prayers answered today, with all seven of my siblings arriving. Thankfully, the largest of the three ponds has been frozen for the past month, and it's perfect for ice skating."

"God has really been working in our lives and that of our family this past year, Lori Anna. Barry was able to tell Loretta his feelings of regret and sorrow, and Loretta now knows Barry tried to find her all those years ago. Loretta said she forgave him when she got saved, but she was finally able to tell him to his face, although I know it was difficult for her. I'm glad I was there to witness the scene when they came face-to-face."

He took her hand and continued. "There's something else that came out of the past three months, which was purely unexpected, at least for me." Taking a deep breath he slowly exhaled. "I feel the call to preach, Lori Anna. Twice while you were in the hospital God spoke to my heart, and now since you've been home the pull has been stronger. I've even pursued information from Belmont University in Nashville. How do you feel about being married to a preacher?"

With her palm she cupped his cheek. "I want whatever God calls you to do. I think you'll make a fine preacher."

"I wonder if this has something to do with Dad. He did turn seventy-five this year. I'm not saying that's old, but maybe God is transitioning me to preach in the Christmas Hotel chapel. As you say, we'll just need to wait and see. I already have my Bachelor's degree in business management, so it won't be as if I'll be starting over at the university. I'll still be able to manage Christmas Hotel. In fact, I need to prepare some nice Christmas bonuses for all my assistant managers. They've certainly stepped up to the plate while you were in the hospital. Yes, Lori Anna, you are so correct. We've been blessed."

At ten o'clock, Ken and Loretta arrived with their three girls, and shortly after, Barry and Diana drove up with their four children. Bella, Fritz, and the seven pups joined the group outside. The dogs and pups were a great way to open the conversation. While Chris and Lori Anna made introductions, the pups jumped at ankles, receiving attention from the excited children.

The adults stood back from the children to talk. Diana whispered to Lori Anna, "When you offered for Jessica to choose the first pup, Barry and I were grateful. The dog she grew up with, and *all* the children loved, died of old age eight months ago. I wondered how the children would take to a new dog, but seeing them playing with these pups I know they'll welcome the new puppy."

"Ken and I felt the same way," said Loretta. "Our dog died this past year, too. I just wonder how the kids will choose. All the pups are so cute."

Barry and Diana made their exit first. "We're off to Nashville for Christmas shopping, while all of you ice skate," said Barry. "Are you sure you want them to stay until two o'clock? That's a lot of children for the both of you *and* your baby."

"I thought the same thing," added Ken. "Loretta and I can visit another time with Mom and Dad, and stay here to help you. Lori Anna, they may tire you."

Lori Anna shook her head. "No, we want you to go on with your plans. I feel fine, and all the children are young adults. We'll be okay. I want to get to know my siblings. This is a wonderful Christmas gift for me. We won't be skating the whole time. Chris and I have made lunch for the nine of us. We just need to heat it up. We'll come in at noon and eat ... and then choose the two pups." She whispered the last sentence, so only the parents would hear.

After changing Olivia's diaper and bundling her in her snowsuit, they headed toward the pond with their skates tied together and dangling over their shoulders. Chris decided to leave the pups in the house. "It might be hard keeping them off the ice," he explained to the children, so just Fritz and Bella followed them to the pond.

When they arrived, Chris asked the children, "Have you ever skated on a pond versus an ice rink?"

They looked at each other and shook their heads.

"Well, the main thing to remember is the ice will have some bumps. It won't be smooth like in a rink. However, on the plus side, you get to skate in the wonderful outdoors."

"It's lovely on your farm," agreed Jessica. "I've always wanted to live on a farm."

"Me, too," added the other six.

"Do you have horses?" asked Jason, one of the twins.

"Not at this time," said Chris. "I did once have a horse. I've been thinking about more horses. I'd like Olivia to have a pony when she's a little older."

Emma was the timid one, maybe because she was the youngest of the girls. However, her face brightened and her eyes rounded. "A pony?"

Lori Anna hugged her. "Yes, a pony. Chris and I would love to invite all of you back, especially when we get these horses. Would you like that?"

Julia answered first. "Yes, ma'am!"

Lori Anna laughed. "Please call me Lori Anna. I'm only six years older than you, Julia. You make me feel old."

They all took seats on the boulders that Chris had placed strategically around the pond a long time ago. "I don't think anyone wants to sit on the ground to lace their skates."

"Where did you find these small boulders?" asked Jessica, while lacing her skates.

"Actually, they were found years ago when these fields were cleared for farming. I found them lined up in a fence row. I used my tractor to move them here. They make great seats for fishing. I stock the pond with catfish in the spring after the thaw. By the end of autumn, all the fish are caught and eaten."

"We've never fished," said Jeremy the other twin. "Some of my friends fish with their dads in the summer."

"Well, maybe you boys can come back in the summer and fish with Lori Anna and me. Even you girls," added Chris. "I'm sure you'd like to bait a hook with a wiggly worm. If Lori Anna can do it, so can you."

Emma's eyes rounded. "Yuck!" She closed her eyes and shuddered.

Lori Anna laughed, "It's not so bad, girls. Chris taught me, and I found fishing fun and relaxing."

The twins, Jason and Jeremy, were the first on the ice and the first to fall. Their older sisters ventured onto the ice next. The two sisters skated together, holding hands, and then they each paired up with one of their brothers. Jenna, Rebecca, and Emma soon joined them, while Chris and Lori Anna watched.

Olivia was still strapped on Chris's back in the backpack. Chris removed the backpack and pulled the legs out to turn it into a chair, while Lori Anna spread out the blanket. Olivia bounced up and down in her chair and stared at those on the ice. Chris and Lori Anna agreed to take turns skating so one of them could always stay with Olivia.

"Lori Anna, your siblings are great kids."

"I agree, Chris. This is a wonderful Christmas. I thank God for his love and mercy that I'm here at this moment." She looked up at Chris with tears glistening in her eyes.

He hugged her close. "I'm happy to be sitting here with you in this moment. I'll let you skate first. Before you go, I have a question. Have you noticed how Bella has been following Jessica around since she arrived? It's almost as if Bella senses Jessica's somehow connected to you."

"I was going to say that earlier, but I thought it might sound strange and rather eerie."

Following an hour of skating, they headed indoors for lunch. The kids were fascinated by the wood stove and ice box. Chris explained both to them.

Jessica walked around the kitchen eying and touching all the unfamiliar items. "I feel like we're receiving a history lesson today. Is it all right if we come back when we have more time? I want to learn more about the iron stove."

Lori Anna hugged her. "I hope you'll all come back and visit, and any time. We're family." Lori Anna looked around at all her siblings. "Okay, we have thirty minutes before your parents return, and Chris and I have a gift for each family."

"You don't have to give us a present," said Jenna. "Just being here with you is present enough."

"Well, this is something extra special, and your parents have approved," said Lori Anna. She placed her arm around Jessica first. "I wouldn't be here right now if it wasn't for you, Jessica. You saved my life."

"I couldn't let you die. Anyone would have done the same thing."

"I'd like to think that," interrupted Chris, "but unfortunately, *anyone would have done it* is probably not the case. Lori Anna and I appreciate you did this for her, not even knowing her. You went through your own pain when they extracted your bone marrow. You could just as easily have said no, but you didn't. I don't believe everyone would have been as brave as you, Jessica."

"Words of thanks can't express what I feel," added Lori Anna. "You gave me back my life. I would like for you to pick the first puppy to take home for you and your family." She turned to Jenna, Rebecca, and Emily. "I haven't forgotten my other siblings, so start deciding, because you get to choose next."

Whoops and hollers from the children filled the room. Chris knew the word excitement didn't come close to the happiness displayed from the children. Jessica discussed with the twins and her sister, and they chose a male puppy that looked like Fritz. Jenna, Rebecca, and Emma already had their eye on a female pup which looked like Bella. First whispering among themselves, Jenna then turned to Lori Anna and asked, "Would you mind if we name our puppy Annie?"

"Not at all, girls. I'd be honored."

All seven children were playing with their pups when the parents arrived.

"Diana and I thank you both. You've made our four children very happy."

Ken echoed the same sentiments for his and Loretta's three daughters.

"Enjoy your pups," said Lori Anna.

Chris laughed. "Bullet and Gabe's DNA is now spread to Hamilton, Ohio and Lexington, Kentucky." To the children he added, "I hope you'll return in the summer for fishing, and have a very merry Christmas."

Chapter Thirty-Eight

Christmas Love and Mercy

"Rejoice evermore. Pray without ceasing. In every thing give thanks: for this is the will of God in Christ Jesus concerning you."
1 Thessalonians 5:16-18

Christmas Morning
December 25, 1988
The Wright and Stanley families, Christmas Hotel guests, and about two hundred of the people of Franklin gathered the next morning in the Christmas Hotel dining room for the weekend selection of omelets prepared by the Christmas Hotel chefs.

Christopher looked around at his family, picked up Jerilyn's hand, kissed it, and smiled at the next three generations around the seven tables pulled together. His heart constricted with overflowing love for each and every one of them. He swallowed the lump in his throat before he spoke.

"Jerilyn and I have been blessed by our Lord beyond measure." He looked fondly upon his loving wife, before his gaze returned to his family and friends. "When Jerilyn and I first met back in December of 1941, there were just us, five-year-old Lily, and Ken and Carrie Emeline in the womb." He laughed. "Back in those days there was no way of knowing for certain about twins until they arrived – or their sex for that matter. Our blended family has been blessed by our Lord throughout the years. I thank Him for each and every one of you. I *think* there are thirty or more of us Wrights, but I've lost count. We'll soon need a bigger dining room and chapel at Christmas Hotel."

The chuckles of his family filled the room, joined by the people at the nearby tables who overheard.

"I love you all so very much," Christopher continued, "and the Lord has provided a very special message for me to preach this morning."

The waiters interrupted with the serving of all the omelets. The food having been served, the family held hands and Christopher bowed his head. "Let's pray. Dear Heavenly Father ...."

Following breakfast, everyone gathered in the chapel for the Christmas message. Lydia Grace and her husband Jacob sat at the organ and played Christmas hymns while the parishioners filed into the small chapel. Soon, the people had to spill out into the lobby. Chris had installed lobby speakers eleven years earlier when he finished college and began work at Christmas

Hotel fulltime, to allow overflowing crowds to enjoy the service.

Christopher addressed his congregation. "Last night on Christmas Eve, we read Matthew's account of the birth of our Savior Jesus Christ. Please stand in honor of the Lord for the reading of Luke's account in chapter two verses one through fourteen." Christopher read aloud the fourteen verses.

"You may be seated." Christopher paused to look around the chapel at his family, friends, and Christmas Hotel guests, many who stayed at Christmas Hotel as a yearly celebration. "I don't know about you, but this story stirs my heart, no matter how many times I read it. I sometimes have to stop and dwell on the fact of how much our Lord loves us ... me.

"About seven hundred years before the birth of Jesus Christ, His birth was predicated by the prophet Isaiah. I will paraphrase the story. Isaiah addresses the 'house of David,' meaning the family and descendants of King David, and speaks of a virgin pregnant with a child, and giving birth to the child. Isaiah says this in the context of this virgin birth being a sign from God.

"So Jesus is born, as predicted, and the event is recorded here in the Book of Luke. There are many prophecies about the coming of Jesus in the Old Testament, but I just singled out Isaiah's prophecy. I find this amazing, don't you?"

Heads nodded, and there were several "amens" of

agreement around the chapel.

"My sermon today is 'What does this baby mean to me?' I know He will grow up to give His life for me, so that I will have eternal life with Him. I say for me, because if I was the only one who would accept Him as the Christ, He would have still died just for me."

He paused a moment. "Most of you are aware of events that have happened in the lives of my family over the years. At breakfast, I spoke to my family about our family's amazing blessings from our Lord Jesus. You all know my beautiful wife Jerilyn." He waved his hand toward Jerilyn and smiled. "Jerilyn and I will have been married forty-seven years on New Year's Eve." He waited until the applause was finished. "Through the years, we have raised five beautiful children of whom we adore. They married well, they all have Christian spouses, and they have given Jerilyn and me fourteen grandchildren to date."

He looked at Chris and Lori Anna. "I suspect there will be more in the future." Lori Anna blushed, and the congregation chuckled. "We now have a great-grandchild, compliments of Brian, the oldest child of Lily and her husband John ... and of course Brian's wife, Christine, had something to do with giving us this beautiful great-grandson Nicholas."

Christine smiled at both her husband and baby Nicholas on her lap, and the crowd chuckled again. "I predict more children in their little family, too."

Brian smiled and gave his grandfather a thumbs up.

"However, the events for our family have sometimes been painful. As most of you know, we had a child kidnapped from the hospital a day after birth, whom we did not see again for eight long years. However, she has grown up to be an accomplished pianist, has married an accomplished pianist, and they have given us our wonderful grandson, Anthony, who is on his way to becoming an accomplished pianist, too.

"Carrie Emeline's first husband died in war, and it took a while for her second husband to accept the gift of salvation, but Marcus finally surrendered his life to Jesus Christ. Marcus now helps foreign war veterans who come home with the terrible affliction of post-traumatic stress disorder."

He paused again, took a deep breath, and slowly exhaled. "We now come to the year 1988, and one year ago tomorrow my son Chris married the lovely Lori Anna Stanley. They began their honeymoon in January; a nearly three-week celebration in Bellingham Bay, Washington where Carrie Emeline, Marcus, and their children live. Two months after their return, they discovered God would bless them with a baby in October, and that was exciting and another celebration for all of us. However, the excitement changed to worry and despair, when we discovered Lori Anna had leukemia."

Christopher noted the anxious faces of many of the

hotel guests, who were unaware of this painful event. "However, out of that discovery came a more profound faith in Jesus Christ for all of us. Yes, He had given all of my family His greatest gift: the gift of salvation, but now our family would again be sorely tested. We clung to Him in prayer for Lori Anna that she might be healed. More than one of us questioned Him and asked ... why, Lord?

"The leukemia pronouncement was made in late August, and at that time Lori Anna was also nearly eight months pregnant. A bone marrow donor was needed, and soon. The search was made through the National Bone Marrow Donor Registry. However, the nation-wide registry is so new there are not many people signed up." He looked out again at his congregation. "I hope this week you'll all get registered, and if you need to know how, Chris will be passing out the information after the service.

"But let me get back to Lori Anna. There was no match through the registry, and we asked God again ... why? Well, as some of you know, Lori Anna was adopted, and the best match would come from a full-sibling. She did have three half-siblings, and they along with Lori Anna's biological mother were tested. Again, no match, and we again asked God, why?

"Brian Demeter, our private investigator in the family, tracked down Lori Anna's biological father. On a lighter note, if you ever need a P.I., Brian is your man." Christopher paused while the crowd chuckled and smiled at Brian.

"Lori Anna's biological father was tested, but no match. However, he had four children, and the oldest was a match for Lori Anna. Lori Anna's miracle occurred when this girl wanted to help her unknown half-sister. *And* we discovered that the whole family are Christians!"

A round of applause broke out in the chapel and in the lobby. "Yes, do clap, but clap for our amazing Lord Jesus. This precious baby we just read about in God's Word, grew up to be *our* Savior. In conclusion, out of this terrible and painful ordeal, Lori Anna now has four more siblings she's getting to know. I think of Romans chapter eight and verse twenty-eight, 'And we know that all things work together for good to them that love God, to them who are the called according to his purpose.' Our Lord and Savior, the great Healer was revealing the why all along. He let us know He is always in our presence.

"We already knew He's above us and doesn't have to explain the why, but we were the ones always wanting to know the why. Trust, forgiveness, love, and mercy were just some of the things He afforded to us. I want to say that this year, Christmas love and mercy and His grace came down for Lori Anna and all of our family. Lori Anna is in remission, and we give Jesus, the precious baby born, and placed in a manger nearly two thousand years ago, all the glory."

At that, the audience in the Christmas Hotel chapel and lobby were on their feet clapping and shouting praises to Jesus Christ. Tears streamed down their faces as they looked over at Lori Anna who was hugging her baby close, and Chris's arms wrapped around the both of them.

"Please be seated, because there's more. Something else wonderful came from this ordeal. He called Chris to preach."

Christopher waited for the next round of applause to subside.

"I will quote first Peter, chapter five and verse ten, 'But the God of all grace, who hath called us unto his eternal glory by Christ Jesus, after that ye have suffered a while, make you perfect, stablish, strengthen, settle you.'

"Yes, Chris and Lori Anna suffered for a while, but while Lori Anna bravely fought leukemia, Jesus provided Chris with strength and the knowledge that he was to preach. I found out yesterday Chris will be going to seminary in Nashville, but what Chris does not know is that the other Wright family members prayed together last night regarding another matter. I'd like Chris and Lori Anna, and of course baby Olivia to come up here."

Chris and Lori Anna looked at each other in obvious bewilderment. While standing in front of the congregation, Chris's brother and sisters smiled at them. "I'd also like Jerilyn, Lily, Ken, Carrie Emeline, and Lydia Grace to come forward, too."

Christopher waited until all were in place, surrounding Chris and Lori Anna. "As most of you know, ever since Chris was a toddler following after Jerilyn and me, he's always wanted to manage Christmas Hotel. He gradually learned every aspect of each area of Christmas Hotel. He even added a few things appreciated by many of our guests, such as the gym and the darkroom in our basement, but most importantly, to the pleasure of the Christmas Hotel guests, his phenomenal age-twelve decision to place mistletoe above every doorway." He paused for more laughter from the congregation.

"The Hoys, who were the original owners of Christmas Hotel, said the passing of the Christmas Hotel baton should be prayed about, and then passed to God's chosen Christian couple. They passed the baton to Captain Jacob and Mary Bazell, who in turn passed it to Jerilyn and me. Jerilyn and I are now passing it to Chris and Lori Anna Wright on this Christmas. It is on this day, in front of our family and congregation and the guests and staff of Christmas Hotel, and all of Chris's siblings, Jerilyn and I place this document of complete ownership in the hands of Chris and Lori Anna Wright."

Together, Christopher and Jerilyn handed the

folded deed to them. Another thunderous applause broke out in the audience. While Christopher waited for the clapping to subside, he shook Chris's hand and Jerilyn hugged Lori Anna.

"Merry Christmas, son," whispered Christopher. "May God bless you both and continue to shower blessings on those who visit Christmas Hotel."

Chapter Thirty-Nine

Giving Back

"Thy sun shall no more go down; neither shall thy moon withdraw itself: for the LORD shall be thine everlasting light, and the days of thy mourning shall be ended."
Isaiah 60:20

Midnight
December 26, 1988
At midnight, long after Olivia was tucked in for the night, Chris and Lori Anna bundled up in their winter coats, scarves, hats, and gloves. Chris locked the front door and opened the kitchen door, flipped on the back porch light, and then flipped it off. The moon was full. Fritz, Bella, and the remaining puppy followed them out the door.

Holding hands, and carrying the baby monitor, they walked ten feet to the log bench Chris's dad had made for them for their first anniversary. On the back of the bench, written in script, was spelled out *Chris* on one side, and *Lori Anna* on the other, with a big red heart in the middle. Seated on the bench, watching the dogs playing in the light snow, they snuggled together with his arm around her, and looked up at the moon and the stars.

Chris turned her face to him and tenderly kissed her. When he released her, he whispered, "Happy anniversary, Lori Anna."

"Happy anniversary to you, too, Chris." Snuggling back together, Lori Anna placed her head on his shoulder. "What shall we name Olivia's pup, Chris?"

He studied the puppy, frolicking in the snow with her parents. "Mom and Dad are naming their pup Bobby. Lydia Grace is naming her pup Sadie. Lily is naming her pup Ginger. Brian is naming Nicholas's pup Artie, and the Spencer children are naming their pup Jake. We know Jenna, Rebecca, and Emily chose the name Annie for their pup. Our pup is a beautiful combination of her parents with Bella's long golden hair, but with Fritz's contrast of black and brown mixed in. I think she'll have a regal appearance when she's grown, so she needs an elegant name to suit her. How about ... Phoebe?"

"Phoebe, huh. Okay, I like that. Here, Phoebe." The pup strutted toward them, and they laughed. "She likes Phoebe, too, Chris. Phoebe it is."

For the next ten minutes they sat in silence, listening to the sounds of an owl hooting and the occasional bark of Fritz and Bella, mixed with playful yips from Phoebe.

"I can't believe we own Christmas Hotel, but I can't deny it's always been my dream."

"I'll help you with the mission of Christmas Hotel, Chris, and someday we'll be the ones to pass the baton."

"It's certainly been an amazing year, and my dad said it best: Christmas love and mercy and His grace came down and met us this year."

"God has been good to us, Chris. His grace met us in so many ways. We must give back. I'd like to help others with serious illnesses. I can raise money for wigs where needed, and take family pictures at Vanderbilt Hospital. I know I can get permission to take Bella with me. She's well-behaved, and the children would love her, and so would the adults. I'd like to set up a weekly visit after the first of the year. When Olivia is older, she can go with me, too."

"That's a marvelous idea. You'll be using your photography for something very important. You're right, Bella would be wonderful for the children. You and Bella will give them something to look forward to each week."

When they reentered the house, they headed straight to Olivia's room, softly opened the door, and watched their daughter who was sleeping peacefully, her little arm hugging one of the newly purchased stuffed animals. Her Charlie Brown Christmas tree partially lit the room. They tiptoed over to her, kissed her cheeks, and tucked the quilt around her.

Closing her door, they returned to the living room. "Lori Anna, I have a surprise for you."

He walked to the cassette player and pressed a button. Lori Anna smiled when the song, "Somewhere Out There" played.

Beside the twinkling lights of the Christmas tree, Chris twirled his wife and drew her into his arms. Swaying to the music of their song, he said, "Merry Christmas, my darling wife. Happy anniversary ... and look up."

She smiled when she saw the mistletoe he had strategically hung from the ceiling light fixture above where they danced. After they kissed, the final lines of the song played: "Somewhere out there, if love can see us through, then we'll be together somewhere out there; out where dreams come true."

Look for the New Edition of
Christmas Hotel Series Book Six:
Christmas Hotel Reunion
Coming November 15, 2019

.

"Grace be with you, mercy, and peace, from God
the Father, and from the Lord Jesus Christ, the Son
of the Father, in truth and love."
2 John 1-3

About Saundra Staats McLemore

Saundra Staats McLemore is a member of the American Christian Fiction Writers (ACFW) and the Ohio chapter of the ACFW. Saundra is also a member of Landmark Baptist Church in Dayton, Ohio. After thirty-three years, Saundra is recently retired as President/CEO of McLemore & Associates, Inc., a nationwide sales and marketing business she built in 1984.

Saundra's passion has always been history, and she enjoys reading historical Christian fiction. Saundra's novel *Abraham and Anna* was endorsed by two of her favorite authors: Richard Paul Evans (author of *The Christmas Box*) and Jeanette Oke (author of the Love Comes Softly series). Saundra has two series published: The two-book inspirational eighteenth century Staats Family Chronicles and the six-book inspirational Christmas Hotel series. Saundra is currently writing her ninth novel: *For the Love of Ali*.

Born and raised in the state of Ohio, Saundra is married to Robert, and Anthony is their only child. The other two members of the family are the cat Charley, and the mixed-Treeing Walker Coonhound Sadie.

Author's Notes

Although all my books are works of fiction, I do like some real people to "visit" my stories.

Dr. L.F. Beasley was a practicing physician in Simpson County, Kentucky from 1934 until he retired in April, 1975. He served in WWII beginning sometime in 1942. He made house calls until he retired, delivered many babies, and conducted many surgeries. He died in 2011 at the age of 103. His mind was good; he drove his car until age 99, and played golf into his late 90s! He did not like his given names, therefore he went by his initials L.F., and so I will not reveal his given names either. (Information provided by his daughter Barbara Beasley Smith of Franklin, Kentucky)

Christmas Hotel, the first book in the Christmas Hotel series was inspired by an article from January, 2008, in the *Franklin Favorite*, the newspaper in Franklin, Kentucky. The article spoke about a diary left behind in the now razed Keystop Motel in Franklin. The diary, dated 1873, possibly belonged to a young girl named C.E. Bazell from Rock Camp, Ohio. An Ohio assistant librarian traced the diary to a girl named Carrie E. Bazell who lived in Rock Camp with her parents until the late 1800s. Carrie E. Bazell died March 20, 1884 at the age of twenty-one, according to a brief obituary.

Look for *Christmas Hotel Reunion* the sixth and *final* book in the Christmas Hotel series. (New Edition) available November 15, 2019.

Reviews are always appreciated. If you so desire, please post an honest review at Amazon.com and Barnes and Noble for *Christmas Love and Mercy*, and I thank you!

Information as of this Writing

The Bone Marrow Foundation
515 Madison Avenue, Suite 1130
New York, NY 10022
Phone: 212-838-3029 or 800-365-1336
Fax: 212-223-0081
TheBMF@BoneMarrow.org

American Cancer Society
www.cancer.org
Phone: 1-800-227-2345

Organ donor registry:
Register by State at U.S. Department of Human Services
www.hhs.gov
www.organdonor.gov/becomingdonor/

The Leukemia and Lymphoma Society:
3 International Drive, Suite 200
Rye Brook, NY 10573
www.lls.org
Phone: 914-949-5213 or 914-949-6691
Depression Hotline: 1-630-482-9696

Crisis Call Center: 800-273-8255

Suicide hotline: 1-800-784-8433

Suicide Prevention Hotline: 630-482-9696

Abortion/Adoption Hotline Information:
National Right to Life
Phone: 202-626-8800
www.nrlc.org
or *Focus on the Family:*
Phone: 800-232-6459
www.focusonthefamily.com
help@focusonthefamily.com

Family Talk:
Phone: 877-732-6825
www.drjamesdobson.org

National Adoption
Phone: 800-923-6602
www.nationaladoptionhotline.org

Life Issues Institute
Phone: 513-729-3600
info@lifeissues.org
Anger Management Hotline:
Crisis Call Center
Phone: 800-273-8255

Christmas Love and Mercy

Discussions and Questions
for Book Club

In the following questions, please either answer for yourself or try to see the situation through the eyes of a young man or woman you know well.

(1) How do you feel about Chris Wright's whirlwind romance with Lori Anna, a woman thirteen years his junior? Do you or anyone you know have as great an age difference? Were there mixed emotions as to what Chris experienced? Would you have fought your feelings, as Chris did?

(2) Have you or a member of your family or a friend experienced the dreadful disease of cancer in any form? Did you or this person turn toward or away from God?

(3) Thankfully, Lori Anna's pregnancy was viable when the leukemia diagnosis was made. Have you known

someone who was pregnant at the time of any cancer diagnosis? What decisions were made?

(4) Lori Anna asked Chris to spend more time with Olivia and less time with her when she was in isolation at Vanderbilt Hospital. She thought it best for her daughter. Would you have been able to honor her requests?

(5) What do you think about Loretta's decision to confront her rapist? Could you have done that, even though it happened more than twenty years earlier? Could you have forgiven him? Was Loretta right or wrong never to tell Barry that a child had been conceived that night?

(6) What do you think about Ken and Loretta's decision to tell their girls about Lori Anna and how she was conceived? As a parent, how would you handle the situation?

(7) When Barry and his wife Diana discovered that Lori Anna was conceived the night of Barry's assault on Loretta, they had a decision to make. The author did not add the details to the story, but how do you think they would tell their four children? How much information would you provide?

(8) Jessica Spencer turned out to be Lori Anna's bone marrow match. Knowing this would be a painful procedure, could you make the decision to do this for someone you didn't know?

(9) Lori Anna turned out to be an older sister to Jessica, and Jessica thought she was her dad's first child. Have you known of a situation where a birth order was upset? How did the child who thought he or she was the oldest accept the information?

(10) What passages strike you as insightful, even profound? Is there a bit of dialogue that is funny or poignant that summarizes Chris, Lori Anna or any others in the story? Is there a particular comment by Chris or Lori Anna that states the book's thematic concerns? Do you feel Chris and Lori Anna and others grew and matured by the end of the story?

(11) Do the characters seem real or believable? Can you relate to their predicaments? To what extent do they remind you of yourself, or others, in the past or present?

(12) Did certain parts of the book make you uncomfortable? Did this lead to a new understanding of awareness or an aspect of your life you had not thought of before?

(13) What is the book's most important message? Why do you think the author wrote this book?

(14) Discuss loneliness, fear, anger, trust, and other emotions felt by the Chris, Lori Anna, their parents or Loretta.

(15) Is the plot engaging? Is this a plot-driven book: a fast-paced page turner? *Or* did the story unfold too slowly with a focus on character development? Did you find the plot predictable? What did you think of the plot development? How credible did the author make it? Was the ending satisfying? If not, why and how would you change it?

Sneak Peek Book Six *Christmas Hotel Reunion*

Chapter One

Decisions

"Remember ye not the former things, neither consider the things of old. Behold, I will do a new thing; now it shall spring forth; shall ye not know it? I will even make a way in the wilderness, and rivers in the desert."
Isaiah 43:18-19

Monday Morning
June 01, 1998
Chris looked in on his mother. She sat in her home office, staring at the screen on the Brother Word Processor. At times, such as these, he wished he could see into her mind and know her thoughts. She had not completed a manuscript in two years. Her days as an author had ended, and the words on the pages were now jumbled ideas and full of typos. Chris pulled the door closed leaving his mom to her thoughts. He needed to see his dad.

Retracing his steps, he walked back into the homey living room and looked around. A conglomeration of family pictures sat on the mantel, walls, and baby grand piano. He could mentally picture his dad, and sisters Lily, Carrie Emeline, and Lydia Grace playing the piano and singing. He and his brother Ken would harmonize with them, as the two brothers did not play any musical instruments. The gift of playing musical instruments was passed down from his grandmother to only his dad and three sisters.

His parents' dog, Bobby, lifted his head from his extra-large doggy bed. Bobby struggled to his feet and wagged his tail in greeting. The poor old dog was now afflicted with arthritis but never missed a chance to greet Chris. He was the only remaining pup alive from a litter a decade ago. "How ya doing, ol' boy?" He petted the dog and scratched him behind the ears. "You go lie back down." Bobby hobbled back to his bed and flopped down, expelling a loud groan.

Chris figured his dad was in the workshop, so he headed out back. The screen door wobbled and creaked when he opened it. *I need to fix this door for Dad.* He found his dad in the workshop, but not working on a project, as Chris was accustomed. Dad sat on the edge of the workbench, feet braced on a sawhorse, chin in hands, elbows propped on his knees, and looking out one of the open windows.

It was a pleasant day, so Dad had the shop's AC turned off and the windows wide open. A slight breeze crossed the shed, and all three overhead fans turned.

The radio played music from the forties, and Chris heard one of his parents' favorite songs, "I Know Why (and So Do You)" playing.

Dad turned when the squeaky old door opened, and Chris watched him discreetly wipe the tear from his eye. "Good morning, son," he greeted in a croaky voice. Clearing his throat, he asked, "What brings you here today?"

Dad slid from the workbench, and the two men hugged. They sat on one of the wood benches his dad had constructed. Woodworking, once a hobby, and now a small business, was at times too much for Dad. His main requests and specialties were in his intricate birdhouses and decorative outdoor benches. Today, his hands were empty. Chris's father worried about the health of his cherished wife. This wasn't the first time he'd found his dad lost in prayer or thought. "Dad, I hope I'm not interrupting."

"Chris, a visit from you is never an interruption."

"Are you worried about the trip to Carrie Emeline's, and the cruise to Alaska? If you don't think Mom is up to the trip this year, we'll all understand. When all of us kids gave you those tickets for the Alaskan cruise on your anniversary, Mom was better. Now she doesn't always know everyone or her environment. We won't have hurt feelings if you don't think you should go."

Dad raked his fingers through his hair – one of the habits Chris had acquired from his father when he was anxious or nervous. "I don't know, Chris. I'd like to try and make the trip. We'll fly to Carrie Emeline's first, and then I can decide whether we should board the ship or not. I can always give the tickets to Carrie Emeline and Marcus. They'd appreciate the vacation to Alaska, so the tickets won't go to waste."

Chris ran his own fingers through his hair and exhaled. "Lori Anna and I have been discussing you and Mom. Maybe Lori Anna and the children and I should move in here. I think you could use some help."

With one eyebrow raised, Dad grinned. "Do you think I'm an old man and no longer capable of taking care of the house and your mother?"

Chris felt the heat rise in his face. He didn't intend to embarrass his dad. "No, but I worry about you overdoing things. You *are* the youngest eighty-five-year-old I know. However, the doctor told you to take it easy after your heart attack. I know it was mild, and it's been two years, but I have yet to see you slow down. Lori Anna and I conferred, and we agree it's best. We want you to want our help. Would you be okay with us moving in with you and Mom?"

Dad blew out his breath. "I've considered this, too. Yes, I'm okay with it, son. I had always hoped one of you five children would take over the family home. When would you want to move here?"

"We can be packed over the next two weeks, and move in before you leave on the trip."

"What about your farm? You have horses, cattle, barnyard animals, and crops. You added on two bedrooms when you adopted Abigail and Michael, and Olivia was raised on the farm. Your three children are attached to their home. Would you sell everything?"

"No, we wouldn't. I've been in contact with Lydia Grace and Jacob. Lydia Grace has always been fond of my home, even before I was born. She and Jacob have agreed to move here from New York and take over the farm, freeing up Lori Anna and me to move here and help with Mom. Olivia is nearly ten, and she'll be a big help with Mom. She's very mature and wants to be a registered nurse or a photographer someday." He chuckled. "What a wide range of career choices."

Dad shifted on his seat and nodded his head periodically. Although his dad was now elderly, he was still handsome and still tall with a straight back. His once dark brown, wavy hair was now gray and cut short.

"Yes, Chris, Olivia is a very perceptive child and whatever career she chooses, she will excel. I agree that Olivia will be a great helper for her grandmother, and I also realize your sister has loved your farm even longer than you have. Your mother and I will enjoy having Lydia Grace, Jacob, and Anthony close by."

"I thought you'd like that part, Dad. In reality, the children will adjust just fine. Olivia loves the visits with the patients at Vanderbilt Hospital, and she helps when Lori Anna photographs the patients for social reasons, as you know, rather than medical. Abigail at seven and Michael at five are mature for their ages, too. They enjoy helping on the farm, and they can continue to do so after school and in the summers, if they want."

"What about you, son? Will you adjust? You've poured your heart and soul into your pastoral duties, Christmas Hotel, your family, *and* your farm. You've done an admirable job. I must warn you, taking care of your mother is heartbreaking. I never know when she'll be coherent. She's *usually* fine until the evening, but not always. They call it sundowning, but you know about the term."

Chris looked around the workshop where he had spent many years working beside his dad. He smiled. All his dad's tools were laid out in precise order and cleaned to perfection, as always. Breathing deeply, he inhaled the pleasant smell of the clean air and the wood shavings on the floor. He recalled a conversation he and his dad had with their dear friend, the retired Dr. Beasley. As Dr. Beasley explained in layman language, "Sundowning is a term coined due to the timing of the patient's confusion. A multitude of behavioral problems begin to occur when the sun sets. Sundowning generally occurs in the patient's middle stage of Alzheimer's and often patients understand this is not normal. Jerilyn does realize when she begins to fade away, as she calls it. Sometimes the confusion is like a curtain coming down from one moment to the next."

His dad continued, "However, Chris, it doesn't mean her mornings and afternoons are *always* lucid. She has her good days and bad days. The hardest part is keeping her away from the oven and the range top. She still wants to cook. I thank God I discovered the pot of beans on the stove when I did last month. All the liquid had boiled away, and the pot burned and had just caught fire. I was able to put out the flames before the kitchen burned. Now, I keep a baby monitor in whatever room I leave her, and I have the extension with me at all times." He pointed to the workbench where the monitor sat.

"Dad, it's because of situations, as you just described, Lori Anna and I want to be here. We'll be able to take some of the pressure off you, so you can relax as much as possible. We want you to enjoy your time with Mom. It will also give you more time to spend with at least three of your grandchildren."

"That alone will give me great pleasure, Chris. I appreciate you and Lori Anna wanting to do this. It's going to be a sacrifice on the part of your family."

"Not nearly as much of a sacrifice as you and Mom have done for me through the years, and you know Lori Anna loves our family home. She's always said it's the prettiest home in Franklin, and I agree. However, I'm also a bit prejudiced."

"I agree, too, Chris."

"Is it a deal, Dad?"

They shook hands. "It's a deal, son."

"Thanks, Dad. I think this is a good plan for all of us."

Christmas Hotel Reunion
available November 15, 2019